UNMANAGEABLE

UNMANAGEABLE

LESLIE MCADAM

HeartEyes
Press

I hope you put this note in a drawer
and forget about it.
Then find it again and know I still love you.

Greeting card by Scott Malone

SCOTT

I'm like a cat burglar … but the only thing I'm gonna steal is his heart.

Yeah, yeah, okay. That's a cheesy line. But I revel in groan-worthy lines, and I'm not kidding about the cat burglar thing. Adrenaline is coursing through my veins as fast as the Winooski River spilling over a dam, and I'm feeling like a felon.

Probably because I'm, like, breaking and entering—or entering, anyhow. Edsel hasn't given me a key, but he hides one under a fake rock by the porch. Easy peasy.

With my heart in my throat, I slip through the front entrance of his one-story house in the Old North End and shut the heavy door behind me.

While my current activities resemble a cat burglar's, the similarities end quickly. I'm giving, not taking. Also, judging by Cary Grant in *To Catch a Thief*, cat burglars wear black from head to toe.

I'm about to get naked.

Setting down my reusable grocery bag of supplies, I survey the scene. My boyfriend's living room is nicer than mine—most are—although it's in a plain brick house not far from downtown. Nothing really special about it except the fact that he resides here.

But special is what you make of it. I just want to make him happy.

I *flove* surprising my boyfriend, and my tummy's all aflutter thinking about the word *boyfriend.*

This is the longest relationship I've had in … ever. Sure, he's spent most of it out of town on business trips and a volunteer search-and-rescue mission, but he's coming back tonight and I'm going to show him *exactly* how much I missed him.

First things first. I get out the package of rose petals I bought at the Burlington florist. They were pricier than I expected, but he's worth it.

Walking backward, I sprinkle a trail of petals down the short hallway to Edsel's bedroom, like Hansel and Gretel on a mission from Cupid. After flinging handfuls on the bed as artistically as I can, I look around the room. It's a tad messy, so I pick up his clothes from the floor. I examine a patterned shirt. Not sure I've seen him in this one before.

I shrug and throw it into the hamper.

Once the room is tidy, I survey the scene and clap my hands once. I'm amped and giddy and tempted to fling myself onto the bed and make rose petal snow angels.

Focus, Scott.

Carefully avoiding the flowers on the floor, I tiptoe back to the entrance, lock the front door, and grab the rest of my supplies.

A few moments later, champagne is chilling in an ice bucket, next to two flutes and these great chocolates imported from Napa.

Is it imported if it's from the same country?

They're a luxury, yes, but how else do I celebrate someone so special? That's what credit cards are for.

Tapping my lip, I wonder if I should have gotten one of those chocolate fountains that you dip marshmallows in and then feed them to each other. And strawberries? But they're out of season …

Candles! I pull them out of the bag, along with matches, and light them, then turn the bedroom lights off.

I check my phone. He's supposed to be home any minute now.

One final thing.

Quickly, I strip down, folding my clothes and stacking them on the floor by the bed. Won't be needing those any time soon, wink-wink. I may not *be* particularly buff, but I look good *in* it.

Then I fasten a silver glitter bow tie around my neck and arrange myself on the bed in the classic Burt Reynolds centerfold position: on my side with my head in my hand, showing off the tattoo on my hip. He said he likes my tattoo … he being Edsel, not Burt Reynolds.

I exhale and try not to fidget. Must not make rose petal snow angels, because strewn about, they're so decorative.

Like me.

Music! I grab my phone and put on the romance playlist. "The Girl from Ipanema" starts up, and I hum, thinking about Brazil and warmth. But a chill comes over me. Vermont's fall is nippy.

Well, if a boy is going to be nude, he may as well be comfortable. Trying not to disturb the floral display too much, I head to the thermostat in the hallway and adjust it.

Oh, Edsel's going to be so surprised! I'm so excited!

Returning to the bed, I get back into position.

As the minutes tick by, I quiver with anticipation, and I start panicking that I got the date wrong. Or the time wrong.

But when he sent me his itinerary a few weeks ago, Google automatically uploaded it to my calendar. I checked his flights. He should be getting home at any moment.

Finally, the key sounds in the lock, the front door creaks open, and my heart rate increases tenfold.

He's here!

I'm about to call out to him when I hear him say, "I can't *wait* to get you naked."

I'm going to respond that I'm already naked, when a deep male voice responds, "I want to fuck you so hard you feel me for days."

Wait.

What?

Chills erupt all over my body, even though the heater's on full blast. Did he bring someone home for a threesome? Because I guess I'd be into that, although I'd prefer to have just one love for the rest of my life.

Then it hits me. That cheating *bastard*.

I grab wildly for my clothes, scattering flower petals everywhere.

Edsel's voice echoes down the hallway. "What the fuck is this?" Then, "Oh, shit."

"What?" says his companion.

"Hang on a second. Let me deal with this."

I have my boxers on and one leg into my corduroys when my now ex-boyfriend turns on the light and walks in, eyes hard, auburn hair mussed.

"What are you doing here, Scott?"

I pull up my pants and fasten them hastily. I don't understand why Edsel looks so angry. We've been together three whole months. I wanted to do something nice for him.

But I guess I got it all wrong.

I want to sob, but instead I hold up a shaking hand as I reach for my argyle socks. "We're done."

He puts his hands on his hips. "What the actual fuck, dude? I told you I needed a break."

I stick my toes in one sock. "I thought you meant you were going away for work."

"I did go away for work." He puts a fist to his forehead and sighs. "We aren't exclusive. You're like Walter Mitty—creating these fantasies that just aren't true. You need to live in the real world."

"No, I don't," I mutter, putting my foot in the other sock.

"Scott, when someone tells you they aren't interested, you have to listen."

"You never said you weren't interested."

He groans and rubs the back of his neck. "Fine. I'm telling you now. I don't know what goes on inside your head, but

4

you can't just break into my house like this. Or anyone else's."

"Ed, you might need to get a restraining order," his companion says, entering the room.

I get a look at my replacement. His lips are kiss-stung, and he's everything I'm not. My body type is kinda "gets by on ramen." He likely consumes nothing but steak, because he's huge, with muscles. I'm sure if he turned around he'd have a perfect, solid ass like that shiny CGI character from *Deadpool 2*.

Dammit.

With one swoop, I snatch my shirt, coat, phone, keys, and wallet, stick my feet into my unlaced boots, and hiss, "You asshole. I never want to see you again."

"Then that makes two of us, sweetheart," Edsel says, his hand on his hip.

Shoving past them both, I run into the bracing air, the wind stinging my tear-filled eyes. I'm still shirtless, wearing the bow tie. And now I don't remember where I parked my car. I had to drive around, because this neighborhood never has parking.

I groan, which turns into a yelp from the chill, so I keep running, looking for my car.

When I finally find it and put my key in the ignition, it doesn't start. Because it's a 2003 Hyundai that hasn't been serviced in … approximately forever. I should get it looked at—if I had the money for repairs. I know a good mechanic, but I can't expect him to work for free.

For now, though, there's a trick. Wiggling the key, I pump the brakes, and with a groan, the engine turns over. I get going and creep back to my house, coasting as often as I can because the fuel light is on. I can fill it up when I get my next paycheck.

Whenever that is.

My not-trusty vehicle sputters out of gas about three blocks from my house, so I pull over to the side. The neighborhood isn't that great, but it's not like I have anything valuable in the car.

I take a moment to take off the bow tie, fix the laces on my boots, and put my shirt on, and then I zip up my jacket. I lock my car and jog to my house in the dark night, thankful that all the hiking I do keeps me in shape.

When I get to my cruddy apartment—part of a charming, falling-down 1930s mansion that's been carved up—I bound up the stairs into the common hallway.

"Is that you, Scott?" My ninety-seven-year-old neighbor opens her door a crack.

"Hi, Mrs. Olson. How are you?" As anxious as I am to get home and lick my wounds, I need to be polite.

"I was hoping you could help me with the Facebook."

Despite the day, I grin. I adore Mrs. Olson. She doesn't complain about aches or pains in her body, nor any gossipy issues with her large set of friends. Nope, her issue is Facebook. I hope to someday be ninety-seven with Facebook as my biggest problem. "Show me what's going on."

She lets me inside. Her mail is on the floor, having been stuffed through the slot in the door, so I pick it up and set it on her front table. Her warm apartment is in much better shape than mine—but then, her son owns the place.

I follow her into her living room, where there's a tidy desk with an older desktop computer that her kids set up.

After she shows me how she can't log on because she's forgotten her password, we reset it together, and she's back in business.

As I go to leave, she reaches for her purse, but I hold up my hand. "No, ma'am. This is me being neighborly."

"I pay the Johnson boy to water my plants. I should pay you for helping me figure out this damn machine."

I shake my head. "It's fine. I want you to enjoy Facebook. Send me any of those recipe videos you find."

"Then thank you. Have a good evening."

"You, too." I close her front door behind me. When I get to my place, I gather up my own mail, and *criminently*, there are a lot of "Final Notice" envelopes. I toss them on the counter. I can't deal with them right now. There's too much month at the end of the money. Every month. Freelance writing doesn't pay the bills.

Throwing myself on my couch, I let myself process everything I've bottled up since Edsel unlocked his door.

I'd thought I had something going with a search-and-rescue hunk who made me feel like I was his entire world.

Apparently not.

I look around at my place—futon that serves as both couch and bed, rickety wooden table and chair I picked up on the side of the road that's both desk and dining set, laptop that goes to the blue screen of death with the worst timing—and compare it to Edsel's home, where everything works.

Maybe I'm not good enough for him.

I'm tired of being lonely, but I need to not date anyone for a while. Because that's how I get tangled up in these crappy situations. I want so badly for someone to love me that I keep thinking *this* guy is the one. But I'm always wrong.

Getting up off the sofa, I put on a beanie. My apartment is freezing, because when I turn up the thermostat, I can't afford the bill. I open the cupboard. Looks like Cup O' Noodles for dinner again.

But I'm going to eat it on china, by candlelight, with a glass of two-dollar wine. And I'll take a bubble bath afterward.

Pulling out a pan to boil some water, I think, enough is enough. I can't live like this anymore.

New Scott is going to job search with a vengeance and get out of this shithole apartment.

And more importantly, new Scott isn't going to fall for the next guy he meets. Because it always ends in disaster.

LUKE

"Hey, Daddy, looking for some fun tonight?"

The whiskey sears a path down my throat and warms my belly. House music blares in the hazy light of this New York City nightclub. I gaze at the twink who's sidled up to me at the bar, one hip cocked to the side. Then I give him a long once-over. His body language says he's ready and willing.

Okay. Just, "Don't call me Daddy," I growl.

The guy bites the tip of his finger and bats his eyelashes, swiveling his whole body. "Sorry, Daddy."

I pinch the bridge of my nose. Do I want to go through with this? The guy is cute, and I came here because if I don't touch someone soon I might shrivel up from loneliness. But I don't want to deal with this crap. "I'm serious. Not my thing."

He raises his eyebrows. "Uh-huh. Okay." He leans toward me and smiles. "You're hot." He smells … okay. Like cologne. I dunno what kind. Not bad, but not what I'd pick.

Still, he looks at me like he knows what this is about. It's transactional.

I never used to do things like this—bar hookups—but after what I've been through, it's good enough … I guess.

Shoving back my stool, I stand up next to him. I'm a good six inches taller than him, and at least fifty pounds heavier. Probably fifteen years older, too. Better be sure.

Bending to speak in his ear, I ask, "You legal?"

He grins. "Yes, but we can pretend I'm not."

I groan and scrub my hand over my face. "Fuck, I don't play these games. You know what? Never mind—"

"Wait," he says, looking me up and down and changing his tactics. "I'll stop. I didn't think. I mean." He gulps. "You seem like you're a little tense. I could help with that, if you like."

Nodding once, I frog-march his skinny-jeaned ass down the hall to the bathroom. The thumping music gets quieter when the door closes behind us, and the stall at the end is empty. Once we're inside it, I jam him against the wall, his front to the cold tile of the trendy bathroom.

"Fuck, yes," he hisses. "Please."

"Drop 'em," I say in a low voice right next to his ear. Then I nip at the lobe.

He moves quickly, undoing his pants and shoving them down to his knees. I take supplies out of my pocket and roll the condom onto my hard prick, then slide a lubed-up finger down his crack. "How much prep do you need?"

"Minimal."

"Good." I kiss the back of his neck, then proceed to breach his hole, wiggling my finger inside him. He's telling the truth, and it doesn't take long for his body to relax. "You'll feel me afterward, that's for sure. Are you okay with that?"

"Yes, Da—" He clamps a hand over his mouth and moans as I line up and press into him. Then he puts his hands on the wall, bracing himself. "Sorry. I forgot."

My irritation lessens a little bit at his apology, but that dynamic is not for me.

For … reasons.

Being inside him feels good. I have a robust sex drive that I can't ignore too long or I get twitchy and even more irritable than usual. He's almost the right height for me, and I press him roughly against the wall, then caress his hips. While I like manhandling guys, I don't want to really hurt him, and I want to make sure he gets off.

I reach around to stroke his cock, and he moans more loudly. "Fuck."

"Good fuck?" I ask, pulling out and pushing back inside him.

This. This is what I needed. My body craved touch. I don't want to think about how lonely I've been.

"Yes, good fuck. Damn, your thick cock."

I keep fucking him while I jack him, and when I'm getting near, I rumble, "You gonna come?"

"Definitely," he pants. After a few more strong thrusts, warmth pulses over my hand. I shove into him a final time, letting my release wash through me, then slump against him, my forehead to the top of his head.

Thank fuck. I needed that.

A toilet flushes, and I realize we've been overheard. But what we're doing is fairly common in this place. It's a wonder we're the only ones getting it on in here right now.

After I catch my breath, I pull out.

Reaching for some toilet paper, I wipe off my hands, then clean off his belly as he hastens to tug his pants up. I'd barely nudged mine down—just enough to get my cock out. After getting my clothes situated, I get rid of the trash and step back.

We study each other.

"Thanks," he says dazedly, his hair mussed, his cheek red where it was pushed against the wall, a happy glow on his face.

"Yeah." I nod. "Thanks."

We stand there awkwardly, and I wonder if I should kiss him, but nah. I open the door and let him out first. We both go to the sinks to wash up, and I inspect my face in the mirror.

Same dark hair. Same dark eyes. Same stubble with a little silver starting to show. Same emptiness inside.

What the actual hell has my life turned into? I was never like this before things imploded.

I can't deny that a random fuck helped, though. I'm less restless than I was when I arrived. At least I got this need out of my system.

For tonight.

A little voice coming from somewhere in the vicinity of my heart, though, tells me hookups like this won't ever be enough.

The next night, I'm at my desk in a glass-and-steel prison of my own making, surrounded by other glass-and-steel prisons in Manhattan. Investment banking never sleeps.

No one else is here but our janitor, George, who is emptying the trash cans from the cubicles in the center well and the offices that line the windows. When he gets to my office, I pick up my trash can and hand it to him. He tips it into the bigger bin he's wheeling around.

After he dumps it out, he pauses. "Please tell the partners thank you for the flowers for my wife."

I nod. "I will." I take the trash can from him and flick my eyes to my computer screen. But he lingers, so I glance back again. "Can I help you?"

George swallows thickly. "I also wanted to say thank you to whoever for the gift card for food delivery. It was very generous."

"Mmm."

"Will you tell them thank you?"

I bite my lip. "Sure thing."

It was me, but I'm not going to admit it. His wife had a difficult pregnancy. The rest of the office chipped in for a huge flower arrangement to be sent to the hospital. Waste of money. George and Denise are hard workers and deserve some help. The practical thing to do was give them meal delivery for a week. That way she could concentrate on feeling better. I don't need credit for doing the sensible thing, although now I'm suspicious that my secretary told him it was me.

He stands in my office for another moment.

"Anything else?" I ask, frowning.

"No. Just. Thank you, sir."

"Luke is fine."

George gives me a tight nod and carries on with his work. I return to mine.

After I get another company's analysis done, I'm interrupted again, this time by my phone lighting up.

Kira: *We need to talk.*

I sigh, push back from my desk, and text back, spinning my chair so I can look out at the night.

Luke: *That's never a good way to start a conversation.*
Kira: *How else do I say that we need to talk?*

Grinning, since I can picture her exasperation, I relent.

Luke: *Now is not a good time.*
Kira: *Tomorrow?*

If there's one thing my ex-wife is, it's persistent.

Luke: *Fine. What's it about?*
Kira: *Addi.*

My heart seizes up. This is why I answer Kira's texts immediately.

Luke: *Call me now.*

My phone rings.

"What is it?" I ask.

"I'm fine, thanks for asking." Kira's amused voice fills my ear. It hurts to hear, which is why I favor texting. "How are you?"

Kira and I are better friends now that we're divorced than we ever were as a couple, but she nevertheless reminds me of my biggest failure. My pain doesn't matter when Addison is involved, though. "What's going on with Addi?"

"Relax. Addison is fine. She's enjoying riding lessons with the money you sent."

"Okay." I'm not sure where she's going with this. I stand and look down at the lights and movement on the bustling streets below.

"You always give her too much."

But not enough of Daddy, is what I know she's thinking. I close my eyes.

Kira and I worked out our divorce in an avalanche of good manners. She has custody of our six-year-old daughter because, okay, yeah, I'm very old-fashioned about some things, and I think it's better for a child to be with her mother. Plus we didn't want Addi to see us fight. I visit with Addi at scheduled times, but she lives hundreds of miles away in Vermont for most of the year.

Kira takes a deep breath and lets it out. "So. I got an assignment today."

"Where?"

A pause. "That's the thing. It's in Myanmar. For at least three months, maybe six."

Again, my heart seizes up. "I don't want you going to Myanmar," I snap.

"Good thing you have no choice in the matter." Her voice softens. "Sorry, that came out wrong. I wanted to talk with you about it. It's a chance of a lifetime, following a long-term story about Americans who've been imprisoned there."

"I still don't like the idea of you going halfway around the world to somewhere potentially dangerous."

"I know."

We're both silent a moment.

Because I know her well. Investigating an important story is her dream. It's the reason for her journalism degrees and internships.

I'm also aware of all the opportunities she passed up once she got pregnant.

Dammit.

My heart sinks.

"About Addi ..." I prompt.

She clears her throat. "Right. We need to decide what to do with her. I can't take her with me."

"No, you can't." My voice takes on a low register I reserve for times when I'm super pissed. I begin to panic at the thought of her taking my child out of the country. *Hell, no.* "Is she going to stay with your parents?" While I trust Kira's mom and dad, they're not my favorite people.

"My mom's been slowing down lately. It's not a good idea to have them watch a small child for that long. I just don't think they could keep up."

"So it's me." My mind starts racing. "You want me to transfer her to a school in Manhattan? I needed to get her on a waiting list when she was in the uterus."

"No. Actually ... I was wondering if you could come back here while I'm gone."

My brain fuzzes out. "You want me to do what now?"

"I was wondering if you could take some sort of sabbatical or at least work remotely until I return." Her words come out in a rush. "Move back to Burlington temporarily. Live in my house. That way we can maintain Addison's routines and structure. It'll minimize disruption."

Her words stun me, and for a moment I have zero to say. "I c-can't watch her," I stutter. "There's no way. I can't just quit my job, and she wouldn't—"

"You've never been able to leave your job. But when is it going to be enough money for you? You already have plenty, and you know it. If you took time off, the world wouldn't stop spinning.

And if you can't stand the thought of doing nothing, then keep working—just do it remotely." She pauses and exhales. "Look, I wouldn't be asking this of you if there were another good solution. There isn't. It's not like I can take her with me—"

"God, no."

"And I've been waiting *years* for this kind of opportunity. Addi's old enough that I can finally follow my dreams." Her voice drops to a whisper. "I've worked for the chance to investigate a story like this my entire life, and I've done my part with sole custody. You're her father. It's time you act like it for more than a month in the summer and every other weekend."

I know she's right.

Her words rip at my heart, because I'm fully aware of the balance she strikes between her passion and being a mother.

But. "Fuck, Kira. Insulting me, when we agreed that you having custody was best for her, is not the way to convince me to leave Manhattan."

"Do you have a better idea?"

"No," I mutter. And even if I spent time thinking about it, I'm sure she's right. I want my daughter to have the best childhood possible—which is why she stayed with her mother. But Kira has her own ambitions, and I guess this is her time to achieve them.

I can't kill her dreams, which means either Addi comes here and we disrupt all her friends and schooling or I move there and learn to deal.

It's not like I have something—someone—keeping me in the Big Apple anyway.

Kira's voice is quiet. "Just. Think about it."

"Yeah, okay."

We talk a while longer, but the whole time my mind is racing, trying to figure out logistics. I can't fucking take time off. But work from home? Maybe I could do that.

I hang up. Since the evening is shot, I gather my things and go home to my loft.

My sleep is restless. My baby girl is calling for me in my

dreams, but I can't reach her. I'm battered by rushing water, while she sits alone on a horse on a high overlook like in an old western movie. I'm helpless to get her down or to save myself.

Then my dream shifts to Kira wearing fatigues, holding an AK-47 in one hand and a steno pad in the other.

I wake up in a cold sweat. Fuck, I do *not* want Kira getting hurt. But supporting her is the right thing to do. And maybe I can keep Addison safe.

First thing the next morning, I text Kira.

Luke: *I'll move back.*

I just hope I don't fail at being a parent the way I failed at being a husband.

Two weeks later, I pull up to my ex's house in Burlington, Vermont—a house that used to be mine—and for a moment I can't breathe, the ache in my chest physical. This house represents everything I wanted … and lost. Returning feels like regression. I'm embarrassed and out of place, like a kid who flunked third grade and has to repeat, spending every day with constant reminders of how I didn't achieve what I set out to while everyone else moved forward.

My daughter's face appears in the front window, and that both endears her to me and pisses me off. Because I'm not someone worth waiting for. She should quit that.

Gingerly, I get out of the car and approach the front door. Addi flings it open. "Daddy!" she cries, running to throw her arms around me.

Addison has her mother's long, curly hair. We all have dark hair and eyes, although the shape of her eyes is more like mine than like Kira's.

"Hey, girl," I say, my voice sounding gruffer than usual. Her head comes up to my stomach, so I reach down and lift her up into an embrace. "There you are."

She snuggles against me, which makes a lump form in my throat.

Her mom looms in the doorway. Kira looks good, her trim body neatly dressed in a cashmere sweater and white jeans. She's always so put together and self-assured.

I suppose, looking back, maybe her independence is one of the reasons why we broke up. Maybe I needed a partner who needed me.

"Hey," I say, giving her a quick peck on the cheek.

"Hey." She gestures for us to come inside.

"Let me show you my room, Daddy!" I set Addi down, and she tugs on my hand. "I got new pictures on the wall!"

"I can't wait to see." I lock eyes with Kira, who nods that it's okay for me to immediately bail on her. Our daughter is the priority, not Kira and me sorting our shit.

In the hall, we pass a big family portrait, and my body tenses up again. Kira, Addi as a baby, and I sit in a formal studio, dressed up and serious.

Yet another monument to my failures.

Since I last saw it, Addi's room has transformed into a fantasy little-girl bedroom. Not the princess kind, but the enchanted-forest kind, the walls adorned with a large tree, red mushrooms with white spots, and all kinds of animals. There's a canopy bed with tree branches for posts. It's whimsical and fairylike, with a bookshelf and cushy rocking chair, a child-sized table and chairs, and stars painted on the ceiling.

I don't know shit about home decoration, but this is awesome.

"Wow," I say. "Your room is something else."

"Right, Daddy? I love it. Will you play fairy king with me?"

I stroke her hair. "Later, pumpkin. Right now, I need to talk with your momma."

She nods and bites her knuckle. "Momma is leaving, isn't she?"

"Yeah. That's why I'm coming to stay with you for a while. Until she's done with this job."

"I wish you could both stay," she says quietly, and my heart just fucking sinks.

She was a baby when we separated, so she's never had both of us at once.

"I know, baby," Kira says, appearing in the doorway, unshed tears shining in her eyes. "But it's important for Momma to go and do this story. We can talk on video whenever you want."

Tears well up in Addi's eyes, and I couldn't feel any shittier if I tried. I never want her to be sad. She walks over to Kira, who picks her up.

"It's going to be hard, baby," she says, "but this is really important to Momma. And it'll give you a chance to spend time with Daddy."

Addi snuffles into Kira's blouse, and I stay back, not knowing what the hell to say or do.

Normal parents see their children daily. Normal parents know their child's quirks, their likes and dislikes, how they see the world. For me, Addi is like a fixed point on a wheel, spinning around to meet up with me at different points in her life, but each time she's older and different.

I can handle this two ways. I can complain, or I can treat this as an opportunity to get to know my kid and be the best dad I can.

I choose the second.

Except.

Not five days after Kira leaves, I'm wringing my hands at a crying first-grader, a house full of toys and dirty clothes and dishes that I can't seem to get to no matter how much I try, and a pile of overdue work. This is unmanageable.

I need help.

3

SCOTT

"Dude," I whine as I pick up a menu at Vino and Veritas, "my life is out of control."

My friend slides into the booth across from me, a sympathetic expression on his face. "Tell Uncle Murph everything." Davey Murphy is a tiny bundle of energy, with dark blue eyes and neat, dark brown hair. He clasps his hands under his chin and bats those eyes at me like I'm telling him the most important and interesting thing he's ever heard.

He's on duty, working as a bartender, but the bar isn't too busy right now, although there are a few patrons quietly enjoying the offerings from the new chef's menu.

I had a thing for Murph a while back, and we even got together a few times. But the last time I came over with amorous intent was … memorable. In some ways I was the catalyst for him getting together with his boyfriend.

Jason and Murph were platonic roommates until the day I showed up at their house in the rain with a picnic basket and a few bottles of wine (because: me). After Murph had put my soaking wet clothes in the dryer and we were kissing on the couch, a very pissed-off Jason came home, went all jerkface on us, and tried to kick me out before storming off himself.

Turned out Murph liked his roommate and his roommate liked him, but they hadn't told each other that very important fact. And in Jason's case, he hadn't even figured out he liked guys at all.

Now they're all happy ever after, and I'm happy for them. Over the past year, Jason's even become my friend—or at least he doesn't mind me, since without my harebrained idea of having a picnic in their living room, he and Murph might not have gotten together—and we can laugh about what happened. Most days, at least.

Murph and I were never meant to be, but he's remained a friend who provides a supportive ear to my complaints about my lack of a love life.

"You were right," I say.

"Of course I was. About what?" He gives me that charming Murph grin.

I settle back in the booth and laugh. "You just assume you were right?"

"I'm always right." I give him a look, and he corrects himself. "*Mostly* always."

"Fair," I say. "But you said I should dump Edsel, and you were prescient." Hell, he said I shouldn't date Edsel in the first place.

"Prescient?"

"I specialize in fancy words."

"But not in relationships."

"Ouch." I make a pained face. But I can't get mad at Murph, because I know even his bitchiest comments don't come from a place of malice. A divot on the edge of the table becomes very interesting, and I talk to it instead of him. "I wanted to surprise him, and, well, he ended up surprising me."

I glance back up and see Murph's curious expression. With aching shame, I tell him what happened—from my aborted three-month-anniversary party at Edsel's place to my own home papered with debt collection notices.

"Oh, Scottybear. You need to get your life together, my friend. Living this way isn't sustainable."

"Yeah, I'm realizing that. I wish I were like you. Bills paid. A sweet boyfriend. I'm jealous of your happiness."

The kindness in Murph's eyes is a little too much to take. "Hey," he says quietly, poking my hand where it rests on the table. "You're going to find the right guy. There's some hopeless romantic like you out there, waiting to take you for a ride in a horse-drawn carriage off into the sunset or whatever."

"Fat chance," I mutter. "All I find are cynics. Or guys who are taken."

"Okay, *that's* not the way to find a boyfriend." He sighs. "I have this philosophy about life where I think, 'It can't be only me.' I'm not the only boy who likes *Rick and Morty* and also glitter and sangria and nachos. I just knew there was someone somewhere who'd appreciate my quirks, so I wouldn't have to be alone."

I blink. "*Okayyy*. Cool philosophy."

Murph rolls his eyes. "What I mean is, it can't be only you, either. There's someone looking for you, my little turtledove. I know it. Mark my words. You'll find him."

I wish I had Murph's confidence. Before that dustup with Edsel, I was positive he was the one, but now my optimism has left me, never to return.

"What do I do while I'm waiting for 'the one'? And how do I solve my money issues?" My voice cracks. "I might lose my place."

"How can I help?" He bites his lip. "Do you need to borrow some money?"

"No." My tone comes out much more forcefully than I intend. But *hell no*. "I'm not getting into more debt, especially not to a friend. I just need to put my job search into hyperdrive. I have to get myself a job that pays more than the greeting card gig."

"Now, *that's* a solvable problem." Murph's eyes light up, and he claps. "What do you want to do for work? What skills do you have?"

"None."

He glares at me. "You have to be good at something."

"Well, I'm very good at arranging romantic dates, but that's not exactly a salaried position."

He tilts his head to the side. "You could be a wedding planner!"

I scratch the back of my neck. "Actually, that's not a bad idea." My shoulders slump. "But I don't know how to break into that business. And I need money fast."

"Who needs money fast? You're still job hunting?" A body hovers over us, and I look up to see my friend Jeremy Everett. After he and I got a tiny bit sauced one night here at V and V, he adopted me as a member of his booklover gang. Like Murph, Jeremy's a force of nature, only he's a bit more reformed fuckboi and a bit less princess. He runs a hand through his halo of dirty-blond hair. "You could sell plasma. Or sperm."

"Hey," I say, scooting over in the seat to let him in. "And, um, no."

"I'm not gonna judge," Jeremy says, holding up his hands. "You gotta do what you gotta do."

"Even if I were desperate enough to bring the product of my ham candle to market, I'm pretty sure I don't want to pass on my genetic material. The recipient might end up in as dire straits as me."

"*Product of your ham candle*?" Murph and Jeremy say at the same time.

Shrugging, I hide my smile.

They burst out laughing, and then Murph clucks his tongue. "I've had about enough of 'Bag on Scottybear' time. No more, okay? We're problem solving."

"Fine." I grimace. "Just no, uh, dissemination of my, um, semen. For profit. I mean, I don't have a problem with it, but it's not for me."

They crack up again, and now we're getting looks from around the bar. Vino and Veritas is all chatter and good vibes, but there is a point where you can be a little too loud. We might be getting there.

"Do you have to get back to work?" I ask Murph.

He checks his phone. "I have a couple minutes left of my break. And this is more entertaining than that time Jason and Tai lost bets to me and Emmett and had to stand on the street corner across from city hall in Speedos holding signs that said, 'Love me, love my Nantucket Nad Bucket.'"

Jeremy raises his eyebrows. "I missed that one."

"You did," Murph and I say together.

I shake my head to clear it. "Back to the task at hand. No selling bodily fluids or parts. And no, Jeremy, I'm not going to college of any kind, clown or otherwise." He has some weird clown thing I don't understand. Although, truth be told, I probably would like college if I tried it. But I haven't had the funds for tuition, so I've never applied.

"Your loss." Jeremy nudges me with his shoulder. "You're a good writer. Can you do more of those freelance writing jobs? Maybe for something other than cards?"

"Yeah," Murph says. "Ads for those come up all the time. I see them when I take website jobs."

"I can look, sure. Although I'm pithy, and I think they pay by the word."

"So be verbose," Jeremy says. Like it's that easy.

Murph unlocks his phone. "Well, let's see what's listed in local hiring." He navigates on his home screen and then starts scrolling, sucking in his lip as he reads. Jeremy gets out his phone, too.

After a moment, I realize I should be doing the same … except I can't, since my phone is out of data. Because I can't afford anything beyond the most basic setup.

"Here's one," Murph says, showing me. "They're looking for someone to help with farmwork. I guess it's seasonal? Over at Shipley Farms. They're a client of Jason's."

"My immediate thought is I'm much too pretty to do farmwork, but I can't be such a diva."

Murph grins at me. "I'm the diva, not you. Let's put it in the maybe column."

He pulls the pen from his order pad and writes "Farm boy" on a V and V napkin. Then goes back to searching on his phone. "Hmm. This one is looking for a dishwasher."

"I could do that."

"Where?" Jeremy asks.

"The diner that's about a block away. Okay. We'll see if we can submit your resume—" Murph scrunches his nose. "Oh, shit. As I'm saying that, it's updating and saying the position is filled. Sheesh. Competitive job market."

"Can I see your phone?" I ask.

"Sure."

He hands it to me, and I start scrolling. "Baker, no. Part-time cashier. I could do that. Dental assistant. Nope, not qualified. Nanny." I pause. "Nope."

Jeremy elbows me. "Why not? Don't you like kids?"

"I like kids. Quite a bit, actually. Since my parents were the von Trapps, and I'm the second oldest of nine, I have a lot of experience corralling youngsters."

"*Nine*?" he and Murph say together.

I nod, used to this reaction. "They were busy. I've never been a paid babysitter in my life, though."

"I don't know," Murph says thoughtfully. "I think you'd be a blast with kids. Let me see it." I hand him back his phone.

"And you don't have a criminal record, right?" Jeremy says.

I shudder, thinking about what would've happened if Edsel had called the cops on me. "Nope. But they'll find out my credit score is only slightly higher than my weight."

"If they ask," Murph says, as if it's the most obvious thing in the world, "tell them that you're having a rough time financially and really need the job, then turn the conversation to what *you* can do for *them*. How you like taking care of kids and you can come up with all sorts of fun things for them to do. How you're safe and have practical experience."

"That's true," I say. "So do I send them an email?"

"Nope," Murph says, studying the listing. "It says to call. Do it before I have to go back on duty."

"What, now?" All kinds of butterflies flap around in my tummy.

He mock glares at me and checks his phone for the time. "What are you waiting for?"

"You can do it," Jeremy says.

"But what if they want someone who's licensed?"

He turns and faces me, putting his hands on my shoulders. "They want someone to watch their kid. You're perfect." His boyfriend, Aaron, walks in, and he scoots out of the booth. "I see the love of my life. But you got this."

"Thanks. To both of you." I smile at him as he hurries off. *Gah*, everyone has a date. Then, letting out my breath, I enter the number and call, Murph watching over me like I can't properly adult. Which, to be fair, I can't.

This sexy, deep voice answers. "Hello?" Murph's eyes widen, because I'm sure he can hear it.

I clear my throat. "Hey, um. I'm calling about the nanny ad? I'm an experienced babysitter. I can be your nanny. Or manny. Or whatever. Some people don't like the term manny, but I don't think I'd have a problem with it. Were I to get the job, I mean. And my name is Scott Malone."

Smooth, Scott. Smooth.

"What are your qualifications?" The voice makes me shiver in a good way.

"I'm certified in first aid and CPR. And since I'm from a large family with a busload of younger siblings, I've spent almost my entire life caring for children."

"Do you have kids of your own?"

I can't help my bark of laughter. "No, I'm not in a relationship."

"What does that have to do with it? I'm not in a relationship, either, but I have a kid," the grumpy voice says.

Interesting.

"Sorry. I do genuinely like kids. I can send you a résumé." That I would have to create posthaste.

He sighs loudly, and something about the exasperated yet struggling sound makes me want to reach through the phone and soothe him. Even though I don't know him. "I never thought it'd be this hard to hire help, but yes, that'd be great. Is this the number to reach you at?"

"Yes." For now. Until it gets shut off.

"Why don't you come by the house for an interview?"

"Sure. When?"

"What are you doing now?"

"Now?" I say, thinking rapidly. I'm supposed to go to a football game with my dad tonight, but I have time until then. Murph nods his head repeatedly. I mouth, "My car is in the shop." I went back for it shortly after the Edsel incident, but when it took me nearly ten minutes to get it started the next time I wanted to go out, I decided I couldn't put off the repairs any longer. It was too much to hope the jiggle-the-key trick would work forever, and I need transportation.

"You can borrow mine," Murph whispers.

Nerves make me feel like I'm on a Ferris wheel. "Sure," I say. "I'm in downtown Burlington. Where are you?"

He gives me the address, we end the call, and I set down my phone. "I'm scared."

Murph smiles. "Don't be. He must be desperate if he's having you come right away. You need the job. He needs a nanny. Win-win."

"Thanks. For everything. Helping, encouraging. Lending me your car."

He waves me off. "My pleasure." He slips the key out of his pocket. I note his key chain says, "Don't even think about touching my man," and I laugh.

I hold it up. "This new?"

"Yeah, isn't it cool?" Murph reaches over and covers my hand, his eyes searching mine. "I know the world seems

26

desperate right now. But it's all going to be okay. Walk in there with swagger. Like you're delivering him exactly what he wants. Yeah, you're going there in a borrowed car and clothes from Second-Hand Rags, but ..." He lets go of me and trails off. "Just ... okay. So you're in a bad place. Don't let that color the way you're moving forward. Show him you're the best person to care for his child. He can trust you. Be honest and yourself. He's bound to like you. You're fun, and you have the most adorable nose."

I touch my nose. "You think my nose is adorable?"

"It's perfect." He squeezes my shoulder. "Go get 'em, tiger. And bring me back my car in one piece."

"I will." We get out of the booth, and I grab Murph and pull him into a hug. He's wiry, all lean muscle and bone, but he still feels solid. Like he's a friend who'll always be there for me. I need to return the favor. "Thanks. I owe you."

Jeremy gives me a thumbs-up from where he's snuggled with Aaron. I can do this. *I can.*

Jason walks in, and Murph's eyes light up. "When you make it big-time, don't forget to thank the little guys," he says with a wink, then sashays back behind the counter. "Break's over for me. When you're done, come back and give me a full report. I want to know if that voice is from a guy with a face made for radio ... or if he's as sexy as I think."

He waves me off just as Jason wraps his arms around him. Murph squeaks and cuddles into him. It makes my heart long for what they have.

"They are too happy," mutters Tara, an employee in the bookstore, as I leave.

"Can you blame them, though?" I ask.

"Not at all."

I exit with Murph's keys in my hand, hoping something will go right for me. When I get to his car, I laugh. His license plate frame says, "Dragons don't believe in you either." Shaking my head, I get in and start the car. Unlike mine, the engine turns over immediately and everything works. Yet another thing for me to be jealous about.

It's a cool, glorious fall day, and I drive past a series of hiking trailheads before I get to the neighborhood I'm looking for and find the turnoff to the secluded address. It's not that far from town, but it feels like it's a world away, a compound nestled in the trees. I follow the winding driveway to a sprawling, one-story farmhouse that's something out of a dream. It's painted all white with dark green trim. There's a wreath on the door made of fall leaves, and the whole place looks very well-kept and classic New England.

In the driveway are a new Range Rover, a Mercedes SUV, and a Subaru. So, yes, these people can afford me.

Honestly, if they even pay minimum wage, that would be better than the pennies I'm making piecemeal at my job.

I park Murph's car and get out, zipping up my jacket and straightening my hair. When I walk up to the door, it's quiet inside.

Holding my breath, I knock.

LUKE

"Daddy!" Addi calls.

"Yeah, baby," I say absently, typing as fast as I can. I just gotta get this email done.

"I'm bored. Come play with me."

"In a minute."

My fingers hover over the keyboard, because now I forgot what I was going to write.

Dammit.

It's not her fault. She's a child. But I'm used to being able to do things on my own, without interruption.

Small feet patter into Kira's office, which I've taken over for my time here. I look up and do a double take. "Umm, Addi?"

Part of me wants to laugh. Part of me wants to get mad. All of me feels like this is a bigger mess, both literally and figuratively, than I thought I was getting into.

"Yeah, Daddy?"

"What did you do?"

"Makeup like Momma."

Her face is smeared with red and green paint.

"Baby, that's not makeup."

"It's make-believe, Daddy."

"Where did you … never mind." I save my email in draft and close my laptop. I'm not going to get that done now.

"I spilled, too. I'm sorry. It was an accident."

Shit. "Show me," I order, trying not to sound too stern.

Addison takes my hand in her paint-covered one and leads me to our kitchen, where paint has dripped all over the floor.

At least it's tempera. I think.

There's a knock on the door.

So. Yeah. This couldn't get any worse.

"Stay here," I order, pointing to her kid's chair in the kitchen. "Let me get the door."

Thus far, I have not been impressed with the candidates for the nanny position. They've either been college kids who don't seem to have a brain in their body or established sitters too set in their ways. The last one smelled like Vicks VapoRub. I don't want someone who is cold and strict, although they do have to be safe and responsible. I want someone I can trust.

I open the door, belatedly realizing that my hands are wet with paint, to a man from a different time.

He's young—in his early twenties, maybe—with a face that I'd say is more cute than handsome. Straight nose, bow-shaped mouth, prominent jawline. He's tall and has overgrown light brown hair. But he's wearing a complete hipster outfit of a collarless dress shirt that's made of some rough linen kind of material, pants with two sets of buttons like a sailor's, and a friggin' waistcoat under his jacket, which he is unzipping. He's got this sweet, hopeful smile.

"Hey," I say, breathless for some reason.

"Hi." He gives me another smile. "I'm Scott Malone. Are you looking for childcare?"

I gulp and nod. "Yeah," I say, although my voice sounds scratchy. "Luke Lagomarsino." Scott reaches out his hand, then thinks better of it. "Sorry. Addison got into paint while I was working."

"Sounds like fun." He grins at Addi, who, rather than staying in her chair, has appeared at my side, studying him.

"Come in," I say, gesturing to the living room, and quickly wipe my hands on a Kleenex.

"I can see how you'd need some help." He brushes past me as if he's been here before and makes his way to the kitchen sink. He smells like clean laundry.

My phone buzzes, and I pull it out of my pocket. "Sh—oot," I say. "Hang on. Sorry. I have to get this. Just—"

"Don't worry," he says. "I got you."

I can trust him for five minutes in my own house without needing to install cameras, no? I may be overly protective, but here's his test.

With a grimace, I answer my phone and walk down the hallway. Although I'm not going to leave my daughter alone with some man I've never met before, I need to be far enough away to take my call uninterrupted.

While I pace, I can see Scott walking around the kitchen, talking with Addi. She seems fine, so I focus on the phone, keeping one ear peeled for any signs of something wrong.

My coworker drones on and on about a report we have due to a client next week, and I go into the office to take notes.

I don't know how long it takes, but when I finish, I return, pocketing my phone.

Then I stare.

Scott is sitting on the floor while Addi fusses over him. Her face is clean. There's a little trace of paint on one side, but otherwise, she's completely washed up. So are my floors.

"How did you do that?" I ask, but Addi interrupts me, handing Scott a bucket.

"Here's your table." She digs in the pile of plastic food and hands him a plastic carrot. "Here's your knife."

He accepts it and winks at me. "Carrots double as cutlery at my house, too. No problem."

His wink does nothing to my insides. Nope.

Meanwhile, Addi drapes a kitchen towel around his neck like a bib and holds a block like it's a waitress's tablet. "And do you want fries with that?"

Scott shifts so he's cross-legged. "Yes. Should I order salad?"

"Yes."

"And mashed potatoes?"

"Yes." She nods seriously.

"And meat?"

"Yes."

Scott spends the next few minutes ordering every food item he can think of: pizza, sardines, a burrito with extra vegetables, ice cream, cotton candy, a cheeseburger, sushi, and six slices of cheesecake. Addi scrunches her face and pretends to scribble on the block, taking down the order.

"Are you going to take my order to the kitchen?" Scott asks.

"Yes." She turns away and instantly comes back. "Here's your food!" She puts down nothing on the bucket.

Despite myself, I'm very amused.

He looks up. "Oh, waitress?"

"Yes, sir."

"Can I please have an extra glass of milk, too."

"Yes. Coming right up."

She scoots off to the corner and then comes back a moment later with … nothing.

Scott picks up the carrot and feigns cutting up the nothing with it and a spork he fished out of the pile.

He pretends to eat with relish, and I don't know if he's showing off for me or not—but it's working. "This is sooo good. My compliments to the chef."

She puts her hands behind her back and twists to and fro, pleased with herself.

"How did you get her clean so fast?" I ask, astounded.

He grins. "My parents were trying to staff a baseball team, I think, and I'm almost the oldest. I spent my entire childhood taking care of younger kids. And cleaning up their messes." Scott stands up, and before I know what he's doing, he's handed Addi a glass of water and given her a book to color in.

I blink, then recover. "I need to talk with Scott," I tell Addi. "Will you be okay for a minute?" It heartens me to see him playing with her. He didn't just dump her in front of the television or hand her a screen—he's encouraging real, creative play. The kind I wish I knew how to do.

So, my snap judgment is as follows.

One: Scott is incredibly competent. He's like Jeeves, with a sixth sense of what needs to be done. This is a very good first impression.

Which leads me to …

Two: Scott is a bad idea. Because I do not need a cute guy around.

I scowl at him.

He clears his throat. "So, I didn't get a chance to introduce myself. I'm twenty-three, a native Vermonter, and my favorite things are sunrises and sunsets." He blushes. "Sorry, that sounded like a dating profile. I'm not. I mean, I am. I'm not." He rubs his face with his palms. "I'm gay. If that's going to be a problem with being around your kid, best you know now."

"No," I say quickly. "That's not a problem. I have no idea why anyone would ever think that."

Scott shrugs. "You never know."

"No homophobia in this house. Trust me."

"Okay. Good." He lets out a breath. "I grew up in Stowe. My parents run a ski lodge." He digs in his pocket. "Here are my first aid and CPR cards. They're current, and I've kept them up for more than a decade. I've had to call 9-1-1 for my siblings more than once when we were out skiing, so I'm pretty cool in a crisis. Especially in the woods. And I just really like kids, I guess."

"Are you going to have kids of your own?" I blurt.

Why the hell do I care?

He snorts, then tries to cover it. "Eventually, yes. But I need to take care of some things for myself before I bring another person into my life. Nothing bad," he says hastily. "I'm just still getting my feet on the ground, you know?"

I nod, remembering what it was like to be young and trying to earn a nest egg. We talk about how this would be a live-in position, and I go through Addi's schedule and the kind of help I need: besides taking care of her, some light housekeeping, errands, and so on. Kira has a cleaning crew come once a week, but I can't seem to get all the rest done on my own.

"I can do that."

I'm overwhelmingly relieved by his confidence. I look at him intently. "The most important thing is that Addison is safe and happy. She gets into things if I can't watch her, and I don't want her getting hurt."

"Of course," he says. "I would never let harm come to her. Are there any particular concerns? Food allergies or special diet, that sort of thing?"

I shake my head.

At some level, I can't believe I'm contemplating inviting a strange man to come live with me and my child. But I guess after this whole scenario of me returning to Vermont, it's not *that* weird. And he—or whoever I hire—would be staying in a different part of the house, with a separate entrance. We remodeled the space when we bought this property, intending it to be for Kira's parents. But so far they're still on their own, and it just sits as a rather nice bedroom suite with a bathroom, sitting area, and kitchenette.

Meanwhile, I'm staying in one of the large guest rooms. No way in hell am I sleeping in Kira's bedroom.

I still need to do due diligence. "Do you have references?"

"I'll write them down for you." He reddens. "I came over here so fast, and I don't carry a list around with me."

If his references and background check pan out, he's got the job. He's the best of everyone I've interviewed, and I have a good feeling about him.

I tell myself the good feeling isn't because of how he looks but based on the way he acts with my kid.

"Should we decide to hire you, when can you start?"

He gives me a big, shining grin. "Immediately."

5

SCOTT

Murph bounds up to me, clapping his hands, when I return to V and V. Jason, Jeremy, and Aaron are gone, but he looks eager to chat. "Did you get the job?"

I shrug and hand him back his keys. "I dunno. I think it went well. He's going to contact my references and get back to me." I cough. "I gave him your number."

"As you should." He twists his hands. "Sooo, what was single dad with a hot voice like?"

"A veritable smorgasbord of masculine pulchritude."

Murph stares.

"Dude, he owes me a new pair of pants, he's so fucking hot," I groan. "I'm gonna think of him as *hotsexyboss* the whole time. If I get the job, that is."

"Yes!" Murph squeals, grabbing my sleeve and tugging me closer. "Tell me. Tell me, tell me."

I sigh. "I think he's straight. The job is to care for his daughter. I don't know the story as to why he has her, but he seems overwhelmed."

"Oh." Murph waves a hand. "You can make him whelmed easily."

"Whelmed?"

"So he's not overwhelm— Never mind. I want to hear the part where he's sexy."

I think about our brief interaction and how I had to battle not to stare at him. "He has the Joe Manganiello smolder thing going on. My height, but bigger and older than me—although not, like, old enough to be my dad."

"So just, like, a *daddy*."

That does funny things to my insides.

He sniffs. "Shame if he's straight. That is, shame for you. Good news for women, I suppose. It's always fun to work with a hottie, even if there's no touchy-touchy. I mean, I enjoy the scenery around here." He gestures to the bar where Tanner, the large, tatted beast of a manager, stands behind the counter, frowning at the cash register.

"Scenery is one thing. It's a bad idea to hook up where you work, though."

"Speak for yourself," Oz says, smirking, as he passes by with a tray of wine glasses. Oz and his partner, Reeve, have both worked at V and V.

"Present company excluded, I guess," I say.

Murph tilts his head to the side. "Did hottie daddy say how much he'd pay if he hired you?"

My cheeks heat up. "Um, no. Actually, I never asked him that. God, I'm really bad at job hunting."

"You have time to learn. Was he nice?"

I let out my breath. "I don't know. He was gruff. But he wasn't mean or anything. His daughter was the cutest thing in the world, and she hung on his every word, so he has to be a nice guy, right?"

"She was cute?"

"Adorable. Imaginative. I want to see her use that creativity to soar."

"So maybe *you're* the daddy in this relationship," Murph muses.

This needs to stop. I'm not going to think about my potential boss that way. I am *not*. "Okay, first, it's not a relationship. Straight would-be boss is probably straight. And second, it's just a job. A way to get myself out of debt—hopefully. If I get hired."

"You'll get hired." His phone rings, and he gets a mischievous look in his eyes. "David Murphy speaking," he says in a smooth telephone voice.

If I weren't so impressed with his ability to pivot, I might laugh out loud. Murph hates to be called David.

I can tell it's Luke on the phone, because the low register of his voice does something to me. I surreptitiously cross my fingers that Murph doesn't torpedo my chances.

"I *do* know Scott Malone. I've known him for a few years, in both a personal and professional capacity."

Professional? I mouth.

Go with it, he mouths back.

"I do websites and graphic design, and Scott provides content."

That's true. I have helped Murph with his *Rick and Morty* blog.

"Yes, he's great. Super creative and fun. I think he'd be great around kids." Murph listens. "No, I don't think so." He pauses. "Scott is very responsible and safety conscious. Everyone falls in love with him. You will, too."

A bark of laughter on the other side of the line and then some more words.

"If you need any more information, I'm happy to provide it."

After he chats with Luke for a few more moments, he hangs up with a big grin. "You're gonna get the job."

"I hope so." I let out a breath. We need to talk about something else. "Are you going to the game tonight?"

He smiles. "Yes! Jay Jay and I will see you there."

"Fantastic." I turn to leave, then pause. "Oh, I put in a few gallons of gas. Sorry I couldn't fill it up, but I replaced what I used. And I got you this." I hand him a chocolate bar I picked up for him at the gas station.

"Pfft." Murph brushes me off. "It's fine. You're a friend.

There's no ledger of who does what for whom." He holds up the chocolate. "And thanks!"

"I don't want anyone to feel taken advantage of."

"You could never do that," he assures me.

"I don't want to take more than I give."

"Okay, sugarplum. You were there for me when I needed it. I'll be here for you. Things will get better. I promise."

With that, he goes back to work, and I stroll out into the brisk autumn sunshine. Soon the leaves will start to turn. This is one of the most romantic times of the year: sweater weather, with the scent of woodsmoke perfuming the air. Then again, I'm known for seeing *everything* as romantic.

Except, perhaps, mud season.

———

I'm sitting next to my dad in the stands at a high school football game. My uncle—his brother—is head coach, so we try to make as many of the games as we can.

My dad *loves* football. But what he loves even more is trolling for dates for me.

Some dads, when their kid comes out to them, pretend it didn't happen. *La, la, la, let's just go on our merry way.* Kind of a *Don't ask, don't tell.* Well, more like, *You told, but we won't talk about it.*

Not my dad.

My father has never met a stranger, so he chats with everyone, everywhere he goes. He's taken it upon himself to find me the perfect man. Now that he knows Edsel and I are a thing of the past, he's applying himself to the task with renewed zeal.

It's hilarious, because there couldn't be a more heterosexual male—but that doesn't stop him from introducing me to anyone he thinks might be gay.

If it weren't so charming, I'd get mad. I can't count the number of times I've watched my dad, in his Patriots jersey, trucker hat, and jeans, sidle up to guys and ask if they're looking for a date. Half the time they're straight, and he's had to deal with some pretty extreme reactions. When he gets one who is into guys, they study him, likely thinking he's some kind of bear looking for a boy toy. But he just chuckles and goes, "No, I'm happily married to Aimee, but have you met my son?"

Then he propels me forward like I'm the showstopper proto-type vehicle at the car convention rotating on a dais for all to see.

Again, if it weren't so cute, it'd piss me off, but at this point I just roll with it.

Murph and Jason are sitting to my left, so my dad starts chatting with the person to his right. I hear him say, "My son Scott likes Red Vines, too. Don't you, Scott?" as he nudges my side.

As if I'm not right next to him. And as if I'm five.

But I'm pretty sure he's trying to hook me up with a high school kid, and that's a hard pass.

"Dad, he's jailbait," I whisper.

"No! Really?" He studies the guy, wrinkling his nose in confusion. "How old are you?"

"Twenty-one."

"See?" Dad puffs out his chest. "I told you. Would you like to date my son?"

"Dad!" I try not to be sharp with him, but it kind of comes out that way. "I can find my own dates."

"You can," he says placatingly, patting my arm. "But you don't. So you need a little push from your old man. The right guy will see that you're everything they want."

"I have a girlfriend," the guy says.

"Too bad," my dad says. "If that changes, come find my son." He stands. "Gonna get some snacks."

"Is he always like this?" Murph asks, snuggling into Jason, after my dad makes his way down the grandstand.

"He is. Having Dad in my corner wasn't something I counted on when I came out, but he's perpetually my matchmaker. The worst was at a funeral when he tried to hook me up with the priest."

Murph snickers. "I'm jealous. At least he pays attention to you."

"Too much attention. He wants me to have the same kind of love he has with my mom. One of those long-term pairings that get stronger over the years."

"You're lucky." Jason leans forward. "My dad's barely past pretending I'm straight."

"He tolerates me now," Murph protests.

"He likes you, but he still wishes I were dating some girl."

Murph kisses him. "Do we care?"

"We do not," Jason murmurs. Then he looks up at me. "Seriously, though, be grateful. Having a dad who's interested in your life can be annoying, but trust me, it's worse if they disapprove."

"That doesn't mean I want to date every guy he picks out for me."

"No, but … unconditional acceptance is a gift not many of us have."

"Speaking of which," I mutter, looking up.

My dad is back, a full tray of nachos in his hands and a geeky professor type trailing behind him. The guy isn't bad looking, actually.

"This is my son Scott," Dad says grandly, gesturing to me, as he hands Murph the nachos. "He's gay."

I choke back a laugh that's almost a sob. "Dad! That's not my only quality."

"It's an important one. You two can go on a date." He grins and motions between us.

I say, with all the sincerity I can muster, "I am so sorry my father strong-armed you into coming over here."

The guy has a nice smile. "I came willingly once I saw who he was talking about."

"Ooh," Murph says, passing my dad back the nachos, and I blush.

My dad preens, now crunching on a cheese-covered chip.

"Well, let me have your number," I say. "I can call you."

"Let me have it," my dad says, yanking out his phone. "I'll make sure he does."

"Dad!"

The guy chuckles. "I don't mean to pressure you. I just think it's hilarious that your dad is your wingman, and I think you're cute. If you want to go out sometime, let me know. My name is Dennis."

"Nice to meet you." I shake his slim, cool hand.

I swore I wouldn't fall for the next person I met. But … I could go out.

Murph raises his hand. "I know just the place for a drink."

Jason shoves him with his shoulder. "Always advertising."

"Vino and Veritas is great!"

So now I'm making vague plans with a nerdy professor to go to V and V—he's never been. Meanwhile, I'm hoping I have a chance at a nanny job.

Dennis goes back to his friend group, and my phone buzzes. At first I think Dennis is texting me already, but it's the mechanic's shop giving me a call. I answer.

"Hey, Scott, your car is ready."

I stand and make my way to a less crowded area of the bleachers. Even though I don't want to know the answer, I ask, "How much did the damage come to?"

When he tells me, I clamp my lips shut to avoid shrieking. To be fair, it's not a high price. It's a very reasonable price, which is why I entrusted my car to this shop. But it's too expensive if you're broke, like me.

He can read my silence. "If you need time, I'm sure we can do a payment plan."

The sun breaks through the clouds. "Really?"

"Sure. We're closing up for the night now, but I'll leave the key under the floor mat, and you can make a payment tomorrow."

I let out a breath. If I do a little bit more work, I might be able to pay it off in a few months.

Hell, I need this job more than ever.

"That would be great. Thank you so much." I pocket my phone and return to my dad and friends.

After the game, my dad drives me to pick up my car. It seems to run, which is the best I can say for it. I'm always disappointed when I get my car back from a mechanic. I have an irrational hope that I'll get a better one instead. Oh well. They're mechanics, not magicians.

When I get home, key in hand, an eviction notice is taped on my door.

Shit. Did I forget to pay rent?

Now that I think about it, did I pay rent *last* month?

Probably not. And while Mrs. Olson is kind and her son is fair, I've used up any goodwill I had with him, since even on a good month I tend to be a few days late. I rip the notice off, not wanting to read it, and go inside.

I add it to the growing stack of unopened mail, unpaid bills, and threats to my well-being in the kitchen. It's too much, and I don't know where to start dealing with it. My logical brain tells me that sometimes when I open the bills, they aren't as bad as I fear. Still, I have so much anxiety about money and have had enough experience with my past sins—I mean financial decisions—adding up to be so much worse than I expected, that now I'm completely gun-shy.

So I sweep them all aside and concentrate on what I *do* have: a roof over my head, although I'm not sure for how long. Clothes. A bed. A few books. A computer. And food. I think.

I open the cabinets and pull out a jar of two-buck Peanut Delight and some dead bread from the bakery outlet.

Staring at it, I'm disgusted with myself. If I eat nothing but old bread and shelf-stable peanut butter, I'll end up getting scurvy.

Fuckity fuck.

I look around at my place, my heart sinking. I'd thought I was at rock bottom before, but this might be it. My head spins, and I get a sour taste in my mouth.

I put my head down on my wrists and let the tears come.

Eventually I crawl into bed wearing two pairs of sweats and socks because it's so cold. I have to get a job. I have to get out of here. I can't live like this anymore.

And somehow my prayers are answered. A few days later, my phone vibrates with a call, and a gruff voice offers me a nanny position making more money than I've ever earned in my entire life.

"I accept," I say immediately, and begin to pack up, looking around this place with contempt. I'll miss Mrs. Olson, sure, but that's it, and I can make sure to visit and help her with "the Facebook" whenever she needs it.

I'm about to start a new adventure. New Scott is going to get back on his feet.

6

LUKE

Goddammit, Scott's even cuter than I remembered … and it's pissing me off.

I did my due diligence. I trust but verify. His background check showed that he has a terrible credit score but no lawsuits or criminal activity. I can't hold not having money against someone, especially when they're young, and there were no other red flags. His references panned out; therefore, he was the logical winner.

But if I'm being honest, I threw logic away and am operating on feel—which to me is about as comfortable as jumping into Lake Champlain during a snowstorm.

Bottom line, I think Scott Malone will keep my daughter safe and help her grow. And he'll enable me to actually get some work done in the office.

So I'm standing on my front steps with my hands in my pockets, watching him pull up in some godawful car and rethinking my decision. Because no way in hell is he taking my daughter anywhere in that death trap.

Once he turns off the engine, Addi bursts out from behind me and bounds over to him. He extracts himself from the car and kneels down in front of her, saying, "Hey, Addi! We're going to have so much fun together! I got this for you." He hands her what looks like a toy horse.

She takes it and clutches it to her chest, then giggles and twists in place, not knowing what to do with his attention, until she succumbs to his enthusiasm and starts jumping up and down. "Okay! Yay!"

He's on his knees in my gravel driveway, and he glows in the late autumn sunshine, his light brown hair showing glints of golden and darker brown. I suppress a groan.

This was a bad idea. I'm *not* going to notice that he's sexier than I remembered. Because that's irrelevant.

I just need to get laid. *With someone else.*

"Why don't you show me where my room is?" he asks Addi, then glances up at me as if to ask if that's all right.

"Go ahead," I mutter.

Scott stands up, turns back to his car, pulls out a small paper bag, and hands it to me. "I got you a few treats from the bakery."

I open the bag and see two maple crullers. That was thoughtful of him. "How did you know these are my favorite?"

"Lucky guess? Or maybe they're everyone's favorite."

He flashes me a smile, then picks up a duffel bag in one hand and offers Addi the other. Together they race into the house, leaving me in the dust. I pull a beat-up gym bag with a faded Stowe High logo out of his beat-up car, which is filled with boxes and bags. It looks like he raided a dumpster behind a supermarket, because none of them are proper moving boxes, but I grab a big one and haul it inside, the bag slung over my shoulder and the bakery treats balanced on top of the box.

When I get to the mother-in-law suite, he's already looking around and whistling. He turns to me and beams. "Really? This is mine?"

His smile rearranges my insides. It's like being hit with pure happiness.

I swallow and nod, setting down his things. "Yep."

He drops his bag, and Addi tugs him around the room

pointing out the television, sitting area, kitchenette, and bathroom. And the bed. Fucking hell.

I'm just thankful he'll be living in another part of the house from my bedroom. I wouldn't be able to handle sharing a wall with him.

"This is so much nicer than my apartment," he says in wonder. "And before that, I never had this much space to myself."

As he inspects the room, opening drawers and the closet, I can't stop watching him—his enthusiasm is fascinating. He's like a little kid himself, in some ways.

When did I get so jaded?

He catches me staring, and I cough. "Help yourself to any food in the kitchen. You don't have to eat in here. It's just if it's convenient."

"Thanks!" Scott turns to Addi. "Are you hungry? Do you need a snack?"

She nods, and he looks up at me. "Want me to fix her something?"

I grunt my approval.

He grins. "I got this. You can go back to work."

It's Sunday afternoon.

I resist the urge to harrumph, even though this is exactly why I hired him—so I could get work done and Addi could be taken care of. But I'm not totally willing to let him be unsupervised with my child yet. And it *is* the weekend.

We all return to the main part of the house. I wonder whether I need to give him the same explanations about Addi's care Kira gave me before she left, but Scott seems to know exactly what to do. After a moment, I retrieve my computer from my office and come back to set up shop at the kitchen table. I don't mean to be overbearing …

Nah. I do. I want to watch him.

While I check my email on my laptop, he pours her a glass of milk in a plastic cup, brings out fruit and Vermont cheddar and crackers, opens some cabinets, and in a few minutes, sets the result before her. He's cut the cheese into hearts and stars and put them on the crackers like they are pieces on a checkerboard. And he somehow turned the apple into a swan.

I fucking hired Mary Poppins.

Addi giggles and claps.

I blink at him. "You're making me look bad."

Again, he bathes me in a warm smile that makes me feel things I haven't felt in a long time. Like belonging. "I'll never make you look bad. You can't be replaced."

I only wish that were true.

My laptop chimes with an incoming email, and I decide to go back and work in the office after all. He can handle this. I hide away until the scent of tomato sauce and spices wafts through the house. I don't know how long it's been, but Scott and Addi have been quiet the entire time.

Following my nose, I see Scott cooking spaghetti and meatballs, Addi perched up next to him on a stool, "helping." He's humming a Lost Frequencies song I've heard quite a few times. It's annoyingly catchy. He and Addi are wearing matching aprons —he must be using Kira's—and the domesticity of it hits me somewhere deep.

This is what I wanted with Kira. A family where everyone did nice things for each other. Where we worked together to teach our daughter how to be a human.

And this is what we never had.

I don't say much at dinner. Scott mostly focuses on Addi. I can't tell if I'm relieved or grouchy about it. The food is delicious, though.

After, Scott insists on doing the dishes, so I draw Addi a bath, help her put on her nightgown, and tuck her into bed.

As I'm doing so, Scott appears in the doorway, a gentle smile on his face. "Want me to read to her?"

I almost say no, but then I catch Addi's expression. She can't get enough of him. So I scoot over and awkwardly listen while he reads to her, not wanting to leave but not feeling comfortable enough to participate. He finishes the story, smooths her hair, and glances up at me with a smile. "Sweet dreams," he says to her.

"Night, Scott."

"Night, baby," I say, kissing her forehead while Scott stands to the side.

"Night, Daddy." I switch on her night-light, arrange six stuffed animals, turn off the overhead light, and shut the door behind me. Once in the hallway, I resist the urge to slump against it.

Scott raises an eyebrow. "We made it through the evening."

I nod. *How many more to go? Am I always going to be this uncomfortable being her full-time dad?*

"I'll go get the rest of my things."

I follow him back to the front door, where he heads to his car in the dark. "Need help?"

He shrugs, so I take that as a yes and help him move in.

"Thanks for getting right to work," I say, "but you can take the time you need. I can handle her while you move in." I think.

"You hired me to work, not to decorate. I can set up my space on my own time. It won't take long. I don't have that much stuff."

"Yeah, okay."

I still feel bad about it. Instead of saying anything, though, I just leave him to it.

I can feel his eyes on me as I retreat.

A noise jostles me out of sleep in the middle of the night, and I startle to a sitting position.

What was that?

I slide out of bed and throw on a T-shirt and a pair of sweats. While my first reaction is panic, I calm myself. The alarm is set. No one's screaming. I have a child and a new employee in the house.

I rush to Addi's room, thinking maybe she fell out of bed. I crack open the door, but she's sleeping soundly, her night-light showing her chest rising and falling.

That eases my frantic heart somewhat, so I keep going through the house, headed for the living room.

When I get to the kitchen, Scott has his back to me, and he looks adorably rumpled. The light over the stove is on, casting a dim glow over my new employee. He's delicious, his lean arms sticking out of a T-shirt and his ass rounding out plaid pajama bottoms. He looks like he's ready for Sunday morning cuddles and mimosas.

And where the hell did *that* thought come from?

He's piling turkey on a sandwich not quite to Dagwood heights, but close enough. I'm not surprised he needs a midnight snack; he didn't eat much at dinner.

I knock on the wall so as not to startle him, but he jumps anyway. "Hey," I say.

Something about his sheepish look tugs at my heart. "I'm sorry," he says. "I, um."

"I said you could eat if you were hungry, and I meant it."

Scott swallows hard. "Thanks." I can tell he wants to say something more.

"Go ahead."

"Want some?" He gestures at the sandwich, which he has taken the time to put on a plate and slice on the diagonal.

I shake my head. "No. I should go back to bed—"

"Stay." He gives me a shy smile. "I mean, I wouldn't mind the company."

"All right." Might as well. I'm awake, and I should get to know him. I fill two glasses with water and pull a stool up to the bar, and he sits down next to me and digs in. I don't miss how ravenous he seems.

What's he been doing before now? He seems nice and earnest, but lost. I don't know how to ask about his situation without being nosy.

So we sit in silence for a while, the only sounds the occasional clink of our glasses on the counter and his chewing.

"Are you from here?" he asks, finally. "Burlington, I mean."

"Yeah." Then I realize I shouldn't be so curt with him. "I grew up here, but after my divorce I took a job with the Manhattan branch of my company. Kira stayed."

"Was this your house?"

I nod.

"And she's doing some journalist thing somewhere?"

"Yeah."

"It must be tough being back here."

I laugh. "You have no idea."

He goes back to his sandwich and, after a moment, says, "I just broke up with my boyfriend. Though it wasn't that serious. Or it was more serious for me than for him. Story of my life."

"How so?" My curiosity gets the better of me.

"I always think the other person is more into me than they really are." He groans. "Maybe I'm in love with the idea of love, but I'm never going to find it."

Ouch. "You just haven't found the right guy for you. I'm sure he's out there."

I'm not sure why I sound like a motivational speaker.

But confirming that Scott is single is even more dangerous than simply having him around.

Because if he's available, and I'm stuck in this town …

He chews quietly, and I have to shut down that train of thought.

My new nanny has to get to know my daughter and her routine. He doesn't need to know me.

Standing abruptly, I pick up my glass and set it in the sink, then turn on my heel. "I was just wondering what the sound was. Gonna go back to bed."

"I'm sorry for waking you," he says softly. "And I'll be sure to get Addi up in time for school."

I grunt in acknowledgment and return to my room.

Where I stew in my own juices.

Because what was I thinking? It's hard enough to be back in Vermont, in this house I helped buy, with the family photos I'm in … and then disappear from. The ones that are just Kira and Addi get to me.

I can't change the past, though. Right now, I need to do the best I can with my daughter, let Scott help me so I can do my work, and otherwise leave him be. I can't let him become more than that.

Still, he's tempting.

Too tempting.

SCOTT

As I watch Luke's retreating back, I wonder—not for the first time in my life—if there's something fundamentally wrong with me. Am I so unappealing that unless he has some legit, functional reason to speak with me, he has to get out of the room?

Even though he said he wasn't homophobic, once I mentioned my no-boyfriend status, he booked out of the midnight kitchen like someone was offering maple crullers next door.

But he was trying not to surprise me when he came in, which gives him some points, and he didn't seem mad that I was raiding his kitchen, for which my hungry body thanks him.

Maybe, then, he just wanted to go back to bed.

I sigh and take another bite of my rather exuberant sandwich —which is really my dinner, since our dinner was the first meal I'd eaten today. Not that I'd tell Luke that. He doesn't need to know my circumstances. Those are in the past.

Plus, I need to stop confiding in him like he's a potential friend.

He's my boss. Nothing more. Yes, he's *hotsexyboss*, but I can ignore that.

Still … I was not expecting my new, standoffish boss to look so human, so approachable in the middle of the night.

During the day, Luke was intense and sometimes intimidating. In the middle of the night, wearing a soft, heather gray T-shirt and sleep pants, he seemed ... vulnerable. The only other hint at his vulnerability in the short time I've been here has been a softness in his eyes when he's around his daughter. That he schools quickly when he's talking with anyone else.

Luke's looks, though, just do it for me. His eyes are a deep umber color that's almost prismatic, with layers upon layers in them. They're mesmerizing. And his physique? *Yum.* From the precise way his hair is trimmed at the nape of his neck (which I got a great view of when he filled glasses of water for us) to his broad shoulders and narrow hips and waist, he's gorgeous. He's shaped in the classical male form, and whenever I see him, electricity crackles across my skin.

But I'm not supposed to be lusting after him, and I thought I'd given myself the proper talking-to: he's almost assuredly straight, and in any case, I'm probably just a kid to him. And even if I'm not, new Scott has rules.

So my love life with my new employer can exist where *all* of my love lives reside: in my mind only.

I finish my meal, wash the plate, set the kitchen to rights, and return to my room, pausing before I slide back into bed to take it all in. Luke's ex-wife's house is the opposite of where I just came from. This place is *Architectural Digest* country-home posh, with quality furniture and divine bedding and everything well chosen.

After crawling into the world's most comfortable bed—especially if you've been sleeping on a flat, crappy futon—I turn off the light and listen to the noises of this house: a few creaks, the heater turning on, an occasional owl hooting outside. So very different from the constant rumble of cars on my old, busy street. It's all somehow both new and eminently familiar. Like I'm home.

I can't think of this as home, though, because it's temporary. I'm only employed until his ex-wife gets back.

Still, with my belly full, staring into the dark in this homey environment, I feel safe. I've been living in survival mode for so long. Now I have a stable food supply, housing, and a job that should last long enough for me to figure something else out.

I just hope I don't do something to fuck it up.

———

Nerves awaken me at dawn, and once I'm dressed, I help Addi get ready for school. Together, we choose an outfit. Then I fuss with her curly hair, consulting a YouTube tutorial for tips, and make her breakfast.

While she's sitting at the kitchen table drinking her orange juice, Luke appears. I ignore the sleek way his wet hair is combed and how he smells delicious. He's dressed for the office, even though he's working from home, in a slim-cut dress shirt and flat-front slacks.

His feet are bare, though, which feels way more intimate than I'm ready for.

"Daddy!" Addi holds out her arms, and he gives her a hug, dropping a kiss on the top of her head, which causes a weird sensation in the pit of my stomach.

Huh. I'm jealous. *Of a child.*

Stop it.

I beam. "Good morning!"

Yes, I'm a morning person. While I don't think he is, he turns his attention to me, and his eyes are kind as they roam all over my body, making my cheeks heat. He smiles back. "Thanks for getting Addi ready."

"You're welcome," I say cheerily. "Would you like some coffee? I made a pot."

He nods and grunts. Ah, we're back to Luke-speak. He sits down next to Addi to read the news on his tablet. At least I assume it's the news. Maybe it's webcomics.

I head to the coffee maker. "How do you take it?"

"Cream, two sugars."

That surprises me, because I figured he'd be all, "Black coffee gives you chest hair," but who am I to judge? Maybe he has some secret sweetness inside. He accepts the mug I offer him with a look I can't interpret. It isn't annoyance or impatience. I send Addi to go brush her teeth while I wash her breakfast dishes.

"If you want to ride along, I can show you where her school is," he says after he takes a sip. I'm noticing that he's reluctant to give me the reins, but I don't blame him for wanting to keep an eye on me. "Then you'll know the way. I added you to the list of authorized adults who can pick her up."

"Oh, I can take her. I know where it is." Addi told me all about her class yesterday, and I googled where her school was to be sure. I grab the lunch I made and put it next to her backpack.

He frowns and digs in his pocket, then hands me the key to the Range Rover. "Use my car." He gestures to where I parked. "I put you on my insurance. Used the info on your tax form."

"Excellent. Want me to get anything for you while I'm out?"

Luke pauses. "Actually, do you mind stopping at the grocery store? We could use some things." He stands and goes to his room, then returns with his wallet. "I'll get you a card, but here's some cash for now. Just stock up on whatever you like to eat." He gives me $200. As he hands it to me, a spark zings across my skin.

What *is* it about him? Why can't I be around him without wanting to climb him like an electrician on a light pole? Thankfully, I have some control and just say, "Happy to do it."

Addi and I drive to school, and I walk her to her classroom and introduce myself to her teacher. I proceed to the grocery store, where I have to force myself to make choices without looking at the prices. I'm so used to eating like a broke college kid at the end of the semester that putting fresh fruits and vegetables in the cart is a luxury. Being able to buy real, healthy food makes me again feel like I'm … coming home.

When I pass the floral aisle, a display of peach-colored dahlias makes me stop and stare. They're so beautiful.

I *have* to get them for the house.

Actually, I'm getting them for Luke, because everyone

deserves flowers. I'll tell him I'm teaching Addi how to arrange them. I use my credit card to buy them—like I buy everything these days—and separate the receipts so he can see I'm not squandering his money.

When I return, Luke's holed up in his office. I put away the groceries and, for now, stick the flowers in a vase I found. While I have a book to read for book club, I should do something that might generate some income. After tidying Addi's room, I spend part of the morning setting up my suite—basically putting away my clothes and books—and then take my laptop to the couch in the front room. There, I start working on a new card design while I enjoy looking at the leafy maples turning fall colors.

I'm so absorbed in my work that I don't realize it's past lunchtime until my stomach rumbles. I haven't heard a peep from Luke, so I decide to make a meal for the two of us. I heat up tomato soup and make toasted cheese sandwiches, then put together a tray with a plate, a mug of soup, and a spoon rolled into a napkin.

Luke looks up, eyes unfocused, when I knock on his office doorframe.

Every time, I swear, *every time* I see him, my attraction grows.

But I shut it down. "I made you some lunch, if you'd like." At his blank expression, I add, "You do eat lunch, don't you?"

"Yeah," he says, his voice hoarse. "Thanks."

I set everything down on his desk and step back.

He fingers the napkin. "Looks good," he says, then furrows his brows. "Is this what you've been doing?"

"After I went grocery shopping and put everything away, I worked on cards for a while."

"Cards? Like solitaire?"

I smile. "No, like greeting cards. That's my other job. I write freelance for a few different companies."

Genuine interest plays across his face. "How does that work?"

"I get paid for the submissions they accept. I'm lucky to get three figures for one. So I have to submit all the time."

Luke stares at me. "You must really have to hustle."

"I'm not that great at hustling, actually. Most of my time writing cards is spent staring into space. Hence why I needed this job."

He studies me with what I'm beginning to learn is his "Scott is amusing me" look.

I like his "Scott is amusing me" look.

It might be even better if he were doing it with my lips around his cock, but I can keep that thought to myself.

My boss is my boss.

My boss is almost assuredly straight.

Straighty straight straight straight.

Maybe if I repeat that to myself enough times, it will sink in.

And I want to touch him.

Oops. Dammit, Scott.

I excuse myself and go back to work.

A little while later, I pick Addi up from school and take her to Lost Acres Morgans. We have some time before her riding lesson starts, but not enough to go home, so we stop at a park for a snack and a break.

"How was school?" I ask.

She chatters about everything she did today while she eats sliced apples with peanut butter and drinks some juice. When she's finished, she asks to play on the swings, so I tell her she can do it for ten minutes until it's time to go.

Addi runs to the other kids, and I sit on a nearby bench. I check my phone and find a new text.

Dennis: *Even though your dad pushed you into this, I'd still like to meet if you want.*

I don't know how to answer. New Scott needs no man. But I don't want to be rude. And maybe Dennis could be a friend.

Or a hookup. Being around Luke has definitely led to some pent-up sexual energy. Maybe a nerdy professor is the way to release it.

Scott: *I'm working right now, but when I get a day off, do you want to do something?*
Dennis: *Yes, please.*
Scott: *Ok I'll let you know.*

A woman arrives with three children, one of whom is Addi's age and joins her on the swings.

"Your daughter is energetic," the woman says, sitting at the opposite end of the park bench.

"Oh, she's not my daughter. I'm the babysitter."

She gives me a reevaluating look. "Well, you seem to have everything under control," she says, like it's a surprise. "I'm sure you'll be a fantastic father when it's your turn."

I'm not ready to be a father anytime soon, especially given my financial status. Eventually, though, once I have my shit together, I'd love to be a dad.

I check my phone. "Time's up, Addi!" I call. "We need to go ride horses."

The woman looks at her enviously. "Riding lessons, too?"

"Lucky kid, right?"

"Most definitely."

I hold Addi's hand in mine, my backpack with the remnants of her snack in the other, and we load up to go to the stables.

Once there, Addi walks straight up to a man in jeans and boots. "Hi, Mr. Caden!"

"Hi, Addison. Are you ready to ride Lady today? Or do you want to ride Max for a change?"

"Lady, please."

"You got it." He takes her over to the tack room, and I follow. "I haven't seen you before," he says. "Are you Addison's father?"

"No, I'm the nanny. Scott Malone." I shake his hand.

"I'm sure we'll be seeing a lot of you, then. My brother Ty owns this place, but he's in Oklahoma for nationals. I'm filling in for her lessons."

Addi puts on her helmet and "helps" Caden saddle up a small black horse who seems practically a pony but is the perfect size for her. As I watch the joy on Addi's face when she makes her way around the ring, I wish Luke were here.

Because I'm not the only one who wants to be a good father someday.

8

LUKE

Scott and Addi burst into the house after her riding lesson, full of noise and energy and fresh air. Cheeks flushed, hair windblown, Addi leaves her riding boots in the hallway and deposits her helmet and other gear, then races off. Scott chases behind her, imploring her to clean up first—and actually succeeds with little fuss.

From where I'm sitting at the dining room table, I shake my head. I'd moved out here with my laptop because the house was quiet, but also because it makes me feel like I'm part of a family rather than hiding from one.

In Manhattan, my office and loft are sterile places where nothing lives except me. No plants, no animals. Just shiny surfaces with no fingerprints.

With these two, there's mess. Mess that gets cleaned up, thanks to Scott's competence, but mess just the same.

What's surprising is how the disorder is growing on me. I thought I'd be annoyed, but I'm more amused than anything else. The house cleaners will catch whatever we miss.

Addi wheels back into the dining room, her face noticeably cleaner. Scott follows and pours each of them a cup of water. She climbs up into my lap and wraps her arms around me.

That's another thing I'm not used to. Physical affection, even from a child. I lean into her, feeling her weight. "Hey, girl. How was riding?"

"So much fun! I got to ride Lady again, and she's my favorite. Can I get a horse, Daddy?"

I groan and catch Scott's eye.

He grins and shrugs, mouthing, *Not my idea.* And my god, he's stunning, his hair sticking up from the elements and his perfect nose still pink from the cold.

"No horses for now," I mumble. Even though I'd give her anything, and I think she knows it. "You'd have to take care of it."

"I could take care of it! Mr. Caden said I'm good at it." Addi hops off me and accepts the drink from Scott.

"You wore your helmet, right?"

"Yes," Scott assures me. "They followed safety protocols. She seems to know how to act around horses."

"Good." I'm sure Kira checked the place out before signing Addi up there, but something about being here makes me hyper-protective.

"Need anything?" he asks. When I shake my head, he goes down the hall to Addi's room, and I can't help watching his tight ass as he moves.

Fuck.

I can't think about him that way. I shouldn't.

I'm going to ignore these thoughts about him. I'm not going to let myself give in to this attraction.

Brain can override heart. And I don't even know if it's my heart talking or my dick. Probably the latter, and that can just shut the fuck up. It can only get me in trouble.

Still, it's been a while, and my sex drive is raring to go. I'm going to have to have Scott babysit Addi while I go out.

I don't know why the idea of a quick fuck isn't as appealing as it normally would be.

Still, I have to do something.

Tugging out my phone, I re-download a hookup app and sign in. Might as well get back on the market.

I sigh, gather up my things, and take my work to my office.

Later on, when I come out to see what Addi and Scott are up to, I find them in the living room. Scott's wearing a red cape, clearly draped on him by Addi, since it hangs unevenly. He's sporting a tricorne and holding a foam sword in a Puss in Boots swashbuckling pose, and he looks even more ridiculous because she's also given him a huge pair of fake sunglasses.

Addi is studying him intensely, as if critiquing his technique. "No, Scott. You need this, too," she says, handing him a shield.

He holds it upside down, and I can see him grin and try not to laugh. "Do I have it right yet?"

She heaves a put-upon sigh. "No."

Scott grins and turns the shield around, then adopts a different stance. "Like this?"

Addi nods. "Yes." She sits down in front of him with a crayon and a piece of paper and begins drawing something.

I clear my throat, and they both jump. "Hey, guys. What are you doing?"

"I'm the artist, and Scott is my model," Addi says.

Scott explains, "We were watching an episode of *The Muppet Show* where Miss Piggy was posing for her portrait. It gave Addi some ideas."

"Ah. Gotcha." I make myself comfortable on the recliner. "Can I watch?"

"Yes, Daddy," she says.

As I study them, Addi makes a big production out of drawing Scott, although as far as I can tell, he has really long straight legs, a box for a body, and a huge head. A triangle is off to the side, which I suppose is the cape.

Modigliani, eat your heart out.

But while I should be fascinated by my daughter's focus on her art project, I'm more fascinated by Scott and the way he takes her so seriously.

I remember, as a kid, wanting to be taken seriously. Wanting an adult to listen to me.

I can see her learning how to be an artist. How to order someone around—er, I mean communicate effectively. How to have a vision and watch how it manifests in real life.

That's pretty deep, Luke. Maybe she's just being a kid and you don't need to make everything such a huge deal.

As I watch Scott, I realize he hasn't moved a muscle, even though the pose isn't natural or easy. How many adults actually do what a kid wants them to do? It must feel like he's given her some power.

I like that.

Seems as if everything is fine here. I excuse myself to return to my office and immerse myself in my laptop.

When I come up for air—the house again smelling delicious from whatever Scott has in the oven—I walk into the kitchen, where Scott and Addi are doing something with flowers. "Hi, Daddy!" she says, doing a telltale dance.

"Go to the bathroom," I order.

Scott hides a smirk. "Remember to wash your hands."

She trots off, leaving me and Scott alone.

I eye the thing he's working on. It's pretty, but … "Flower arranging?" My tone says, *Really?*

"Yeah! I follow this guy on TikTok who makes the most amazing arrangements. I wanted to try one. It's important to know the fundamentals."

I'm learning that Scott can't help being enthusiastic. I envy his energy. So of course I respond by locking down my interest.

Besides, he's wrong. I raise my eyebrows.

"What?" he asks.

"Flowers do nothing but die. There's no point to them," I grumble.

He frowns. "There's always a point. Just because something is decorative doesn't mean it doesn't have value."

I shake my head. Now that I've dug my grave, I have to lie in it. "Things have to prove their use."

"They do? Do people have to, too?"

Yes. "No." I sound sullen, even to my own ears.

"If you love someone, don't you want to make them smile?" Scott's expression is somewhere between curious and hurt.

I put my hands on my hips. "If I were in love with someone, I wouldn't be all *staring into their eyes* or wanting to clink champagne glasses. I'd just want to, you know, be with them."

Not that I've been in love with someone since Kira. And look how that turned out.

"But wouldn't you want to make them feel special?"

"Sure. But why does that have to mean doing all that cheesy stuff? Why can't it just be, 'We like each other, let's fuck'? Sorry," I add hastily. "I didn't mean to be crass."

He blinks at me. "It's okay. I like fucking. But sex and romance are different things. Sex is easy. Romance is hard."

I shouldn't be having this conversation with him. It's going into dangerous territory. But I can't help but ask, "Why do you say that?" Even though I know my answer, I want to know his.

He peers down the hall to make sure Addi isn't returning yet and lowers his voice. "Sex is *passion*: I want to take your clothes off and rub our bodies together." Fuck, some part of me wishes he was saying that as an offer, not as explanation. "Romance is doing something nice for the other person, something that goes above and beyond what's necessary." He blushes. "I've had plenty of quick-and-dirty hookups. But what I really want …"

"What?" I prompt, not knowing why. Knowing I'll regret asking. Knowing my phone has already started receiving hookup notifications.

"I guess I want to be cherished."

We stare at each other, and the space between us feels charged. He deserves to be cherished. He's a nice guy.

But I'm not romantic. Kira would be the first one to point that out. And it's not like he's talking about me, anyway. "I hope you find someone to cherish you, then," I murmur.

"Me, too." Then he lets out a long breath. "I dunno if it's ever going to happen. It seems like I want something that only exists on the movie screen or in a book. I want my partner to do his part. I'm the one who always does the big thing. For once, I want to be taken care of. Is that too much to ask?"

"You sound like my mom," I blurt. Where did that come from?

He tilts his head. "How so?"

"I don't think my dad has ever loved her the way she wanted him to."

I don't think I ever loved Kira the way she wanted to be loved.

"See?" he says excitedly. "That's the thing. We want to be loved a certain way. And finding someone who will do it the way we want is hard. Or impossible. That's probably why most advice is to love yourself first."

"Yeah." I snort. "I do that."

"I didn't mean with your hand." He gasps. "Sorry. I wish I hadn't said that."

I wish he hadn't said it, too. Because now I'm imagining him naked with his hand on his hard cock, and that mental image will not make it easier to live with him.

He opens his mouth to say something and then shuts it again, and I'm grateful for the discretion on his part. Because I'm not usually this way—talking about feelings and shit.

But something is making me want true love for him, even if I can't have it.

Scott's studying me. I shouldn't encourage him, because I can't get too close. When I get close, bad things happen. I have to remember that he's an employee. I've hired him to take care of my kid. Not to be my friend or confidant.

I need to stay in my lane and keep him in his. If we do that, all will be fine.

One of these evenings, I'm really going to have to pick up someone to fuck before I get even more insufferable. It's too lonely otherwise.

Addi skips back into the room, dragging me from my thoughts. "Daddy, look!" She grabs at the vase to show me what she and Scott made—even though I've had plenty of time to see it already. As she picks it up, it tilts and falls over, sloshing flowers and water all over Scott.

But of course he doesn't get mad, because that's not the kind of guy he is.

Before I can fully register the way his soaked shirt nestles into the ridges and valleys of his chest, he sets the vase and the flowers gently on the counter and checks on Addi, wiping away her tears.

"Sorry," she says, her lips trembling.

He bends down to her height. "It's fine. No worries. We can arrange them again." Then he unbuttons his shirt and takes it off.

So he's standing before me bare chested, with his hair slightly mussed.

And I'm sure my eyes bulge. Because what was hinted at before is now on full display.

Scott isn't a bodybuilder. He's long and lean, with what seems to be natural definition in his abs. While I can appreciate all different kinds of bodies, there's something about the fact that he's almost as tall as me but not as built. Like we're evenly matched, but I'm going to dominate him.

Wait. No.

No one is dominating anyone. He's my daughter's nanny.

"I'll go get a dry shirt."

She nods, and he hurries off to his room.

I watch him go. Again. Because he's fucking hot.

SCOTT

It didn't even take a week of living with Luke and Addi for me to settle into an easy routine.

I drive her to and from school and riding lessons and keep her occupied while Luke works in his home office. He then emerges and focuses on her while I cook dinner.

Can I say I appreciate how he gives her his undivided attention? I mean, it's *undivided*. If he didn't have me, maybe he'd be checking his phone for emails. I like to believe I give them more time together, since I take the pressure off him and allow him to work without distraction.

Can I also say, as a not-only child, I wish I'd been so lucky as to have either of my parents' focus like that? Maybe that's why my dad's the way he is—he's trying to give me the attention I didn't get back then. Better late than never, I guess.

Speaking of my dad's efforts, Dennis texted again, but I told him I was still busy rather than making any plans. Because new Scott isn't falling in love, I remind myself.

And besides, no version of Scott is interested in any Dennis when there's a Luke in the house. Even if said Luke is just for looking at.

Each night when we tuck Addi into bed, there's a while when

the house is quiet. I've been staking a claim to a portion of the couch in the living room to read or futz on my laptop while Luke hunkers down again in his office to do whatever it is investment bankers do at night—play *FreeCell* or finance small countries.

Tonight, I have my book club read in one hand—I'm almost done with it—and my phone in the other, when the group chat pings.

> **Murph**: *Check in, chickadee. We haven't heard you chirp in dayssss.*
> **Murph**: *That's YOU, Scott. You're the chickadee. How's your new job? You still thinking hotsexyboss is straight?*
> **Scott**: *Of course*
> **Murph**: *Gossip around V&V says you're wrong.*
> **Scott**: *WUT?*
> **Murph**: *Apparently Lucas Lagomarsino was one of the first openly bi students in high school here*

My jaw drops.

> **Scott**: *Luke is bi?*

No.
But. I did think he was looking at me …
Shit.
All my assumptions about him were just that. Assumptions. If Murph's gossip is right, that is. I check my phone again.

> **Jeremy**: *<Cheerleading GIF>*
> **Jeremy**: *Yay!*
> **Murph**: *This is so much fun!*

I groan.

> **Scott**: *No, it's not. It's problematic.*

Jeremy: *I barely read and even I've read enough gay romances to know that while they shouldn't, sometimes the boss and employee get together. Or in real life. *Cough* Emmett and Tai *cough**
Scott: *I'm so fucked.*
Jeremy: *Reeaaaally? I'm intrigued.*
Scott: *WAIT. NO. I'm NOT fucked, and that's the problem. I don't want to be. I mean, I do. But I can't.*
Scott: *You know what? Never mind.*
Scott: *I plead the fifth.*
Jeremy: *<Arrow GIF pointing up>*
Jeremy: *Like we'd let you get away with saying that*
Jeremy: *Murph, it's as if he doesn't know us*
Murph: *Right?*
Scott: *FINE. He's hot and I like him and this opens up possibilities, but I don't want to lose my job. I have very important reasons to keep my job. Like, I want to pay off debt and I don't want to be homeless.*
Murph: *And you won't pay off debt or have a home if you get nekkid with him?*
Scott: *I can't afford to jeopardize it.*
Jeremy: *Pretty sure you could figure out how to accomplish all of your goals—financially stable AND sexually satisfied*
Jeremy: *<Cheesy motivational speaker GIF>*
Jeremy: *<You can do it GIF>*
Jeremy: *<Salt bae GIF>*
Scott: *You guys are incorrigible. Yeah, no. I'm not getting together with my boss.*
Jeremy: *Your loss.*
Murph: *I think we need Operation Get Scott a Kiss From His Boss*
Jeremy: *Ooh. YES.*
Scott: *Bye now.*

My friends mean well, but I toss the phone down on the coffee table and glide into the kitchen to distract myself from this conversation, because it was very, very unsettling. Once I've made myself a cup of tea, I curl up on the couch and tuck a blanket around me.

Looking around, I take in how the living area is so charming and open. If I could've dreamed up a Vermont farmhouse, it would look a lot like this, and I'm going to enjoy it for as long as I can.

As I sip and read, my ears can't help perking up whenever I hear Luke's chair squeak. It's become a soothing noise, part of the symphony of the house.

I mustn't pay attention to him, though, so I focus on my book.

I'm not sure how much time goes by before I hear a chuckle and feel his presence. It's good to hear Luke laugh. Tilting my head, I come up for air. Like I do when I'm really absorbed in a book, which I am with this one. Just another page—

"What?" I ask, trying not to sound defensive.

He taps the cover of my book. "You're reading *The Stripper Club*?"

I set it down and cross my arms over my chest. "It's for book club. The series is about a group of male entertainers and how they all find true love. This is the first one." I look up and see his handsome face, knowing that he could very well be into men.

This is very bad.

"What kind of book club reads something like that?" he asks.

"The good kind."

That brings out a full-on smile. "I shoulda figured you'd read romance." Then he does this aborted eye-roll maneuver. Not quite a full eye roll, but it includes a head shake. "Flowers. Greeting cards."

So it's this again. I can't let him get away with dissing everything I love. I sit up. "What's wrong with romance?"

"Nothing. It's big business. Fabio sold how many books?"

I wave my hand. "Oh, honey, he's from decades ago. You have a lot to learn. Romance isn't just about the cover—although there are some delicious ones. Romance is about the feelings." I study him. "Have you ever read a romance?"

Luke stops hovering and sits down next to me, slightly closer than usual. Not that I notice. "No."

"Then you have no basis on which to comment," I decree, like it's a royal pronouncement. I set down the book and look at him squarely. "Do books have no purpose, either?"

"Books have a purpose."

I raise one eyebrow. "And that is?"

"They tell you about the human condition."

I smile at him and tap his knee. "Precisely." Then I shake my head like I'm disappointed. "You know, Luke, you really shouldn't prejudge things."

"It's not a judgment."

"It absolutely is." I grin evilly. "I dare you—"

"To read the book?"

"And show up to book club to talk about it."

Luke rolls his eyes fully now. "I don't have the time."

"Yes, you do. You have a nanny. You can make the time." Raising my eyebrows, I ask, "Or are you scared?"

I know that's a low blow, but I'm gonna take it.

"What the hell would I be scared of?"

"That you might like it."

"Not going to happen. But if it means that much to you, I'll read it. And we'll get a sitter for Addison so we can both go to the meeting."

"If you hang on for just a moment more, I'll let you borrow this copy. I have literally one more page. But you have to promise me you'll keep an open mind."

He stares at me for a long moment. "Yeah, okay. I promise."

"Just to be clear, it's a gay romance. Are you okay with that?"

"Why would that matter? It's the romance I have a problem with, not the gay."

"Okay, good. Well, I hope you don't end up having a problem with the romance, either." I take a deep breath. I want him to confirm what Murph said, but I don't know how to ask it with any finesse. So I might as well just do it. "I initially thought you might not want to read a gay romance because you were straight, but now I heard a rumor that you ... aren't."

He startles. "Where did you get the idea I was straight? I told you there was no homophobia in this house."

"I thought you were open-minded, not queer yourself."

Luke shrugs. "I'm bisexual. It's never been a secret. I dated widely until I met Kira. I was always faithful to her, but after ..." He sighs. "Basically, there have only been guys in New York."

"Okay," I squeak. Because how do you respond to that?

"Sorry," he says. "TMI."

Far from it. It's not enough information. Because now I have all the questions.

On the Kinsey scale, how far to one side or the other are you?

What is your type?

Am I your type?

Because he's *my* type, all growly and classically handsome. But I believe he has this melted chocolate core inside him, otherwise he wouldn't treat his daughter the way he does. He wouldn't be giving my book a try no matter how much he protests.

"It's okay," I say. "I'm good with talking about sex. I like it. Sex, I mean. I mean *talking about* it." My cheeks burn, and I don't think I imagine the flash of heat in his eyes.

"When did you realize you were gay?" he asks.

"I was thirteen. There's only so far an obsession with Josh Hutcherson in *The Hunger Games* will get you before you realize it's for more than the plot."

He chuckles. "Yeah, I liked that one, too. Even though it was such a disturbing concept."

"Well, after I figured my preferences out, I was all tied up in knots, wanting to come out to my parents. I didn't want to talk about it, but I also felt like if I didn't tell them, something was incomplete. Like I wasn't being my full self. So one evening, while doing the dishes, I blurted it out to my mom."

"What did she say?"

"'What?'"

"What did she say?" he asks again.

"She said, 'What?' because in my nervousness, I was apparently incomprehensible and mushed all the words into one. So, I repeated myself and said, more slowly, 'Mom, I'm gay.' Then I burst into tears."

Luke looks sympathetic, and it makes me want to curl up closer to him. I don't, of course. "How did she respond?"

"She said she figured as much and told me she loved me."

He grins. Then his face falls.

"Have you told your parents?" I ask.

"No. I didn't think it was any of their business." He sighs. "They might have guessed. I don't know. I figured the way I'd confirm it was to bring a guy home with me. I think it would be okay. They're pretty open-minded. I just haven't felt the need to talk about my sex life with them. I figure they know I had sex once, since I have a kid. Beyond that, I don't really want to confirm or deny anything. We're not that close. They live in Boston now. They fought for most of my childhood, so I stay away because that hasn't changed. I don't hide from them, but I don't share things, either." He grunts. "Sorry. We got way off topic, and I shouldn't be talking about sex with you."

Please, please, please talk about sex with me. With or without romance.

Trying to play it off, I shrug. "I don't mind, but we can change the subject. So, what do you do with Addi for fun around here?"

Luke frowns.

I almost start laughing. "You don't even know, do you?" I sober quickly at his glare. "I'm sorry. I shouldn't tease you. But there is this thing called 'fun.' People like it. Especially children. It can involve such foolish things as going to a park, or buying ice cream, or"—I fake gasp—"watching a movie. It's a way you can spend time with people who like you." People like me.

While his impenetrable gaze doesn't lessen, I imagine there's a tiny quirk at the corner of his mouth. Like, a millimeter. Maybe less.

"Isn't it your job to take her places?" he finally says.

I blink, taken aback. Because yes, it is. But I thought he wanted to be an involved parent and that I was just here to give him an extra hand.

Maybe I read the situation all wrong.

"Yes, it is," I mutter. I look at my phone. "It's time for bed. Good night."

I pick up my book, and again, I feel his eyes on me as I leave.

———

A few minutes later, I've put on my pajamas and flopped down in bed to read the last page of my book. I'm distracted, though, because in place of one of the heroes, I'm now picturing Luke with another guy. His hot, sexy body wrapped around someone else's. And that someone else looks like me. Oops.

I kind of assume he'd be a top—or at least *on* top—but I suppose I shouldn't be stereotyping. After all, I thought he was straight.

But now that he's confirmed he isn't, my mind is going on a trip to a very sexy place.

The mental vacation, though, is not smart. I have issues with being focused anyway, and now I know he might actually be attainable—in the *he likes men* sense, that is, not in the *attainable for someone like me* sense.

He's so out of my league it isn't funny.

I'm going to get past this little infatuation I have with him. While there's attraction, I don't have to act on it. That's the way I need to play this.

And if my heart is squashed? Story of my life.

I can't help smiling. Okay, so I'm a drama queen. Who isn't? Especially when life hasn't been all that I've hoped it would be.

When I finish my book, I remember I said he could borrow it, and I should hold him to his agreement to read it. I slide out of bed and slip into the hallway, hoping to catch him before he goes to sleep.

The door to his room is open a crack. I knock on it, pushing it open farther, and say, "Hey, Luke?"

Then I freeze.

Luke is reclining on his bed, shirtless, looking at something on his phone. And shirtless Luke is a thing of beauty. He'd inspire an entire line of greeting cards, I'm sure. For that time when you just want to give someone a present: here's *Luke*.

I can't look away from his ripped physique, light dusting of chest hair, and sculpted arms. He even has a tattoo peeking out on his hip, accentuating the line of his V-cut. Fuck, that's yummy.

I have a tattoo on the opposite hip, but I can't tell what his is.

I'm so busy inspecting his body that I don't notice his face. Which is—*wait*—blushing. He's got nothing to blush about.

Unless …

Did he have his hand down his pants?

He did. He's hard. Those soft pants don't hide a damned thing, and I like what I see.

Oh dear. Now I can't seem to take my eyes off the front of his pants.

I gulp. "Sorry. I didn't mean to bother you. Or interrupt. Sorry, sorry. I just meant to give you this." I set the book down on the closest piece of furniture, a chair by the door. "I finished, and now I'll let you … finish."

Luke just stares at me. I half expect him to yell at me, except I've never heard him raise his voice. I don't think he has a temper. Or, rather, I think he keeps everything inside.

I have a feeling that who he is inside is someone I'd like to know. If he'd ever show me.

He clears his throat as if to say something, but my mouth gets away from me and I start chattering. "Were you watching porn? You don't have to answer that. There's no right answer, really. Because if you say no, you're probably lying. Unless you were getting hard to AccuWeather, in which case, go you. If you say yes, you're admitting to watching porn. Which I don't have a problem with by any means. I watch my fair share. But I don't think that's something we talk about in polite company—"

"No, Scott," he finally says, in his deep voice, and he gets the "Scott is amusing me" look on his face again. "It isn't."

"Don't be embarrassed." I can't stop babbling. "You're the sexiest thing I've seen in a long time. At least since I went to see Chippendales."

"Chippendales? Isn't that an eighties thing?"

"Just because it's eighties doesn't mean it's not sexy." My body is reacting to him, and we can't do this. "And, um, you're sexy. Oh, fuck, I said that out loud. I'll just leave you to it."

I turn and flee.

LUKE

Was it porn?

Yes. I was searching for porn on my phone, because I could only talk with Scott so long before my thoughts drifted—as they have been more and more—to him.

Specifically, him on his knees. Him under me. Him on top of me. Me going down on him. As we were talking, I pictured some very interesting scenarios.

Shit.

Normally, my sexual fantasies are generic. They're me with … someone. *Anyone*.

But now I keep thinking about Scott Malone, and it's not just tonight. It's been building since I met him.

I can't get my work done, which is ironic since I hired him so I could work uninterrupted. And I don't really want to go find a hookup, even though I have a live-in babysitter.

While he stood there talking about porn and strippers, I was half a second away from tugging him in here and locking the door behind him. Cooler minds prevailed.

Correction: he left.

A small voice in my head says that he was looking at me as if he wanted to devour me. And that I want to do it right back to him, even if it's wrong.

Now I don't know what to do. I think I need to apologize, although I'm not sure what for. *He* walked in on *me*. But I don't want things to be awkward between us, and getting caught with my hand down my pants is highly unprofessional.

I take off down the hall after him.

When I get to his room, it's the reverse of what just happened: he's looking at his phone and pacing, while I'm in the doorway watching him.

He's so fucking *cute*. Something about his smile and his cheerful eyes makes me ... happy. And he's also hot AF, with a tight ass I want to—

I clear my throat, and he turns toward me with a start.

Now that I have his attention, though, I don't know what to say. I couldn't just let him think I'm some kind of perv. I don't believe healthy sexual appetites are perverted, of course, but I also don't think I should display my erection to someone who may not want to see it. Someone who works for me, who might not even have another place to stay if he left.

"Hey," I say, realizing I'm still shirtless.

"Yeah?" He reddens. "I mean, yes, Luke, can I help you?"

"I didn't," I start, and rub my hand over my face. "Look. I'm sorry for what you walked in on. I don't want to make you uncomfortable."

"Uncomfortable?" He drops his phone on the dresser and takes a step toward me. As I take him in, I realize he's hard. Which brings my erection surging back.

"I'm mindful you're my employee, and I want to treat you right. The last thing I intended was for you to walk in on me like, uh, that."

He looks away and mutters something.

"What did you say?"

Scott locks eyes on me. "I said, I only wish."

I blink at him and tilt my head. "Do you mean that?"

He takes another step closer. "Yep." And another. "You're hot as hell."

I swallow, not knowing what to say.

His face falls, so I hurry to say, "Hold it, I'm attracted to you, too." There. I said it. "And if that makes you feel like you can't—*oomph*."

The oomph comes from Scott throwing himself into my arms and landing on my lips.

I kiss him back hard, gripping his face with both of my hands, and *oh god, he feels good*. I love how he smells like just-folded laundry. I love how matched he is with me, height-wise. As I suspected, we're eye to eye. Or in this case, mouth to mouth.

Scott tastes like toothpaste, his tongue hot against mine. He makes a low moan in the back of his throat, which just does it for me. I love how into this he is, and I can't stop kissing him.

We should talk, but instead, I find myself making out in a way I haven't done since I was a teenager.

His chest bumps against mine, and he pushes me toward the door, but I push him back, and we somehow break apart and eye each other, panting.

"There are so many reasons why this is a bad idea," Scott murmurs, kissing along my neck, mouthing my skin, making me feel *everything*.

I let out a loud groan. "*Fuck*. Agreed." Now it's my turn to capture his lips, and he struggles against me. "There's something here. Between us, I mean. Isn't there?"

"Yeah," he says, his voice quiet. I suck on his neck, and he whispers a quiet, "Fuck."

All I want is to get him naked. I like having my hands on him, and I like the way he's starting to explore my body.

I like being touched.

But this would be more than a hookup, because I like *him*. And we'd have to be very discreet, with a child in the house.

"We should—" I start.

His hands go to my waistband, and one slips under it. He's

tugging it down, about to touch my bare ass, when Addi cries out, the noise muffled but unmistakable.

We freeze, wrapped in each other's arms, and eye one another with extreme concern.

Shit.

"Shit," I say, and I step back and hastily straighten my pants, then run my hands through my hair. Scott looks equally mussed, his lips swollen and his hair a riot around his face.

But we don't take more than two seconds before we're racing down the hall.

In the short time it takes us to get to the other end of the house, all erotic thoughts have fled, and I'm scared shitless something's happened to my kid, although I do have the presence of mind to hope it's just a nightmare.

A very badly timed nightmare.

I beat Scott to Addi's room, but he's hot on my heels. I fling the door open and turn on the light.

She's sitting up in bed, wailing, tears rolling down her face. I careen into the room and sit down next to her, putting an arm around her. "Hey," I say. "Hey, baby. What is it, pumpkin?"

"I want Momma!" she sobs into my side.

My heart sinks to the floor. "I know." I use my best soothing voice. And I try the parenting thing I read in a book about validating what she says by repeating it. "I know. You want Momma."

Instead of calming, though, her sobs turn into shrieks. "I want Momma!"

Her screams increase in volume and frequency until they're at a decibel level that might summon the police.

"Pumpkin, you have to calm down. I know it's scary."

There's a light knock on the doorjamb. I'd been so focused on Addi, I forgot about Scott, but by the look on his face, he's been debating whether or not to get involved. "May I?" he asks.

"Yeah," I say, making a gesture like, be my guest.

My heart is breaking for my daughter, and I don't know how to help her.

But Scott does. He picks her up and sits down, pulling her into his lap, wrapping her up in his arms.

"When my siblings got like this," he says in a quiet voice I can somehow hear over her crying, "it's like their brain would shut off and they'd stay in a cycle."

She's screaming into his ear, but he doesn't flinch. He just holds her tighter, and eventually her sobs start to dissipate.

I feel completely incompetent.

And jealous of my own employee. That's rich.

"We can try calling Momma," I say. "With the time difference, she should be up. Want to video call her?"

Addi nods and sniffles.

"One second," I say, and take off to get my phone. While I'm in my room, I call Kira, hoping she's available. Thankfully, she answers right away.

"Hey," she says. "Where's your shirt? You look a mess."

"Thanks," I bite out. I blow out a breath.

"What's wrong?"

"Addi's really upset. Can she talk with you?"

Kira's face falls. "My poor sweet girl. Of course."

We've done this every few days since she left, but apparently not often enough.

I return and hold the phone out. Addison, still on Scott's lap, takes it greedily. "Momma!" I take a seat next to Scott.

I can see Kira's interest, because she knows who I hired but hadn't talked with him yet. Still, she focuses on our daughter. "Hey, baby girl! It's so good to see your face!"

"Momma!"

As Kira talks, Addi listens, rapt, and the tension begins to ebb from her body.

After a while, Kira's curiosity gets the better of her. "And who is that with you and Daddy?"

"That's Scott."

"Hi, Kira," he says. "I'm the nanny. Nice to meet you."

"I've heard all about you," she says.

Lies. I told Kira about his background, and she gave her blessing. Then, when she tried to tease me about the *he* part, I shut her down.

Now, though, she's not going to let me be. Because she has eyes and can see he's entirely my type.

Finally, after talking for about fifteen minutes, Kira runs out of topics to distract Addi, but just being there has helped.

Scott has helped, too, holding Addi tight.

We promise to let Addi call again tomorrow. We hang up and tuck her back into bed. Scott smooths her hair, and I kiss her forehead, and we turn off the light, closing the door behind us for the second time tonight.

In the hallway, he and I look at each other until he turns his gaze to the ground.

"I think I should go to bed," he says.

And while I want to join him—even just to talk—I don't think I should. I think about how badly that could've gone if Addi had walked in on us. "Um," I say, but he holds up his hand.

"We don't have to talk about it. We can forget it ever happened."

I nod, because he's right.

Although I don't want to forget about it.

In the morning, Scott acts like nothing happened, which is exactly the way it should be.

Right?

Exactly.

Except I find myself tracking his every movement, even more than I did when he first got here—and not because I'm worried about him being alone with Addi, which was my excuse at the beginning. I trust him. He earned that trust quickly, and he takes better care of her than I do.

He's now under my scrutiny because …

Because I like to look at him.

And I start imagining what would've happened if we hadn't been interrupted.

I don't know if getting together with Scott would be a mistake or not.

The part of me that thinks it would be a mistake is the part that's normally in control of my life. The part that doesn't let anyone in. The part that doesn't want to have anything to do with people, because I've learned the other shoe will eventually drop. The part that expects to be hurt, so I leave first or don't even let things begin.

But the part of me that doesn't think it would be a mistake is growing stronger. It's a part that thinks I deserve to feel good and to have nice things, not merely a few minutes of release with someone I only know by their app profile. That I deserve to have someone just for me, who would support me and be in my corner.

I'm starting to hope Scott could be that person. I feel like he understands me, and he doesn't seem to mind my bullshit—he sees right past it. It's like he's Teflon-coated.

I don't think I'm the right guy for him, though. He's a hopeless romantic and I'm … not.

So the two parts of me are at war. When I'm with him, everything seems right, the way it's meant to be.

But when we're apart, I'm plagued by these doubts. Maybe they're old habits. They're certainly annoying.

The doubts win, though. For the next two weeks, he doesn't bring up our kiss, and neither do I. But I can't deny that on some level I want to do it again.

And more.

"Now it's your turn," Addi says.

I don't think they know I'm watching. Scott is sitting on the floor, a kitchen towel draped around his neck like a bib, and Addi's playing barber. She's using her fingers to pretend to cut his hair.

A few weeks of Scott being here, and it's like we never lived without him. Even on his days off, he tends to stick around and help, although I try to remind him he doesn't have to. I couldn't mistake the look of joy on his face when I paid him the first time, though.

I wonder how close to the edge he was living?

He raises his hand and pretends it's a mirror. "Can you take some more off the sides? I like it shorter."

"Yes, sir. We can do that for you."

I suppress a smile. She always seems so serious when she plays. I guess play is serious business. And she seems to always be trying out some new career—restaurateur, artist, hairstylist.

But what warms my heart even more is how into it Scott is. Even when he thinks I'm not looking. He genuinely seems to care about my kid.

Time is our most precious commodity. He chooses to spend it with her.

A chain around my heart begins to loosen. It's creaky. But it loosens.

"Want to read a book?" he asks, once they've exhausted the hairstyling options.

"Yes!" She runs and comes back with a picture book about hot-air balloons that I swear we've read to her a hundred times.

Make it a hundred and one, I guess. She's as into this book as she is into the movie *Up*. Maybe she's going to be an explorer.

"Once upon a time," he begins to read, and she settles into his lap.

I get this pang in my chest. Because he looks *right* with her, like he could be her daddy.

I'm her daddy. I want to interrupt and take her onto my lap. But this is what I hired him to do.

Maybe I can just let her enjoy the simple pleasure of being read to.

"Have you ever been up in a hot-air balloon?" she asks Scott.

"Never. Have you?"

"Nope." Addi looks up and sees me. "Can we go sometime, Daddy? In the air with all the balloons?"

"Not a bunch of little ones like in *Up*," Scott says. "Just one big one."

"Yes. I got that." I hide my smile. "I don't know. How dangerous is it?"

"I'm pretty sure balloon accidents are rare. And it would be so beautiful. I believe they run year-round, weather permitting."

The leaves have been changing, but there's plenty of fall color this time of October.

"Maybe. Do some research on it." I can't believe I'm considering this.

I'd give my daughter anything, though. Even if that means letting her be with someone who's a better parent than me.

I don't like the idea of letting her do something risky, but I'm not sure I have it in me to say no if she has her heart set on it. I growl and head back to my office.

11

SCOTT

As an avid hiker, I've spent plenty of time in the hushed quiet of a forest. It's a good place for me to process my thoughts and get some exercise at the same time.

But not with a six-year-old. Between Addi's questions and her short legs, we've gone approximately a quarter mile from where we parked the car at the Maple Falls ranger station, which is essentially no exercise for me.

Worse, my thoughts are not at all processed. When I'm not answering her questions, I have a running commentary in my head that goes:

I kissed your dad, and I can't stop thinking about it.

Shit, I shouldn't think of him as *your dad.*

I made out with Luke.

He's the sexiest person I've ever seen in real life.

He turns me on like no other person I've ever met.

I don't know how I'm going to keep living with him when I can't touch him.

"What's this?" Addi asks, pulling me from reliving the most glorious kiss of my existence for the seven thousandth time. She's pointing to a yellowish mushroom growing out of a tree trunk in fan shapes, one on top of another.

"That's a condominium for fairies," I say.

She smiles. "Really?" She reaches out a hand, but I gently pull it back.

"You mustn't touch mushrooms. I don't know if this one is poisonous or not. Probably not, but we can't be too careful." I press my lips together. "You really like being out in nature, don't you?"

"Uh-huh!"

"Then let me see if I can get a friend to give you some lessons about what to do when you're in the woods. Would you like that?"

She nods.

Jax, Tanner's husband, is in some line of outdoor work. I bet we could arrange for him to teach Addi outdoor skills, because she could do with some proper safety education.

We take off down the path, bundled up against the increasing cold. In parts of the wood, all the leaves have dropped, so you can tell that winter is thinking about coming to visit. As we go, I start telling her everything I know about hiking—mostly so I can stop thinking about her dad. "If you get lost, the most important thing is to stay still. If you hug a tree and stay put, people can find you. If you keep moving, you might miss them."

"But what if a bear comes?"

"I don't think there are any bears in these woods. If it's not safe to stay still, though, then yes, you can move."

We spend much of the hike studying the trail markers, and I teach her how to tell which way is north by where the moss grows on the trees, along with some other basic safety lessons. "Don't get too close to the edge on these steep parts. It's best to hug the hill. And never go out by yourself," I say. "But it's good for you to have more knowledge. Want to get a book on it?"

"Yes, please!"

The trail we're on is a short loop with a spur off to the water-fall, and soon enough we're back at the car—Luke's car, because he won't let me drive her in mine. (And I don't blame him.)

I text Luke that we're going to the library, and the only response I get is a thumbs-up.

Over the past few weeks, our communications have dwindled to the essential. It's making me itchy, because I'm chatty and I want to talk with him. Not about our kiss. It's clear he wants to forget that ever happened.

But just because I want to get to know him better.

"What do you want to be for Halloween?" I ask Addi as we head up the porch at home, laden with books on wilderness safety and fairy stories. Funny how fast this farmhouse has become home to me.

"A cat," she says.

We step inside and shed our coats and boots. "I was expecting you to say some sort of woodland creature."

"Cats can live in the woods."

I raise my eyebrows. "I'm not going to argue with that logic."

"What's this about cats living in the woods?" Luke walks into the room, shoving his hands into his pockets. God, he looks good in a light blue dress shirt, navy slacks, and charcoal socks. He gives Addi a warm smile and bends down to accept her hug. Every time he does that, a lump forms in my throat.

"Your daughter and I were discussing what costume she wanted for Halloween, and she was suggesting a cat. Thoughts?"

"Do whatever you want," he says.

"I want to be a cat," she confirms.

"We can make that happen." I look hastily to Luke. "Unless you want to be in charge?"

"Go ahead. You'd be good at it. What do we need to buy, Addi?"

She puts her finger on her chin like she's thinking hard, and it's charming. Finally, she says, "Can we get me a tail?"

"I think we could find one in a set that also has cat ears on a headband," I say. "Then we could paint whiskers on you. What do you think about that?"

"Yes, that's what I want."

"Should we get you a leotard? Or maybe you wear leggings and a shirt. What color cat do you want to be?"

"Black."

"Then you could wear all black with your whiskers and your tail and your ears."

"What are you going to be for Halloween, Daddy?" she asks Luke.

I don't miss the flicker of a smile at the edges of his mouth. "Your father."

Addi stamps her little foot. "That's not make-believe."

"Some days it feels like it," he mutters.

"What about you?" she asks me.

"Hmm," I say. "I haven't thought about it. What do you suggest?"

"You should be a cat, too. Only you're a daddy cat."

Luke snorts.

I've been a cat burglar before. So I might as well join her.

"Okay, we'll get two sets of everything." I'm tempted to say three, but I can picture Luke deciding that amputation of a limb without anesthesia is better than wearing a cat costume.

"Yay!" she says and scoots down to her room.

He watches her leave. "Pick something out online and put it on the card. If you want a costume, go ahead and include it."

I swallow and nod. My phone buzzes with a text.

Dennis: *Plans for Halloween?*

Luke is doing that trying-not-to-stare-but-failing-miserably thing.

I chew my lip and look up. "Are we taking Addison trick-or-treating?"

He shakes his head. "Her grandparents—Kira's parents—asked if they could take her out. I said yes. You okay with that?"

"You don't have to ask me about parenting decisions."

"Parenting decisions like whether to buy her a pony, no. That's a decision reserved for me. You seem to like playing dress-up with her, though. Maybe you wanted to go all out. I probably should have asked you before I agreed."

He's sweet. Still, "You're in charge. It's no problem. Addi and I can decorate here, and I can put a costume together for her." I study him. "If she's going to be out, does that mean I can have the night off?"

"Yeah," he says slowly. "Of course."

After another second of debate, I say, "Okay, then I'm going to schedule something that night. Will that work?"

"Sure." A pause. "What is it?" He shoves a hand in his pocket. "Sorry, I have no right to ask."

I grimace as I text. "Just this guy my dad set me up with."

"You're going on a date," he says flatly. "With someone *your dad* set you up with."

"Well, instead of a pony, my dad thinks he got me a stud." I cringe. *Oh my god.*

Luke bursts out laughing but sobers quickly and looks away.

"I don't know the guy," I admit. "But we've been texting." What I want to say is, *I won't go out with him if you tell me you're interested.* But I can only wait around for Luke so long. After all, I'm the one who said we could forget our kiss happened—because I saw the apprehensive look in his eyes that night. He doesn't need me to complicate his life.

He takes a deep breath. "Look, about when we kissed."

"It was a mistake. I know."

His voice drops. "Is that what you think?"

I shrug. I want to shake my head no, but then what will happen?

All sorts of emotions flicker across his face, until finally he nods. "Okay. Have a good time." And he turns and heads back to his office.

After texting Dennis to agree on a time and place to meet, I catch up with Addi in her room and set about making plans for Halloween.

When Halloween night rolls around, I'm just putting the finishing touches on my cat makeup: black nose, whiskers. Addi and I spent the afternoon carving pumpkins and roasting the seeds, and the porch is all spooky and spectacular. I bought candy in case anyone comes by, although this far up the drive, I doubt Luke will have any trick-or-treaters. I used my own money, and I'm so glad to have some in my pocket. My debts still feel like a weight on my back, but I don't have enough saved yet to pay them all off.

The creditors are starting to catch up with me, though. I continue to receive late notices, since I signed up for mail forwarding with the post office. I don't know how I'd explain those to Luke, so I just make a point to always pick up the mail when I'm out running errands. And then put the envelopes in a drawer. I'll deal with them later.

Twisting in front of the mirror, I see my tail hanging over the black leggings I'm wearing. I make a cute cat.

Luke has taken Addison to her grandparents' house, so he's not here when I leave, which would probably be awkward anyway.

But I don't owe him anything—no explanation, no asking permission, nothing.

And I'm not making the same mistakes, now that I'm new Scott.

I got in trouble with Edsel by assuming I meant more to him than I did—or that we had more going on than we did.

Luke and I aren't anything. We're employer and employee who kissed once. That's it.

It sucks, but it is what it is, and I'm moving on.

Dennis doesn't seem like someone I'd fall for anyway, so a date with him won't hurt. It will be fun.

I hope.

When I walk into Vino and Veritas with my cat tail swinging, it's packed wall to wall with people, almost all of whom are in costume. "Grim Grinning Ghosts" is playing, and many patrons are eating from the new menu or drinking cider. I see Murph behind the bar wearing a pointy satin hat with rainbow streamers and an empire-waist princess dress. He does have a solid grasp of his brand. Jason's sitting on a barstool wearing leather clothes and looking like some rugged dude from *Lord of the Rings*. I grin at them and wave, then gesture like I'm meeting someone—which I am.

I'm scanning the room for Dennis the nerdy professor, realizing I barely remember what he looks like and I didn't ask what he'd be dressed as. Given how many people are in masks or makeup, it could be difficult to find him.

I pass a group of my friends who are all sitting at the same table, so I stop and say hi.

Aaron's wearing some kind of hot-farmer getup, complete with a flannel shirt tied above his belly button and a cowboy hat, so I assume the cow next to him waving at me is his boyfriend. I snort-laugh. "That you, Jeremy?"

"It was either this or a clown, and I didn't want to scare anyone."

"You and your clowns." I shake my head.

After I met Jeremy, his group adopted me as part of their boy gang, and because of Briar and Jamie, I'm now part of the motley crew that is book club, as well as their extended group of friends.

We all hug, and Jeremy takes off his cow mask, mussing his hair. He asks, "Join us?"

"I've got a date," I admit.

"With *hotsexyboss*?" he says excitedly.

"No. With this guy my dad set me up with …" I trail off as the crowd parts and I see a guy not in costume sitting by himself at a booth. I recognize the elbow patches.

I chuckle. I probably could've guessed Dennis wouldn't be dressed up. "He's over there. Excuse me, okay?"

They all nod. "Have fun," Jeremy says, and the rest of them wish me well.

"Hey," I say, breathless, when I get to Dennis's table. I sit across from him. "Dennis, right?"

He stares.

I realize he may not have been prepared for me with ears. "Sorry, I'm a cat. I mean, I'm not a cat, this is just for Halloween. You know what? Never mind."

"That's okay," he says. "What's good here? Do you know the place well?"

"Oh yeah! I come here all the time. I'm friends with probably a third of the people here."

"I don't go out much."

"Oh." I'm not sure what to say.

Murph sidles up and pulls out his notepad. "Can I get you boys something? We have Halloween specials."

I gesture at Dennis. "You go first."

"Uh, can I have some sparkling water?"

Murph nods and turns to me. "The usual?"

"Sure."

Dennis stares at me and then looks away. I look back and then clear my throat.

And I find I have nothing to say to him. I, who can usually chat the wallpaper off a wall, can't think of any way to start a conversation. "So, how long have you lived in Burlington?" I finally ask.

"I don't. I live in Colebury."

"Oh."

I pick at the edge of the table, looking anywhere but at him. When I realize I'm doing it, I sit on my hands until Murph delivers our drinks, and then I trace the condensation down the side of my glass. "If you could've dressed up for Halloween, what would you be?"

"Oh, that's a good question. Um. I don't know."

I wait, letting him think. But nothing is forthcoming. "You could be an absent-minded professor. Wear a lab coat and fluff your hair like Einstein."

Dennis smiles. "Yeah, that's a good idea."

And we look at each other.

Our conversation, such as it was, dies, and short of mouth-to-mouth resuscitation—which I'm not willing to attempt—it's done for.

I excuse myself to go to the restroom and check my phone. Nothing from Luke. Not that I was expecting him to check on me, but a boy can always hope.

When I return, I finish my drink and contemplate ordering a second, but I decide not to. I'm driving home, and it seems like I'm driving home early. Tonight's a bust.

I look around the room and see my friends have moved on—not sure if they went to a party or a club, but they're definitely gone.

"I don't think this is going anywhere," I blurt.

He gives me a weak smile. "Me neither. Do you have your eye on someone else?"

"The dad of the kid I'm caring for. He doesn't seem to want me, though," I admit. "Or maybe he thinks he can't date me. Like, thou shalt not date thy nanny. Is that written down somewhere, or is it an urban legend?"

"I'm pretty sure it's an established rule. I'll wish you luck anyway, though. I'm sorry we're not working out, but if you want a friend, I can be that." He gives me a hopeful smile.

"Thanks. I may take you up on that." I shake his hand, leave a twenty on the table—it feels so good to have money again—and make my way out. While I wish my tail would swish, it quietly thumps against my leg. The door closes behind me as I head home to a house with just Luke in it.

12

LUKE

Have I been pacing around the house since I got back from dropping Addi off?

Yes.

Are my thoughts driving me bananas?

Yes.

Can I stop?

No.

After a pass into the kitchen, I beeline to the cabinet and pull out a bottle of whiskey, then pour two fingers into a glass. I throw it back, the burn down my throat making me feel … better.

No. Not better. Just momentarily distracted from the fact that it's Halloween night, my daughter is gone, I'm alone in my ex-wife's empty house while the guy I … want? kissed? … is on a date, and I'm horny as hell. I scroll through the hookup app for the twentieth time.

It's bothering me that this is bothering me. It's not like I'm jealous. He can do whatever the hell he wants.

I pinch the bridge of my nose.

And even if I wanted to, I can't stop him from dating. I have no claim on him.

I need to get laid. I should pick someone close and message them.

I'm about to swipe on a potential match when headlights flash across the front windows. It can't be anyone but Scott, so I take a flying leap, flinging myself onto the couch. While I should grab my keys and leave, instead I sit with my legs stretched out on the coffee table, one ankle crossed over the other. I pull out my phone as if I've been there the whole night and turn on the television. Because it's Halloween, *Children of the Corn*—the original—is playing.

When the door opens, I inspect Scott as he pauses to take off his jacket and hang it up on the hallway hook.

My inner dickhead cheers, because it certainly doesn't look like he's been fucked within an inch of his life. He even still has whiskers on his face—the makeup kind, not the five o'clock shadow kind. So did he not even kiss the guy?

"Oh, hey," he says as he yanks off one of his boots. I hadn't seen him in his costume, but he's still in it—complete with cat ears and a tail.

"Hey." I clear my throat. "Did you have a good date?"

He shrugs, tugging off the other boot. "I guess."

That doesn't sound encouraging. Is it wrong that I'm ... pleased?

I pretend to watch the movie, but really I watch Scott as he goes into the kitchen, tail swinging behind him, pulls out a glass, and pours himself a glass of water, which he downs and sets in the sink. "Want a drink?" He cocks his head to the side, which makes his cat ears tilt jauntily.

"No, thanks." Since I can't seem to take my eyes off him, I give up trying.

He pads over to the couch and smiles awkwardly, wringing his hands. His leggings show off the curves of his thighs and calves and the bulge of his cock. His skintight black T-shirt isn't helping matters. My mouth is watering.

There's no doubt that I need to get laid.

"A horror movie? Really?" he asks. He takes a seat next to me on the couch and plays with his tail, only half watching the movie. But as it goes on, I can see him tense up, and I want to just drag him into my lap.

I'm not missing the fact that we're alone in the house without a pint-sized supervisor.

Can I fix the coolness that's built between us for the past couple of weeks? I should, since it's really my fault. He's too sweet for this world.

"Did Addi have fun?" he asks.

"I think so. She seemed like she was well on her way to getting amped on sugar."

"That's good." He swallows and focuses on his tail, the arm of the sofa, anywhere but the screen.

I look over and burst out laughing when I see his expression.

"What?" he asks, sullenly.

"You look horrified."

"It's a horror movie," he mutters. "I'm supposed to be scared."

I nod, not knowing what to do, but I turn the television down. "How was V and V?"

"Everyone was dressed up." He grins, but it's about half the usual wattage. "My friends had some fun costumes." He rattles off a few costume choices, but since I don't know the people, it doesn't mean much to me.

Still, I enjoy hearing him talk. "Cool."

"I like seeing what people wear for Halloween. I've always been attracted to making something out of nothing. Making things special. I think that life goes too fast, and if you don't make a point to celebrate everything you can, you'll celebrate nothing."

"But you need someone to celebrate with."

We both stare at each other, and finally, he swallows. "Actually, the date wasn't that great."

My heart does a pole vault, but I freeze my expression. "No?"

"Nah. I don't know. I didn't feel like there was anything between us."

"That happens sometimes," I say absently. But what I really want to say is how relieved I am. Arousal courses through my body. He's so near.

And maybe I have a small crush on him. A tiny one. Infinitesimal.

"Yeah, I guess. Maybe I can tell my dad to lay off me for a while."

"Will he?"

"Dunno. Maybe." He yawns, putting a hand over his mouth. "I'm pretty tired. I'm going to bed."

I nod.

He picks himself up off the couch, but I reach over and grab his wrist. We both look down at my hand on his.

"Sorry," I say quickly, letting go.

He furrows his brows. "What are you sorry about?"

"Nothing." I take a deep breath. "Or, rather, I guess I'm glad you didn't hit it off with him. For selfish reasons."

Scott wrinkles his nose. "Selfish reasons?"

"Yeah." My voice is rough.

I can see his face morph from confusion to irritation. "Selfish as in what?"

"As in I didn't want you seeing anyone," I admit.

When he speaks, he sounds exasperated. "Are you serious?"

"Yeah."

"Luke, if you wanted more with me, you should've said something." There's an edge to his tone I haven't heard from him before.

But I don't want to fuck anything up. I need him as a nanny no matter what. "I just ... I don't want to be out of line. I don't want you to feel pressured."

"Pressured about what?"

He's going to make me say it, isn't he? "Pressured to fool around with me because I'm attracted to you. I didn't want you to feel weird about it, but I really like you—"

Scott is on me in a second, almost tackling me, and I grab him at the same time, and somehow we end up mostly on the couch. I struggle to stay upright, and he sits on top of me, kissing me.

The moment our lips meet, all the tension that had been in my body releases. He tastes phenomenal.

I grip his jaw, trying to avoid his cat whiskers, and our tongues tangle together as he runs his hands up my chest and lets out a little moan. He's getting hard against me. My body is responding just as quickly.

That noise stirs me into wanting him even more, although he quickly pulls back, his cat ears askew. "You've been drinking."

"Yeah. I was kind of losing my shit with you being out tonight."

He grins, the drawn-on whiskers on his face tilting up. "Really?" He sounds delighted.

"What can I say? I was horny and jealous of you maybe getting some," I admit. My voice drops. "Or jealous of whoever you were seeing, since they got to be alone with you."

Scott blinks and toys with the collar of my shirt. "Are you drunk?"

"Not at all."

"Good." And he leans in to kiss me again, his hand reaching down to stroke my cock through my pants. This time, my hands come around his ass, only I grab a handful of his tail and grin, holding it up.

"This fucking tail," I say, laughing so hard I fall over, so we sort of wedge ourselves on the floor between the couch and coffee table, with him on top.

I don't know that I've ever laughed while having sex—or whatever it is we're doing.

Maybe I'm too serious. Scott doesn't take life so seriously, and he seems to be doing just fine.

A scream sounds from the television, and without looking, I reach for the remote and shut it off, then kiss him again.

He wiggles his ass flirtatiously. "Do you like my tail?"

"I like your ass," I mutter, pinching it.

"Cool," he whispers, almost nose to nose.

But something is still bothering me, and while I don't want to ruin the mood, I also don't want things going too far without him being sure. (I'm ignoring the voice that thinks we've already gone too far.) I hold his jaw and pull away far enough so he can see that I'm sincere. "So we're clear, no repercussions for your job, whatever you choose. Continuing this or not, you're Addi's nanny."

He grins. "Are you saying I can end up in your bed if I ask nicely?"

"Yeah."

"I'm asking nicely." His beautiful eyes are on mine, and now my dick really surges to life. "Just so *you* know, I'm okay with this. Very, *very* okay."

While I can't say I'm not still worried this is going to go south, my thoughts fly out the window when I notice a wet spot on the front of his leggings. He's leaking precome.

I palm him through the thin fabric. "Fuck, you're hot," I growl, stretching my neck up to kiss him more.

Scott pulls back, looks me in the eye, and swallows hard, toying with my chest. "Let's do this. We're two consenting adults. We find each other attractive. Hooking up while I'm here is no big deal, right? It's convenient."

For some reason, it feels like a bigger deal than a hookup. There's a weird ache in my chest, but I ignore it. "Right. No big deal. And we can stop any time we want."

"Deal."

He kisses along my jaw. "But maybe we don't have to do this on the floor?"

I jackknife up, and he stands, then holds out his hand to help me to my feet. "I'm not that old," I say.

"How old are you?"

"Thirty-six." I know his age from his tax paperwork. I'm not going to think about how much younger than me he is. I'm going to think about how much I need this—and how much I think he needs it, too. I pause before we move down the hallway, rubbing the back of my neck. "You sure you're okay with this?"

"For crying out loud, I'm not a damned virgin. Use me like a rag doll."

With how keyed up I am, we may not make it long. I start to march him to my room, but he isn't a twink in a club bathroom.

So instead, I stop and reach for his hand, tugging him with me.

He comes willingly. When we get to my bedroom, I look at him and grin. "Do you want to keep the makeup on?"

"What?" His hands fly to his face. "Oh my god, I forgot about that. Hang on."

"I'll get you a washcloth," I say, kissing him and walking him toward the bed at the same time—me forward, him backward. "I want you naked when I get back."

He shivers, but it's not from cold, because the house is snug. "I can do that." He grips the hem of his T-shirt to pull it over his head, and I get distracted from my mission, because I really like seeing him undress. Once it's off, he grins at me knowingly. "Thought you were getting something."

"Yeah," I say, my voice like gravel. I spin and head for the bathroom.

The water takes too long to warm up, and while I wait, I imagine him naked. The few glimpses I've gotten of him with his shirt off were tantalizing—skin smooth and unblemished, toned limbs, just the right amount of body hair. I palm my cock through my pants in anticipation.

Once the water's finally hot enough, I soak a washcloth, wring it out, and return to my room.

The sight of Scott lying on my bed naked takes my breath away. As I walk in, he's smiling and stroking his erect cock, his whiskers tilted up.

"Fuck, you're hot," I whisper as I head toward him and sit on the side of the bed. I gently wipe the black makeup off his nose and cheeks. He closes his eyes and lets me do it, and it feels like

I'm taking care of him. I discard the cloth on the side of the clothes hamper, shed my shirt, then turn and really take him in.

While my eyes had immediately been drawn to his cock, I was focused on the motion of his hand, not his body. But now I notice he has a tattoo on his hip.

I furrow my brows.

"What?" he asks.

"What's that?" I ask, pointing. He shifts his arm, and my jaw drops.

"That's my tat. Why are you staring?"

I shake my head, undo my belt and pants, and shove them down along with my underwear. My hard dick bobs against my abs, and I gesture to my own hip.

"Because this is mine."

13

SCOTT

No, Scott. Luke is not your soulmate. Just because he has that tattoo, it does not mean this is meant to be.

I have a lock tattooed on my hip—with a scroll design and a space for a key.

Luke has an old-fashioned key on his opposite hip.

A key that would line up if he ever got his delectable body over mine.

It's not the key to your lock. It's a key. A lock. Get your mind out of the clouds.

"Why did you get that tattoo?" I murmur, my finger ghosting over the soft skin on his hip.

"It's my middle name: Keyes. Why do you have a lock?" He catches my hand but doesn't move it. His erection is right here, and he's big, and I want him.

"What?"

He repeats the question.

"My middle name is Lockhart—it's my mom's family name."

We are not soulmates. We're not soulmates. Not—

We blink at each other and burst out laughing. And somehow what I thought was going to be a hot, sexy session with *hotsexyboss* becomes a tangle of limbs and laughter as we kiss.

His laugh is one of my favorite things. Right in line after those times I see his gooey middle breaking through to show how sweet he is inside. Hell, even his grin at my tail made a mediocre evening exceptional.

Except now his warm, naked skin is all over mine, and *fuck*, this is what I needed. To be touched. To be close to someone.

And the fact that it's *Luke* is not lost on me. He's a wish fulfilled.

The lighthearted moment turns back to smoldering pretty damned quick as Luke grinds against me, kissing me deeply. He leans on one elbow while his other hand traces down my body. I explore his back with my hands, then slide them down to squeeze his ass. I like the way his waist dips in slightly above his hips.

I like the way I feel in his arms, cradled and safe.

I've searched a long time for someone to hold me like that. To anchor me, keep me from going too far off into dreamland.

I'm startled back into the present when he clears his throat. "What the fuck am I going to do with you?" he asks, although from his tone, I don't think he expects an answer.

I answer anyway. "I have a few ideas."

"I do, too, but I don't know what to think of this." His fingers brush my hip over the tattoo.

"I think it's cool?" It comes out more as a question than a statement.

"Me, too." He inspects my face. "So you know, I was tested before I came back to Vermont, and I'm negative."

"I am, too." I got tested at a free clinic after Edsel, because I was worried he'd been cheating on me. Not, in retrospect, that it would really have been cheating, since we were only exclusive in my head.

But that's not what I want to think about right now. I want to think about Luke.

Luke kisses me one more time, then pulls away far enough to study me. I'm memorizing him right back: his dark hair messed up from my hands; his broad, muscular shoulders; his skin tanned and smooth with a dusting of chest hair.

"Look at you," he says, a note of wonder in his voice. With the tips of his fingers, he traces the join of my legs to my torso. "You're magnetic. I've wanted you in my bed ever since you knocked on my door."

"Same here."

With a wicked gleam in his eye, he kisses along my jaw, down my neck, and then continues down until he gets to my tattoo. He looks at it, then closes his eyes, shakes his head, opens them again, and kisses it—a wet, open-mouthed kiss, with his stubble scraping my hip.

Before I can say anything else, he shifts over and takes in my hard cock.

I let out a very throaty moan. "Fuck."

He sucks me good, getting into a rhythm.

"Oh my god, you're a champ at that."

He's inspiring some pretty epic romantic lines right now for a line of not-safe-for-work cards. Like, "Will you please fucking finish me off already before I explode?"

Those will be very posh, fancy cards that'll surely sell well with the stuffy crowd.

Luke pops off and leans back again to gaze at me. "You good with coming this way?"

"Am I good with this?" I mutter in wonder. Like he needs to ask. He *has* to know what he's doing to me. But in case he needs positive reinforcement, I say, "*Yes*," and then I can't control my loud gasp as he takes me in his mouth again.

It's heavenly. There's something about the wet heat and soft-ness of a tongue in such an intimate area that's hedonistic and so fucking pleasurable I can't handle it.

My boss is going down on me, and he knows what he's doing —long pulls and pulses around the crown of my cock. A steady rhythm that makes me lose myself in it. My dick is the center of my attention right now—and his mouth the focal point.

I didn't think Luke would be so gentle. I figured he'd be more demanding—which I'm totally up for, incidentally—but this blowjob is a revelation. It's him *giving*, and as far as I can tell, he expects nothing in return. He's not even touching himself—he's just lavishing me with attention—and, fuck, I'm loving the hell out of it.

Don't think about the L word, Scott. The only L word you should be thinking about right now is Luke.

I'm not going to last long. I warn him that I'm about to come, in case he doesn't want my release, but he doesn't pull away, and soon I'm bursting into his mouth, the orgasm taking over my body and racking it with aftershocks. He keeps milking me until I can't stand the stimulation anymore, so I push him off me and lie back, panting.

The world is a very fine place after all, methinks.

Luke looks up at me, wiping his mouth with the back of his hand. He grins, his lips swollen and red.

He's the sexiest person I've ever seen.

I'm at a loss for words. I don't want to say something like thank you, because that feels weird. I don't want to tell him that it was the best ever, because I don't want to imply he needs to always be this way.

So I scramble up and push at him, and we sort of twist so I'm on top of him and then spend a few moments making out. His hard dick is trapped between us, and I reach down and grip it, wrapping my fingers around his length. It's huge in both ways—longer and wider than mine—and he's uncut.

He makes the best noise—a pleasured grunt that morphs into a "Fucckkk, yes, please."

As his hands run through my hair, I echo his journey down my body, kissing and sucking along his sternum, his pecs, his rib cage, all the while slowly jacking him. I make my way down to his belly button and happy trail.

But while just a few moments ago he reduced me to nothing more than moans, he's—for Luke at least—chattering up a storm.

"Scott, fuck, that's so good. How'd you know I like to be touched there? Oh god, yes, please."

I lick his tattoo and kiss it.

"So damned sexy," he mutters, carding fingers through my hair.

When I get to his dick, I catch his eyes and lick a wide stripe up his shaft, his hot, salty skin tasting clean.

"Yessss," he hisses. "Fuck, that feels fucking amazing."

I want to show off for him. Make him feel as good as he made me feel. Make him want to keep me around.

I double down and bob on his dick, sucking the way he did to me, and now I'm getting the harsh intakes of his breath, the appreciative gasps, the words of praise. "Scott, honey, you're fucking good at that, and you look so damned hot on my cock. I can't wait to see you ride it someday."

I chuckle around his dick but keep my attention on getting him off. Usually I take some time for exploration, but right now I'm single-mindedly focused on making Luke come.

When he warns me, I don't stop until he tips over, pulse after pulse of his warm, bittersweet orgasm flooding my mouth.

I keep sucking until he hauls me up by my armpits, then shifts so he's on top of me again. "You're incredible," he says, wonder in his tone.

I can't imagine why. I'm sure he's gotten blowjobs before. Maybe it's been a while for him, like it has for me.

But I don't say any of that. I just kiss him and enjoy the brush of his naked skin against mine—warm and soft but solid and muscular.

And … all his praise has soaked in at some level. I like the encouragement. I fucking want to please him in every way I can think of.

We roll so we're spooning—he's the big spoon—and I can't believe I'm naked and cuddling with my boss in his bed.

Luke nestles his nose in the back of my neck. "I really fucking loved that, honey."

"Me, too. Do you want to do it again?"

"Now?" He sounds slightly incredulous.

"No, no, no. I mean"—my voice sounds small—"just … again. Sometime when Addi's not around. When we can do this."

He nods. "Yeah," he says, his voice husky. "We can do this again."

We lie there in the dim light of his bedside lamp. I know I should get up and go back to my room, but Luke's said more to me just now than he has in the whole course of most days. I want to keep him talking. "Can I ask you something?"

"Sure."

"Something personal, I mean."

He shrugs. "I don't have to answer."

"True." I take a deep breath and trace the vein on the back of his hand with my finger. "How did a guy like you end up with a kid?"

He lets out a breath. "I always wanted a child. Kira and I … I thought it was love. She told me she was in love with me."

How could she not be?

"She wanted a big wedding, so I gave it to her. We found out she was pregnant a few months into the marriage. But by then, we were realizing that we very much did not have the kind of compatibility that makes a marriage work. We were always butting heads. We just … fell out of love, if we were ever in love to begin with. But I love Addi."

He pauses and stills. I feel him swallow hard. "Hey, like you said, you don't have to answer," I start, but he interrupts.

"It's okay. After we had Addison and it became clear that Kira and I weren't going to work out, I did some soul-searching. I knew Kira wanted custody. While I did, too, it was more important to me that Addison have a peaceful childhood. My parents fought constantly, and it was a miserable way to grow up. I thought it would be best for Addi if I … ceded control, which is not at all in my nature. To me, that seemed to be the smarter, more solid choice."

"So you sacrificed yourself for your kid."

Luke is quiet a moment. Then he says, "I can't imagine what it would have been like if I'd set out to demonize Kira. If we'd battled for custody."

"But dads have rights, too."

"Here's the thing about rights: it's a choice whether or not to exercise them. I chose not to."

"I don't understand that."

He sighs. "It made sense at the time. Now that I'm here, I'm fucking gutted at how much I missed. I should've been around more. It wasn't that I didn't want to fight for her. It was that I didn't want her to grow up surrounded by acrimony. And beneath that, I was afraid she wouldn't become a good person if she was around me too much."

I'm shocked. "Luke, you're a great dad."

He makes a derisive noise.

"You are," I insist. "You just needed some practice. That's all. She loves you."

No answer.

"You can give yourself a break, you know," I continue. "All Addi wants is your undivided attention, which you give her. She'll remember when her daddy listened to her."

"I wish what you're saying were true, but I feel guilty for all the things I didn't do—and scared she's going to figure out that I'm a shitty parent."

That makes my heart hurt. "What on earth is bringing on all this insecurity?"

He tightens his arms around me. "Guess I'm tired."

"I think you might be a little sad, too, because you missed out on part of her life. That's understandable, but it doesn't mean you ruined anything. Kids are resilient. Trust me, I've been around plenty of them."

"How many kids do your parents have?"

"Nine."

"Nine!" Luke makes a choking noise. "Catholic?"

"Nope. Just … Actually, I don't want to think about my parents and sex. Let's say the results speak for themselves and leave it at that."

He squeezes me. "Fair. And you're the oldest?"

"Second oldest. I have one older sister, Minerva, and then seven younger siblings: Aurora, Iris, Ariadne, Hercules, Zeus, Daphne, and Apollo."

Luke whistles. "How the fuck did you get named Scott?"

I shrug. "Dunno. I'm the most fanciful one, too, so it really doesn't make any sense at all. Maybe the lack of a mythic name meant I needed to come up with a mythic life."

"You weren't the true leader of the pack, and you didn't get the attention of being the baby. Were you kind of lost in the shuffle?"

I furrow my brows, although he can't see it. "Um. Yeah. I guess. How did you know?"

"Birth order's a real thing. Just because someone is the oldest doesn't always mean they're independent, but it often does. And the middle child is often forgotten."

"We have seven middle children."

"Even more so. As second oldest, your function was, what? Built-in babysitter?"

"I guess. Yeah." I blink. "That probably has something to do with why I'm the way I am, you know? I got overshadowed at home. Everyone knew we had a huge brood, and that was it. I always wanted someone to think I was special on my own. I want to be someone's world."

"Makes sense."

"Yeah." He yawns, and I sit up. "I think it's time for me to go back to my room." I start hunting for my clothes, realizing I flung them every which way instead of folding them neatly like I usually do.

I want him to ask me to stay, even though I don't think he will. Because this is just physical. Nothing more.

As I slide my T-shirt back on, I look at him.

He clears his throat. "I gotta line my tattoo up with yours one of these nights."

I laugh. "I'm ready when you are. Though, you know, we went about this all wrong."

Luke frowns. "How so?"

"Usually I'd ask for a commitment before getting matching tattoos."

His frown deepens.

My hands fly up. "Dude, I'm kidding. We discussed this. We're two consenting adults. I'm just making a joke."

He nods, mollified. But I still need to make sure I follow my own rules.

I'm not falling for Luke, no matter what.

LUKE

Scott shuts my bedroom door behind him, and I hear him clicking off the lights as he heads to his suite. Meanwhile, I stare at my ceiling.

What the hell have I done?

The past couple of weeks really got to me … and boiled over. What's worse, being naked with Scott was fucking amazing. I want to do it again.

But actions have consequences. Have I ruined things?

Hopefully not. Scott and I live under the same roof and both want the same sort of no-expectations hookup. This should be simple.

So why do I want to tell him he can't get together with anyone else?

It doesn't make sense. I never give hookups more than one night, so being exclusive isn't even an issue. I haven't been in a relationship since Kira, and there are so many reasons why Scott and I shouldn't consider one. He's too young, for one thing. And I guess I never figured I'd be in a meaningful relationship with a man. I might have some prejudices to work through.

Although the wife, kid, picket fence thing didn't work out so well for me the first time.

Still, I want to get out of bed, go down the hall, and hold him all night long.

I can't. That would set a bad precedent. So I ignore the gnawing ache in my heart and the empty space in my bed and flop around, trying to sleep.

After tossing and turning for hours, I turn my light back on and pick up the book he loaned me. If I can't sleep, I might as well be able to talk intelligently about male strippers at his book club.

The next morning, I oversleep, which I never do, and wake to voices. Addison's grandparents must've brought her back, and Scott's up and taking care of her even though today's his day off.

I slump into the kitchen to the sight of a just-showered Scott cleaning up from breakfast. He gives me a shy smile, but I'm distracted by my daughter.

"Morning, Daddy!" Addi says cheerily, with a milk mustache, as she takes the last bite of her cereal.

"How was trick-or-treating?" I ask.

"So much fun! I got lots of candy."

"And I hope you left it at Grandma and Grandpa's house." I stoop to kiss the top of her head before passing Scott to pour myself a cup of coffee. I want to kiss him, too, but not in front of my kid.

I don't have anything against Addi seeing affection, but I don't want her to think that Scott is … what, exactly?

I also don't want to answer that question.

He beams at me, handing me the sugar and cream for my coffee. "Good morning, Luke."

I shake my head. "How are you so awake?"

"Morning person. Want some toast?" He gestures to the loaf by the toaster.

"Sure." What I really want is to press him up against the cabinets and explore his body. I want his mouth on my cock.

Yeahhhh. So.

With those thoughts at the forefront of my mind the moment I see him, I think it's safe to say last night did not satisfy all my urges in regard to him. Nowhere near.

Scott slides bread into the slots, then brings a damp cloth over to wipe Addi's face. "Go brush your teeth," he says to her, and she nods and trots off.

Leaving him and me alone in the kitchen. I intend to say thanks for the help with my kid on his day off, but what happens is I put my hands on his hips and haul him to me, then kiss him until we're both breathless.

When we break apart, he whispers, "Holy shit. Last night wasn't a dream, was it?"

I kiss his nose. "No."

"Cool," he says dazedly.

"Want me to come find you tonight?"

"Yeah."

It's not like I'm ensuring that we hook up again. It's not like I'm jealous of whoever he sees when he's not with me.

But I want him to remember me today as he's out and about, so I kiss him until my toast pops up.

"Wow," he whispers.

Addi comes bouncing back in. "Daddy, can we get ice cream today?"

"Maybe after your riding lesson."

She grins, because she knows that's basically a yes. Oh well. I butter my toast.

Scott surveys the room, seemingly ready to take off. "Are you good here?"

No. "Yeah. I'll make sure we're on time for her riding lesson."

I want to ask him what he's doing today, but I don't want to be domineering—even though it's driving me to distraction not knowing.

But he volunteers, "I'm just going to see my parents and go to an afternoon football game with my dad. You're welcome to come if you want."

"Thanks," I say, irrationally happy he's not going on another date. "Not sure we'll have time after riding. Go have fun."

"Don't forget to see if Kira's parents can watch Addi so we can go to book club next week."

"Already taken care of."

He grabs his keys and leaves. After I get ready for the day, I drive Addi to the stables.

When we get to Lost Acres Morgans, I do a double take, because I recognize the guy standing outside the ring. I don't think I've seen him since he was a scrawny teenager—and he's changed a lot since then.

Landon Maxwell was one of my best friends. We met in elementary school and hung out until we went in very different directions with our lives. Me with the fancy degree and the wife and kid. Him with … prison.

I'm wary, even though I used to know him down to the way he'd nurse birds with broken wings and get sad when they finally flew off.

Now he's huge, with tattoos peeking out of his shirt cuffs—the kind that make me think he has them all over his body. Landon's also a silver fox now, which makes me feel old, since we're the same age. But his face doesn't look old. He just has graying hair.

Could he really have done whatever it was he got sent away for?

Addi marches straight up to him and puts her hands on her hips. "Who are you? Where is Mr. Caden and Mr. Ty?"

Landon's face breaks into a huge smile that softens his rugged features, and the reaction tempers my initial unease. His eyes flick up, and he startles when he recognizes me.

He greets Addi first. "Caden and Ty are helping other riders. I'm Landon. I'm new. Are you Addison?"

She nods gravely.

"And are you here to ride Max? Or Lady?"

"Lady, please." She watches him closely, but given that he

seems to belong here, she doesn't question it too much.

I'm still wary, though. "Hey," I manage.

He eyes me. "Luke. It's been a while," he says in a voice that's deeper than I remember.

"Yeah."

It's hard to believe we used to know each other so well. Now I don't know whether we have anything in common. And I'm not sure I should trust him—as much as I hate listening to rumors.

Ty, the owner of the stables, comes out, saying goodbye to the family who had a lesson before us, and beckons Addi to head his way. The family walks past me and Landon, and as the mother slips on her jacket, some folded bills fall from a pocket, tumbling to the ground like leaves.

Before I can move, Landon's retrieved the money and followed her, holding it out. "Ma'am, you dropped this."

I watch the woman blink at him in surprise, and she bristles before accepting her money back with a curt, "Oh, I hadn't noticed. Thank you."

"No problem," he says, then comes back toward me on his way, presumably, to the stables to help saddle up Addi's horse. I hold out a hand to stop him.

Because while I don't know him anymore, giving someone back their money is the kind of thing the Landon I remember would do. The least I can do is give him a chance. "Do you want to get caught up? I'm back in town for a while. Want to meet for coffee?"

Landon nods. "I can do coffee."

Pulling out my phone, I ask for his number, and he gives it to me.

"I'm on parole," he blurts.

"Yeah, I heard something like that. But we used to be friends, and I'm wondering what the hell happened. Rather than ask the busybodies in town, maybe I should talk with you."

I can see his whole body relax a fraction. "Okay, yeah, sure. Text me."

When I returned to Burlington, I figured I was pretty much on my own. I certainly didn't think I had any friends left in town. But maybe I do.

I just can't believe Landon would be a bad guy. I suspect he got into something he couldn't get out of. I think I owe it to him to hear his side of the story.

When Addison and I come home from her lesson, I get a message from Kira, who says even though the time is weird, she's up and around to talk. Scott's still not back.

"Ready to call your momma?" I ask Addison.

She bites her lip and nods. I never know if these calls will be good or bad—if they're going to upset her or be reassuring.

I guess that's the thing about parenting. There's no "Verified" checkmark to confirm you did it right. And maybe there is no "right."

Addi and I open the laptop and click into Skype.

"Addi!" Kira says, her face lighting up. "Hello, baby!"

I'd expected to have some emotional reaction to seeing Kira every time we do this: anger or longing or relief. But there's none of that. She symbolizes a lost dream, but it's starting to not ache as much as it used to.

"Momma!" Addison bursts into tears. I hoist her up on my lap and wrap my arms around her. She wiggles to get away, and I try not to feel hurt. I'm not the one she wants.

So I let her sit by herself, and I pull up a chair while she calms down and chats with Kira about trick-or-treating and how the leaves are changing and how she's been going on hikes with Scott and how she wants to go up in a hot-air balloon because he read her a story about them.

"What are you going to do for Thanksgiving?" Kira asks, directing the question to me.

Fuck if I know. "We'll figure something out." Maybe go to her parents', although honestly, Scott sounds like the best one to come up with holiday plans. We talk for a little while longer and then shut down the laptop.

I spend the rest of the afternoon sitting on the couch with Addi, eating popcorn and watching *The Mitchells vs. the Machines*, pretending I can't relate to the dad character who in turn can't relate to his daughter … but who also doesn't want to let her go.

That's how Scott finds us when he gets back from the football game, pink-cheeked and happy.

"Scott!" Addi cries, running to him.

"Hey, guys!" he says, and he joins us on the couch after he takes off his outerwear, Addi wedged between us as we watch a show about an ordinary family that saves the world. We pass the popcorn back and forth until there's just hard kernels left in the bottom of the bowl.

We've tucked Addi into bed, and I close the door behind me. Scott and I took turns reading *The Twenty-One Balloons* to her, since we've moved on from picture books. He's looking at me uncertainly, now that our chaperone is back.

"What do you want to—" he starts, and I step close, grab his ass, and kiss him. He parts his lips willingly. "Okay, you want to do that?"

I nod against him. "I do." I harden from the contact and can feel that he's just as hard, just as quick. We can't get enough of each other—or, at least, I can't get enough of him. "But not in the hallway."

"Come with me," he says. "It'll be quieter in my room."

"We might need to be fast. I don't think she'll wake up, but we wouldn't want to get caught with our pants down."

"Agreed. But I do want the pants down … just not with an audience."

I feel foolish sneaking around to have sex, but I suppose this is part of being a parent. Getting it on when I can.

We take off to his room, and he locks the door behind us. He's on me faster than I can move, and I kiss him back ferociously.

With one hand, I flick open the button of his corduroys—more of his hipster attire—and reach inside his underwear to take his dick out.

"Fuck," he whispers. I drop to my knees, and he gasps. "Luke!"

"You don't want it?"

"I want it. But you don't have to … Okay. Yes. You do." He changes his tone as I start sucking on him.

I love the way he feels in my mouth, this part of him that I can give so much pleasure to. I love how responsive he is.

I'm also realizing that this arrangement of ours may be the most decadent thing I've ever done, because I've never had repeated access to such enthusiastic sex. Kira and I fizzled out fast, but I can't imagine getting tired of Scott.

He pulls me back. "Wait. I want to sixty-nine you."

"Okay." We strip hastily and arrange ourselves on his bed.

As he captures my dick in his mouth, I suck on his, and we set up a steady cycle of sucking and stroking. "Get there," I mutter, needing to come and make him come. "I want us to come at the same time."

"I'm close," he says, and goes back to sucking me.

When he tenses up and lets go, I do, too, releasing into his hot, eager mouth. I swallow down all of his come, loving the way I'm finally getting my needs met.

And he's right there with me.

This could be the best thing I've ever tried. My nanny and hookup all in one.

Except we went so fast that it's over almost before it began.

I want to spend more time with him, but I don't know of any excuse to. When I leave him to head back to my cold bed, depositing a lingering kiss on his lips before I go, I'm back to wondering whether I'm doing the right thing.

15

SCOTT

The following weekend, Addi skips next to me as we walk up to meet Jax at the head of our favorite trail at Maple Falls. The woods are in their last gasp of fall color before winter hits, and I'd bet it'll snow by Thanksgiving, given how cold it's been lately.

"So you are Addison," Jax says, shaking her hand. He has this great accent—I'm told it's Cornish—even though he looks like a California surfer boy.

"I am."

"And you like to hike."

"I love it."

He grins. "Scott here has asked me to teach you wilderness skills."

"Both your daddy and I think it's a good idea," I tell her. I haven't actually asked Luke, but I know he'd approve. He's very much interested in the safety of his little girl, so the more we can teach her, the better.

But thinking about him makes my thoughts spin out into the stratosphere. So while Jax starts down the path, pointing out different kinds of plants, I'm back to thinking about what Luke and I have been doing.

What *have* we been doing?

Apart from "each other," that is.

We've been sneaking quick-and-dirty blowjobs or handjobs, too nervous to linger in case Addi wakes up.

But I wish we *could* linger.

Not your soulmate. Luke is not your soulmate.

And we haven't fucked yet.

Not that everyone does anal, and that's okay, but I don't think that's what this is. It feels like Luke is holding back, and I don't understand why. Is there something wrong with me?

We cross over a stream that has a little bridge, and Jax points down. "While the water looks pretty, sometimes it has bacteria in it, so never drink untreated water."

"What's bacteria?" Addi asks.

"Things that can make you really sick."

Her mouth makes an O. "Okay." And now she's all ears as he explains basic outdoor safety to her.

Addison is all about woodlands and unicorns, but I want her to know how to keep from getting a blister, what to do if she can't find the trail, not to touch poisonous plants, and so on.

While Jax does his spiel, I walk along, enjoying being outdoors and wishing I could spend time with Luke like this. We take the spur to the waterfall, so our hike is a little longer than usual.

When we stop at a large boulder to sit, drink from our water bottles, and catch our breath, I ask Addi, "We need to get your daddy out of the house, don't you think?"

She nods at me. She's so solemn it makes me want to laugh. Jax and I exchange amused glances.

"What do you think we should do?" I stage-whisper. It makes me feel like we're in a conspiracy. Which, I suppose, we are.

"We should take him up in a hot-air balloon! Daddy likes to see things from high up. In New York, he lives in a tall building where he can see down on everything."

I raise my eyebrows. I don't know anything about Luke's life when he's not being a work-from-home single dad. I'll have to ask him about it.

"Hmm." I get down to Addi's level and boop her nose. "I think maybe that's something *you'd* like more than your daddy would." She giggles. "But I'll see what I can do, okay?"

"Yay!" she cheers, and we continue on our hike.

On my next afternoon off, while Luke is working and Addison is at school, I stop by V and V. Murph's wiping glasses with a cloth and lining them up on a shelf when I sidle up to the bar.

"Scottybear!" He rushes around the bar to give me a hug.

"Hey." I bite my lip.

He cocks his head and puts his hands on his hips, looking me over from head to toe. He taps his mouth. "Something's different about you."

I narrow my eyes. "How so?"

"You seem … glowing."

Orgasms will do that. "Fresh air and exercise."

"No. That's the kind of glow you get from a good dicking. Trust me. I know these things."

I shrug, but my hot cheeks betray me.

Murph gasps and points. "You did. You slept with *hotsexyboss*."

I flinch. "I don't think of him as my boss. I think of him as Luke. And we haven't technically slept together."

"Banged—"

"Or even that."

Murph looks confused. "Okayyy."

"We've been hooking up"—Murph's eyes light up—"but we haven't actually had …"

"Butt sex," he supplies.

"That."

He grins. "But you are dancing horizontally with Sir Luke."

I shrug yet again. "I mean, yeah. Just dancing, though. Not the sleeping part."

Now Murph's face drops. "What's the fun in that? You don't get to snuggle with *hotsexyboss*?"

I shake my head. "I think we're using each other. It's just to get off. Nothing else."

He takes a step back and studies me, a finger on his chin. "Yeah, no. You're lying."

"What? No! Everything I told you is true."

"Except the part about it meaning nothing. It means something to you."

"Murph, it *can't* mean anything to me. I'm in love with the *idea* of love. Everyone knows this. So I can't trust my feelings. Just because I get all melty around him doesn't mean a damned thing."

"Hmm," he says, sniffing. "What's it like with him?"

I shiver. "I think I have a praise kink now."

The grin on Murph's face could power this building, and his voice comes out hushed. "He's sweet to you?"

"Yeah."

"Then he has it bad, too."

I shake my head. "That's where you're wrong. He doesn't want to be in a relationship again. I'm just convenient. This is a means to an end. Nothing more." It hurts to say this, but I have to protect myself. Murph starts to reply, but I hold up a hand. "I'm the one who always thinks things mean more than they do. This time, I need to face facts."

"Well, for your sake, I hope you're wrong." He presses his lips together. "Is it awesome to be with him otherwise? I mean, with your clothes on?"

"Totally. It's like he's forgotten how to have fun and is only now starting to remember. I think his kid is making him feel younger. And I hope I am, too. He's smiling more than he did when I first met him, and he's so good with her."

"Then find ways to spend more time with him having fun." He grins. "I know you can do that, Scott. You're the best at coming up with things to do."

"Like picnics in the living room?"

"Yes, like that. You'll think of something. Take him to a football game with your dad, or go to a movie. Hell, just hold his hand at the park."

For a moment, I'm fantasizing about holding Luke's hand in public—which is funny, because you'd think I'd be fantasizing about his cock.

But I have his cock. I don't have his hand … or his heart.

"What if I get hurt, though?" I startle. "I can't believe I said that out loud."

Murph puts a hand on my shoulder. "I know you want to be a turtle back in your shell after such a rude awakening with Edsel. But there's nothing wrong with spending time with people you like. You like both Luke and his daughter, right?"

"Yeah, I do."

"Then have fun with them, with no expectations. Life is for living, Scott. You know this. Don't let one bad experience with an ex knock you down."

———

That evening, I run into the living room, where Luke and Addi are watching a show together, and make jazz hands. "Okay! I've got an idea."

Luke glances up at me, and I can't tell if he's annoyed or intrigued. Since I like the latter better, I'mma go with intrigued. Surely that's his "Scott is amusing me" look.

"What's your idea?" he asks patiently, and props to him that he's not saying it like I'm a child interrupting him.

"We should go stargazing. It's a perfect night for it. Do you want to go look for constellations?" I ask Addi.

"Yes!" she says.

Luke looks at me as if I have stars shooting from my head. "Stargazing?"

"Yep," I say. "Outside. Now that it's dark. We should bring hot chocolate and bundle up and go look. It's a beautiful night."

He blinks. "Do you know how to tell what the constellations are?"

"Yep. You point up and go, there's a bunch of stars. And some more."

That gets a laugh out of him. "I don't know any constellations other than the Big Dipper. I'm just going to be looking at the sky without knowing anything about it."

I put my hands on my hips. "You've never just looked at the stars to contemplate your place in the universe? Think about how vast it all is? Wonder whether or not there are parallel universes? Other Scotts and Lukes and Addisons living in a grand old house wondering if it's all going to work out?"

"Nope," Luke says. "Can't say that I have."

"Then it's about time you did." I tug him up. "C'mon. Get your coat and hat. It's clear out, and the news said something about a meteor shower. We should be able to see it."

I get Addi dressed, and we walk down the driveway into a dark, moonless night. I made a large thermos of hot chocolate and brought some cups. I was laden down with blankets as well, but Luke grabbed them from me. We walk down the tree-lined road to the main one, then cross over to a clear grassy area with a view of the sky.

When we get there, he lays the blankets down, and we all arrange ourselves. Addi holds his hand as she lies down. I resist the urge to do the same and instead lie on the other side of her. Our heads are all together, while our bodies go in different directions on the blanket.

"See?" I whisper. "I was right. It's beautiful out here."

Luke grunts. But he looks up to study the stars—millions of points of light in the darkness overhead, the space both infinite and crushing.

"So, Galileo, show me the stars," he says, and I love the playfulness in his voice. It's something I've only ever heard him direct at Addi.

I point up. "There they are."

He bursts out laughing. "I never would have guessed," he says dryly. "Do you know anything about them?"

"Not really. I think some of the brighter stars could be planets. If it moves, it could be a plane or a satellite."

"Isn't there an app that can show us all this?"

"Yeah, but that takes the imagination out of it. Making it up is more fun. Okay?"

His voice gets gruff. "Sure, we can do that."

"I see a lion," Addi says.

And she goes on to point out more animals than even I could imagine.

The night air is cold, but gloves and heavy jackets keep it from being uncomfortable. The wind rustles the leaves in the trees and on the ground, and in the distance I hear a dog barking.

Right here, though, it feels like we're in our own little world.

And the scene reminds me of something.

"Have you ever seen the movie *Powers of Ten*?" I ask. "It's on YouTube—it's only like ten minutes long. It was done by some people who also made midcentury modern furniture, which I think is kind of random. It's super cool, if a bit retro. It starts with people having a picnic and zooms ten times out. And then another ten times. And then another and another, until you're at the farthest reaches of the universe. Then it zooms back in to the subatomic level, each time going by the power of ten. It really makes you appreciate just how big all this is." I reach up to ruffle his hair and then turn onto my stomach, facing him. "You're a numbers guy. You'd like it."

"You'll have to show it to me." I catch a flash of his eyes in the starlight, and his expression is gentle.

In fact, he looks at me so long, I think he's going to kiss me. It seems like the right moment, out here under the stars.

Stop it, Scott. You're such a hopeless romantic that you think every moment is a moment for kissing. And he's not going to kiss you around his daughter.

"Find me more stars, Daddy!" Addi says.

"You mean a constellation? Am I supposed to be making them up, since I don't know any? I mean, that one looks like a bad tattoo."

"Where?" she asks.

He points, but of course we have no idea what he's talking about.

"Can I have some cocoa?" Addi asks.

"Sure, baby." We all sit up. I pour her some, and we rearrange ourselves, Addi in front of me and Luke behind.

He scoots closer to me and kneels, his hands on my shoulders and his breath whispering on my neck. "Look up." With one hand, he holds mine, trying to show me where his constellation is.

Fuck, he's close.

Fuck, he's *delicious.*

Fuck, I need to move before I roll over and tackle him in front of his kid.

"I think I might see it," I say, and it's the truth. "But I'm not sure it's a bad tattoo. One of the ones over there looks like a pair of glasses."

"Which?"

Now it's my turn to gesture. And as we get closer and closer, I realize what a terrible idea this was, because we're definitely close enough to kiss.

Or maybe it was a superb idea.

"What do you think, Addi?" I ask, to keep my thoughts away from *things.*

"I like the stars. Daddy, do you like being out here?"

"Yeah." He clears his throat and then murmurs, so quiet I almost don't catch it, "I'm starting to remember who I was before I went to New York."

I don't think he wants a response to that. But I like that Vermont is making him less ... uptight, or whatever.

After a while, Addison starts yawning, so we pack up and head back.

Luke spent time with us doing something that had no point other than fun. I love it.

We put Addi to bed, and then he finds me in my room, where we go at it as aggressively as always. When we're done, he's putting his clothes back on and about to leave, but I stop him at the door. "Can I ask you something?"

He eyes me up and down. "Sure."

"Addi asked me again about a hot-air balloon ride, and I looked into it. They're pricey, but I don't think that's an issue for you. Apparently cold weather is a good time to go—for buoyancy." I pause. "And I checked the safety ratings of the local company, and they're very high."

He sighs, but his expression is soft. Maybe that's what an orgasm does to him. "Fine."

That's how we find ourselves up at the crack of dawn a week later, yawning and again drinking out of to-go cups. Luke has coffee, I've got a mocha, and Addi sips hot chocolate. The weather is perfect—chilly, but still and clear.

When we get to the huge field where the balloons are being readied, the silence of the morning is broken by hushed voices in the dark and the noise of burning propane.

"Which one are we in?" Addi asks.

I glance around, looking for the one we booked, which is green and blue—hard to see until they start filling up.

"I can't wait to experience this," I say. "I've never been up in a balloon before."

"I'm so excited!" Addi says. "It's just like in the story!"

Luke looks a bit grim, but he holds her hand as we walk.

We find the one we've reserved and meet the people running it. After a few preliminaries, we climb into the basket, and they fire up the burners. Luke had me book a private ride, so it's just us, but the operator is this huge dude who's about the size of me and Luke put together.

Which is how Luke and I end up on one side of the basket and Addi on the other, closer to the operator, to balance the weight. I can tell Luke doesn't like her being so far from him, but the need to be safe has overruled his emotional objections.

"Hey," I murmur.

He eyes me warily. "Yeah?"

"Are you okay?"

"Yep."

Crossing my arms, I ask, "Are you scared of heights and didn't tell me?"

"I'm not scared of heights."

"So you're okay."

"Yeah," he says, his voice husky. "I've just … never done this before."

"Isn't that the point?"

Luke swallows and tries a smile. "I guess."

"Then do me a favor. Do your best to enjoy this moment."

"Enjoy this moment?"

"You have your daughter here, doing the thing she wants to do." I don't mention that I'm here, too. But I surreptitiously hold his gloved hand in the dark. "So enjoy it. If you can."

He gives me a grimace, but it's less tense than before, and his eyes lock on mine. He looks really hot in a dark gray knit cap. "I will."

The firing of the propane makes a racket. Soon enough, the balloon is straining at its tethers, and the ground crew gives the signal to let it go.

And we take off.

We float up into the air, and it's the biggest rush I've ever experienced.

The ground gets farther and farther away.

Addi squeals and claps her hands.

Phew. I'd been worried she'd be scared. But since this was her idea, I guess not. She seems perfectly content, her hands gripping the side of the basket as she stares in wonder. The basket feels stable, and the operator seems to know what he's doing, so I don't think Luke is as worried as he was before.

Meanwhile, I'm noticing how close he and I are standing. And how this is even better than the feeling on a roller coaster or a plane, because it's so silent and still, just the occasional blast from the propane burners.

Luke lets go of my hand to grip my waist, and I lean into him.

While I'd thought we should do this because Addi had been asking and because Luke needed to do something frivolous, I realize that this is exactly the sort of super-romantic experience old Scott would have adored.

And I start wishing for things I'm not supposed to have.

Like Luke.

LUKE

"Okay," I whisper into Scott's ear, trying not to sound too begrudging. "You and Addi were right. This was a great idea. It's gorgeous up here."

We're soaring over the last of Vermont's fall colors, the cold morning air nipping our faces. But it feels freeing and invigorating … and romantic as fuck.

I'm not romantic, and I don't normally waste time doing shit like this. But the one person I'd do anything for—Addison—asked, and, well, it's getting hard to resist Scott, too.

Much to my annoyance.

Scott has this way of getting under my skin. I don't know what I feel around him. It's simultaneously disorienting and liberating. I like how he takes me out of my usual routine, and while I'll never admit it, I like the things I've done since I met him: reading romance, stargazing, eating ice cream with my kid.

But more than that, I want to touch him. He's right here next to me, his body giving off warmth even though he's in a winter coat and knit hat and his nose is red from the cold.

I want to kiss that nose.

I want to take him home and strip him down.

I want to—

"And there's the field where we will be making our descent," the operator announces, pointing to a flat area ringed with trees.

In much too short a time, our ride is over and we touch down at an hour when most people are starting the day. Addi and Scott are all smiles, and I wouldn't be surprised if I looked happy, too.

"It was pretty fun," I admit, shaking the operator's hand. We all thank him and head for the waiting van that will take us back to where we parked. I climb into the front seat, while Scott and Addi slide in back.

"Did you like that?" Scott asks Addi, as he buckles her into a booster seat.

Addi claps her hands and giggles. "I loved it! You could see all the trees and the cows. It was just like in my books! What are we going to do next?"

I glance at her over my shoulder. "We're going home."

She lets out an exaggerated sigh. "Daddy, I mean the next *fun* thing."

The driver starts the vehicle, and we set off along the curvy, tree-lined highway.

"Scott is the one who comes up with those things," I point out. Addi and I both study him—her expectantly, me amused—waiting for whatever imaginative ideas he'll suggest next.

His imagination might be one of my favorite things about him. And, to be honest, it has a ton of competition.

"Well." He thinks about it. "We have plenty of special things to look forward to. Thanksgiving. My birthday. All the December holidays."

"When's your birthday?" I ask, before I can stop myself.

"December 5. We have to get through Turkey Day first. What are you two going to do for Thanksgiving?"

My Thanksgivings in New York have mainly consisted of swanky restaurant affairs with coworkers, most of whom drank too much, and then going to the office to get some work done while things were quiet. "What do you and Momma usually do?" I ask Addi.

"Go to Nana's."

Crashing Kira's parents' holiday isn't for me. It's one thing to be on cordial terms with my ex. But her parents haven't forgiven me for ruining their perfect daughter's perfect family—even if between Kira and me, it was mutual—so while we're polite during Addison's pickups and drop-offs, it's not like we shoot the shit. Good thing they adore seeing her, because it gives Scott a break.

And gives me a chance to spend time alone with him.

I guess we could find a restaurant somewhere. Unless Scott knows how to cook a full Thanksgiving dinner—which, frankly, I wouldn't put past him.

Scott must sense my indecision, because he reaches forward, squeezing my shoulder. I involuntarily lean into his touch. "Want to come home with me? My parents can always accommodate a couple more guests. They're used to cooking for a crowd. If you're up for way too many of my relatives, lots of noise, and enough food to cater a cruise ship."

"If it's okay with them, we'd love to," I say quickly. Partly because I want to give Addi as many normal family experiences as I can. Mostly, though, because I'm curious about Scott and his enormous family.

As we pass by a Costco near where we started, Scott chuckles.

"What?"

"I think we wore her out."

Addi's fallen asleep, her little head against the window, her dark curls going every which way.

Scott's phone pings. In the rearview mirror, I can see him wrinkling his nose.

"What's up?" I ask.

"It's my dad."

"Is he okay?"

Scott huffs. "He's always looking for a date for me." We lock eyes in the mirror, and I realize my expression is somewhere between pissed off and amused. "What?" he asks cautiously.

"Still? How is that going? Has he found you a winner?"

"Absolutely not. His taste in men is worse than mine, and that's saying something." He quickly adds, "Worse than mine before I met you, I mean. Not that we're … Never mind."

"All good," I say. "No offense taken. I knew what you meant."

"But his behavior is either charmingly endearing or hopelessly annoying, and I can't decide which."

"Okay." I scowl. "I still don't like him setting you up." Although at least his dad takes an interest in his life. I missed out on so much with Addison.

While I'm lost in my thoughts, he asks the important question. "Do you want me to tell him I've found someone?"

I turn and stare at him over my shoulder for a long moment. The driver doesn't appear to be paying much attention to us. Finally, I mutter, "Yeah. I do."

He beams, and my heart melts. Something about him reminds me of all that's good in life.

"Okay," he says quietly. "I'll text him. Just be prepared to meet the nosiest man on the planet at Thanksgiving."

I pull out my phone.

Scott scrunches his face. "What are you doing?"

"Deleting the hookup app I installed when I got here."

He blinks in surprise. "Hookup app?"

"I haven't used it," I assure him. "And I won't."

At least not while whatever we have going on is still going on.

I glance up, and he nods thoughtfully. But I think the idea pleases him.

When we get back to the Rover, we transfer Addi and head home, where she shuffles to her room to take a nap. After she's closed the door, I shove Scott against the nearest wall hard enough that he lets out an "Oomph." I press my forehead against his and inhale his outdoorsy scent. His breath hitches, and he grabs my shirt with both fists and kisses me.

God, he makes me feel *alive*. On some level, I always knew my life in New York was a kind of prison—although given Landon's past, I may have to come up with a different term—but we just spent the morning literally flying in the open air, not even bound to Earth by gravity.

My heart is beating so fast I feel like I'm still soaring.

I wrench myself back with a groan but immediately lean in again to nip at his ear, making him shiver. "Do you know what it was like having you so close to me in that basket and not being able to touch you the way I wanted?"

He bites his lip and shakes his head, then tilts his chin up, exposing his neck. I take the invitation and suck on it, grinding my pelvis against his. I hold him tight and kiss him again, our tongues dipping hungrily into each other's mouths. His hands are hard on my hips.

"I wanted you," I mutter. "God help me, up there in the air, with my kid and a stranger right next to us, I had to fight to keep from kissing you."

"I want you, too. I always want you. I want you inside me." Scott's whining a bit, but I kind of love it, because he sounds desperate.

I study him. His face drops, which makes my stomach sink as well. "Hey. What's wrong?"

"Is there something the matter with me? That you don't want to fuck me."

Scrubbing my face with my hands, I step back and frown. "In New York, it's just been anonymous sex. Fast and dirty and ... I get off, they get off, it's good enough." I shake my head. "I didn't want to treat you like that."

He scoffs. "Hate to break it to you, but we've been trading hasty blowjobs and handjobs this whole time."

"Yeah, but ..." I try to articulate what I'm thinking. "Maybe some small romantic part of me didn't want to treat you like someone I don't know. Wanted to be sensitive to your needs, to take my time with you."

Scott seems to chew on my words. "Hmm." He kisses me.

"I've had plenty of quick and dirty. I'm touched you wanted to wait."

"So you want me inside you?"

"I do," he rasps, and I'm sure my expression goes feral. "But I can wait until it feels right. I want us both to be into it."

God help me, I want it to be special with him. We're kissing again, and I'm a moment away from taking him to my room. "We'll get there." I can't explain why I'm waiting. But it doesn't feel right yet.

I know Scott. I know he likes romance.

I can try to give him what he wants.

And maybe some part of me also wants sex to mean a little more.

We keep kissing, making no move to go to either of our rooms, until Addi's door opens and we jump away from each other.

"I can't sleep," she says, rubbing her eyes. "No nap."

I head over to her and get down on my knees so I'm her height. "You had an exciting morning."

"I can take her to the park and grab some lunch after," Scott says. "Do you have plans?"

"Yeah, I'm going to meet Landon from the stables for coffee. I knew him when we were kids."

"Have fun!" he says, and he helps Addi into her coat.

Seeing them leave makes my chest hurt. But I don't need to do everything with them.

"Hey," I say, as Landon walks into the bookstore part of V and V, his silver hair glinting. He waves at me, orders a coffee, and then joins me at my table. I've been eyeing a flyer for drag queen story hour and wondering if that's something Scott should bring Addi to. I wonder what she'd think about it.

"Hey," Landon mutters, not making eye contact.

I sip my coffee and wait. Because this man is not the kid I

knew—but I'm not the kid he knew, either. Whatever happened to him, I'm not going to force him to talk ... although I do, you know, need a friend.

Which is not something I'd ever admit in Manhattan.

Maybe he needs one, too.

Finally, he looks up and gives me a crooked grin. "Well, this is awkward. It's been, what, twenty years?"

"Near enough."

"Last I heard, you were off to some fancy college."

"Last I heard, you were aging out of foster care." I raise an eyebrow.

He nods. "Life was shit, yeah. Being back is ... an adjustment."

"Tell me about it."

We stare at each other and then both laugh.

"Neither one of us is good at small talk," I say.

"Or talk," he mutters.

"Yeah, well. We have our reasons. All right, I'll start. Kira's from here but a few years younger than us. I started dating her after you and I lost contact. I got an economics degree from Wharton. About eight years ago, Kira and I got married, and we had Addi. We've been divorced longer than we were together. After we split up, I moved to Manhattan."

"So why are you back?"

"Kira's a journalist, but she's always wanted to be one of those international correspondents. She couldn't, because of Addison, but she got offered an overseas assignment and asked if I'd watch Addi while she took the job."

"Shit. Where is she?"

"Myanmar. She's investigating the imprisonment of American citizens."

He furrows his brows. "Aren't you scared something is going to happen to her?"

"Yes, but it's her choice. This is her big chance, you know? She went through all that schooling. She's a crusader, and she deserves this scoop. And she's careful. The news agency has security; she's not on her own."

"Still."

I sigh and take another sip of my coffee. "Yeah, still."

"And are you seeing anyone?"

The coffee goes down the wrong pipe.

"Sorry, dude," he says. "I'm crap at asking about normal shit. Mostly I figure it's none of my business."

"Well, I'm crap at normal relationships. So, of course, I'm kind of seeing my nanny," I admit.

"The hipster kid? Scott?"

"Yup." I flick my eyes up to his. "I like him more than I should."

"He seems nice enough."

"He is nice enough, but he's all wrong for me."

Landon grunts.

"What?"

"How do you know that?"

"He's young and—oh—*my fucking nanny*."

"But you like him."

"Yeah. But it's just hooking up."

"Really?"

I don't answer. Instead, I take a sip of my coffee, and he drains his.

"I think you should maybe not worry about what society thinks," he says. "Not that you asked my opinion."

I give him a half grin. "Yeah, maybe. Now that I've spilled my guts, want to tell me what's happened with you since I last saw you?"

He sighs. "The short version is, I was convicted on two counts each of burglary and grand larceny and sentenced to thirteen years."

That's worse than I'd heard. "*Fuck.*"

"I served eight, and now I'm paroled. I've been out for almost nine months and back in Burlington for about four."

"Where are you living?"

"With my sister."

"What happened?"

Landon studies me, likely deciding how much he wants to say. He looks around and, reassured that no one is paying attention to us, begins to tell his story.

When Scott comes to my room that night, I have a minor crisis. I don't want to give him a hurried blowjob like we've been doing, but while I want to take his ass, I'm not ready for that. Physically, yes. But emotionally? No. I'm scared I'd treat him like my hookups, and Scott deserves more than that. If I'm going to be inside him, I want it to not be thoughtless.

So, blowjobs it is. Except I take my time. Kiss him more. Praise him more.

When he leaves, though, my bed is so empty I can't stand it. After what seems like hours of tossing and turning but is probably twenty minutes, I throw the covers off and skulk down the hallway to his room.

When I get to his closed door, I question my actions. I should just leave him alone.

Instead, I rap very quietly and murmur, "Scott?"

His sleepy voice comes through the door. "Luke?"

I feel very, very foolish. But … in for a pound. I open the door and step inside.

"What's wrong?" he asks, sitting up in bed.

I grin, though he probably can't see it in the dark, stripping off my T-shirt but keeping my sleep pants on. "Nothing."

"Is Addi okay?"

"She's fine."

"Do you need something?"

"Yes."

"What?"

"You."

His sharp intake of breath is something I don't know how to handle. "Get in here, then."

I crawl in beside him and gather his sleepy warmth in my arms. Something about him settles me. I kiss the back of his neck. "Good night."

"Good night."

In no time at all, his breathing evens out. The next thing I know, it's morning, and I'm still holding him.

17

SCOTT

The bookstore side of Vino and Veritas has always felt at least as comfortable and cheery to me as the wine bar side. Maybe more, since I've always loved the written word.

But I'm out of sorts right now, because Luke rocked my world last night.

Not with the sexy stuff. I mean, that was great and all, but we'd done that before. After, though … he came to me. And it made me feel like this might be more than a hookup. I'm pretty sure Luke doesn't cuddle with his fuck buddies.

This morning was divine. It was something I've always wanted: to wake up in the arms of someone I care about. With his legs entwined with mine, his face buried in my neck, and his hard-on pressing into my ass, it was all I could do not to rub up against him like a wanton cat.

The bubble burst pretty quickly, since he got up early and left, likely because he didn't want Addi to catch us together.

Still, he kissed me softly before he got out of bed, so I'm about as confused as I get.

Sleeping with me—actually *sleeping*—had to mean something to him, didn't it? Or am I reading too much into it?

Like I always do.

I gulp and try to pull myself back to the present. Next to me in the circle of chairs, Luke manspreads, deceptively calm, my copy of *The Stripper Club* in his big paw. I suspect he's not at all comfortable being part of Briar's book club. I mean, we're talking about feelings and fiction and stuff far removed from Luke's world of high finance and sophisticated city living. But he covers it well.

We left Addison with Kira's parents. They were going to take her out to eat and go to a movie, so Luke and I have plenty of time. If we were dating, I suppose we could call this a date. Of course, we're not. So it isn't.

And I need to stop wishing otherwise. A hookup is just a hookup, nothing more.

Except last night …

Last night, it wasn't quick and dirty.

Last night, Luke cuddled me.

Briar clears his throat. "So, what did we think of this month's selection, chosen by Lucia?" His boyfriend, Jamie, grins at him.

"I thought it was about time we normalized sex work in this group," Lucia says.

"Absolutely," Betty agrees. She's old enough to be my grand-mother, and she's wearing a T-shirt reading, "FEMINISM IS THE BEST F-WORD." The first time I came to book club, I walked in on her telling Briar how excited she was that mari-juana had finally been legalized in Vermont and how she couldn't wait to try vaping. I sort of wish she were my grand-mother. "I'll start," she continues. "I enjoyed it overall, and I was very taken with the character development and the sex scenes. But the breakup at 75 percent of the book was too contrived for my tastes."

"Ugh. Yes. I hate it when authors do that," Cherry says. She's a Moo U student, I think.

We all nod in agreement, except Luke, who frowns.

Briar picks up on his expression. "You don't mind when that happens?"

Luke shrugs. "I dunno. It's fiction. It didn't bother me. Sometimes bad shit has to happen for people to grow."

"That's true," I mutter. The Edsel debacle got me out of my shithole apartment.

Well, that and the threat of eviction.

"And the makeup sex when they got back together was out of this world," Lilah says. She's the book club co-founder and around Betty's age. A few people laugh.

"What did we think of Sebastian?" asks Bart, one of my favorite people in the group. He's a bus driver, and he has a very calming presence that we need sometimes. Especially when Lucia and Cherry argue. I'd never heard anyone scream "reader-response criticism" across a bookstore until I met the two of them. "It took me a while to warm up to him."

"Ugh, he was such a douche," Emily, Betty's niece, says. "He was so selfish, leaving his baby so he could go fuck all those men."

"Right?" Lucia says. "There's no way Sebastian could've been that good at sex with men if he hadn't been getting some on the side during his marriage. He had to have been cheating on Anna. Heartless asshole."

I look at Luke, and he looks back at me, both of us very confused. "Where did you get the idea that Seb was a cheater?" I ask slowly. "Because I did not read that into the text at all."

"Me neither." Luke crosses his arms over his chest and glares, like he's daring anyone to disagree with him.

"I don't know," Jamie says. "I see him as a good guy, maybe career-driven, and maybe at some point in his life he liked the idea of kids and a wife, but he made some selfish choices. He didn't even co-parent."

"Why do you think he was selfish?" Luke asks, voice steely.

Lilah shrugs. "He's an absentee father. He left his wife because he wanted the freedom to be gay, and she was in the way. He realized he didn't want what he had."

"Wow, okay." Luke scoots forward in his seat and puts his

elbows on his knees, his chin propped on his fists. He can be so very intense sometimes. "I read it way different than you."

"I've been divorced four times, sweetheart. There's always a reason marriages fail."

"Is it possible"—Luke's voice is quiet, but we can all hear him perfectly—"that Sebastian feels so bad about not being able to achieve his perfect family that he self-destructs? Maybe he was a nice guy before he realized he couldn't make everyone happy. Maybe he was never going to be happy with Anna, nor she with him, no matter how hard they tried. And maybe after he got divorced, he said, 'Fuck it, I'm going to go fuck my way through this town because I don't deserve my dreams.'"

We all stare at him.

And I think I understand him a lot more.

"I thought he left his wife for some guy," Emily says.

Luke wrinkles his nose. "Show me where you read that. Why does he have to have been promiscuous during his marriage? I think he was faithful."

"It's not on the page," Cherry says. "I just figured why else would they start the book with him in bed with a stripper?"

"Because it's a book about him and the stripper falling in love?" Luke sighs. "I thought it portrayed so much of the crap men go through. We can't show feelings. We can't be hurt." He sits back. "I thought it showed a lot about the human condition, honestly."

I keep my jaw from dropping open. Because while I figured Luke had some toxic masculinity going on, I didn't realize he was self-aware about it.

And he's not done. "Seb tried so hard to be perfect, but it's impossible. If you're a perfectionist, it often results in depression or self-destruction. Seb's just lucky he met Xavier."

We all nod. "That's true," Cherry says—and I remember that she's studying psychology.

"I mean," Luke adds, "that's just my opinion. You can have your own. I don't wanna step on anyone's toes here."

"Nah, that's what we're here for. Lively debate." Briar grins. "I think we can formally welcome you to book club. You're going to be a good addition."

We all give Luke a round of applause, and he raises an eyebrow at me. My heartbeat goes haywire.

"I can't wait to hear your comments on our next read," Briar continues. "If you're willing to read another romance."

"Yes. I think I judged the genre—unfairly—based on the covers," Luke says. "Although who doesn't like looking at hot men?"

"Those who don't," Tara says, shelving books behind him.

"Fair. I guess all I'm saying is that I'm good with it." He nudges me with his shoulder. "What did you think of the book, Scott? Did you like it?"

"I loved it. I thought their first kiss was amazing. And I'm always waiting for the moment when they finally say, 'I love you.'"

Luke sits back. "So, what's the next book?"

Briar tells him the title of the most viral MMF romance on BookTok right now.

"Oh, I read that last weekend," Luke says, surprising me. "And I took a look at the reviews on a few sites and was struck by how much harder the reviewers are on the female character than the males. The guys are grumpy assholes with almost no redeeming qualities, and reviewers are fawning over them. Meanwhile, the woman has sex with other people before they all meet, and everyone is calling her a slut. It's a total double standard."

I gaze at him in amazement. "Misogyny is a problem. But I didn't think—"

"Didn't think I'd notice it?"

"Yeah, I guess."

Luke huffs. "Oh, I pay attention. I pay more attention than you know."

Briar is looking back and forth between us like this is the most fascinating exchange he's ever seen. Luke clears his throat. "I mean, we can talk about it next time, but I thought the author was really good at drawing parallels between the heroine's needs and the heroes' attributes. And I think making her an antihero—an arsonist with a mission—was a great choice for heightening conflict. Especially since they're firefighters."

"I can't wait to read it," Jamie says.

"Are you sure you've never read romance before?" I ask Luke.

"Yep. But maybe you have me hooked." He grins at me, and I melt a little.

Then I remind myself of all the things I need reminding of.

On Thanksgiving Day, it still hasn't snowed, although all the trees are bare. The rainy drive to Stowe takes about an hour, and we get there plenty early, Addi in the back seat of Luke's Range Rover next to two pies that I baked.

I don't know why I'm nervous about bringing Luke. Perhaps because I'm not sure what we are to each other.

Some sort of hybrid employee-boss hookups/maybe kinda friends?

And perhaps because I don't know how he's going to handle this massive meet-the-parents thing. Because it isn't just my parents, it's *everyone*.

Luke and Addison each take a pie as we walk up to the house, which is an old lodge that's part of a ski resort. Addi steps carefully so as not to drop her precious cargo. I don't bother knocking —no one would hear if I did—but open the door and let us into the entryway, which is lined with hooks and places for boots and skis, much of the space taken up already. We shed our coats and go into the great room, which is a combination living room, dining room, and kitchen.

It's filled with people, mostly my siblings, along with some of their friends and a few other assorted aunts, uncles, and cousins, as well as my grandparents.

Oh god, what did I bring Luke to?

"Hey!" my mom exclaims, hurrying over and squashing me in a hug. "Scotty!"

"Mom," I wheeze. "Good to see you." An even dozen of my family circle around us, but I can only pay attention to one at a time.

After kissing my cheeks, she steps back and surveys me. "You're looking better. Not so skinny." She pinches my cheek.

"Thanks." I wave a hand toward my guests. "This is my—" *Employer? Fuck buddy? Date?* "Uh, Lucas Lagomarsino and his daughter, Addison."

My mom gives them a huge grin and accepts the pies with grace, and the introductions start. I catch Luke's eye, and he looks quite amused by all the hubbub. I let out a sigh of relief.

Soon enough, we're swarmed. My youngest sister, Daphne, is about Addi's age, and she immediately takes Addi under her wing. I look at Luke and shrug. He gives me a warm smile.

My aunts corner him to talk about I don't even know what, but he seems so relaxed and comfortable that I stop worrying about him pretty quickly. I also ignore the fact that he's closer in age to that generation than my own. Other than book club, I haven't really seen Luke interact with many people, and I guess part of me expected him to be antisocial. But he's not at all.

Or maybe it's the inescapable pull of my family. Someone is always up in your business here.

When it's time for dinner, I make sure to sit by Luke. Addi's at the kids' table, which is just as big as the adults' table. At one point, Luke stretches and puts his arm around the back of my chair, and it's all I can do not to snuggle into him. But ... do we do this?

I don't know the rules, and that's stressful.

We make it through dinner without anyone calling us out, which is something of a Thanksgiving miracle.

I don't fare so well in the kitchen when I volunteer to help my dad and my oldest sister with the dishes.

Dad corners me while I'm scrubbing a big pot, up to my elbows in suds. "Luke is your boss, right?"

"Yeah," I say cautiously.

"Because he's not looking at you like that. He's looking at you like you're his boyfriend."

I sigh. "Not that it's any of your business, but we are getting together. I don't think you could call it dating."

"What would you call it? Are you exclusive with him?"

He asked me not to date anyone. "I think so."

"Don't you know for sure?"

"Dad, can you leave my love life alone, please?" I hiss. "I don't want Luke to hear."

"Don't want me to hear what?"

I turn around, and Luke is bringing in a stack of dirty plates.

"Nothing," I mutter.

My dad brings his shoulders back so he's standing at his full height—slightly pouchy belly, Patriots jersey, and all. "What, exactly, are your intentions with my son?"

"Dad!" I snap, my voice sharper than it's ever been with my family. My father doesn't even have the decency to look embarrassed. "Seriously, Dad. Stay out of it."

Luke looks between us with a confused expression that morphs to something softer when he focuses on me.

"I was trying to get him to stop 'helping' with my love life, that's all," I mutter.

Luke, to my surprise, comes up behind me and wraps his arms around my waist, kissing the back of my head. "He doesn't need help. He has me."

I try to pick my jaw up off the floor, but my dad's eyes are dancing. "That answers my question, then," he says.

18

LUKE

Tonight—the Saturday after Thanksgiving—we've arranged for Addison to sleep over at Kira's parents' house because they didn't get to see her for Thanksgiving. We've recovered from how much we overate on Thursday.

And I want him.

I've put off fucking Scott because I wanted to be sure I was in the right mental space for it—the right space to give him everything I could. Besides, I didn't want to do anything too involved when my kid was around.

While it doesn't normally matter that much to me how I get off, and I expect Scott will go along with whatever I suggest, he deserves to be treated right. He deserves *more*.

I'm not going to analyze why I think that, but it's true. He's wormed his way into my thoughts, and I respect him enough to try to give him what he really wants: affection ... and attention. I can do that without dipping into feelings.

So tonight's a perfect night, for eminently practical reasons.

Why do I feel like I'm justifying something to myself? I should just fuck him and quit my dithering.

"Hey," I call, and Scott follows me to the bedroom, where I tug him to me and start taking off his shirt, one button at a time. His breath ghosts against my skin, a whisper.

I love the way heat radiates from him when we're this close. It makes my cock stand up and my heart beat faster.

I don't want to get distracted from my task, but his exposed skin is so kissable. So as I slide his shirt from his shoulders, my mouth traces the areas I've just exposed, dancing along his warm skin, dropping kisses like I have to touch him everywhere.

Because I do.

"Oh," he whispers. "That feels—"

His words are cut off when I reach down and stroke him. "I fucking love how hard you are for me."

"Always."

I drop to my knees. With tender, gentle fingers, he tugs at my hair, then caresses my cheeks. I unbuckle his belt and tear down his zipper, needing to see him. Releasing his hard cock, I take a deep breath. Because, fuck, I am very definitely into this.

I take the tip in my mouth, then go down a little bit and start sucking. I know he likes licking and rubbing at the head, so I ignore the base, focusing all my attention at the crown and just underneath.

Given the way his knees buckle before he catches himself on the nearby chair, I think I'm doing okay.

"Luke," he whispers. "That feels so unghhhhhh."

He releases precome into my mouth, and the salty flavor makes me hum. I love all of this. I love the feel of his soft skin and solid cock. I love the way he smells, clean but with a natural scent underneath. I love the noises he makes. I love it all.

Most of all, I love feeling like I'm in charge of him. I very much want to be in charge of him, especially in the bedroom. But I also want to make sure he's taken care of in other ways.

I'm not going to analyze that, either.

"Luke," he repeats. "This is turning me on too fast. If you keep—"

I pop off. "I want you to come."

"What if I don't want to?"

I startle and pull back. "You don't want to? I'm sorry—"

"I *do* want to. I just don't want to, too *fast*."

"Oh." Relief courses through me, and I wrap my fist around him. "You can come again later. You're always ready. Advantage of being younger."

"Not an advantage," he moans, fucking himself into my hand a few times. "Awkward boners are never an advantage."

"Don't say never. I'm sure we could come up with a way that they are."

"But I'm still going to come too fast."

"Are you really standing here and arguing that I shouldn't give you a blowjob?"

He pauses. "Well. Yes. I guess I am."

"Can you think of a better use of our time? Do you want my mouth or not?" I demand.

"Yes," he gasps, scratching his fingers through my hair again, making me want to arch into him like a cat. "I most definitely want your mouth on me. But I also want to touch you," he says, his voice quiet and pleading. "You're all dressed."

I stand up and smile. "Fair enough." Without any further discussion, I start stripping. In no time, I'm down to my boxers, and he looks at me in appreciation.

"Fuck, Daddy."

I glare at him. "Don't call me that."

He giggles. "It's okay. I'm not into that. I mean, I understand the dynamic, but it's not for me. Still, sometimes you are a daddy. Don't argue. You will lose."

I sigh. "Fine."

Scott shoves a hand into my underwear and slips them off. Then he drops to his knees, and before I know what's going on, he's licking me and then sucking, and I forget what we were arguing about.

"*Fuck.* That feels so good."

He doesn't reply, since his mouth is occupied. And now I'm

understanding why he stopped me. Because I want the rush of orgasm, but I also want the good feeling to go on and on.

I remind myself who I'm with. Scott wants to savor things. He wants to be romanced.

While he can be dirty, I think he's more interested in the connection.

Connection he shall have.

I take his hand, and he pulls off me in surprise. "What?"

"Come to bed, honey," I whisper.

The way his face lights up makes me want to do anything for him. He's *incandescent*. "Okay," is all he says, but his face says far more.

He follows me to the bed, and when we get beside it, I take his face between my hands. I study his eyes, seeing the heat and joy there, and I kiss him. It starts off sweet. I'm trying to be Prince Charming here … although our cocks are touching, so the similarities end pretty quickly.

But then we're fully making out, tongues interlocking in the deepest kisses I've ever had. Kisses that make my body throb, not just my cock. Kisses that make the hair on the back of my neck stand on end. He pulls me to him, and I take handfuls of his perfect ass, then try to do the romantic thing and hold his waist instead. He groans, and we fall onto the bed, him going backward and me climbing onto him, our mouths never separating.

If he wants to be romanced, we'll take our time.

The frenzy is done, and now it's even more intense because it's like each kiss is an event. I don't care where it leads—I'm here for that individual kiss.

I've never experienced anything like it. Time is a living, breathing thing, but it's also crystallized so we'll be able to look back on this later. Moments with him are suspended in amber.

I can't get enough of his lips on me.

And mine on him.

I love the way he tastes. I love the way our bodies align—as well as our lock and key tattoos. I love the way he's so into this.

I'm almost getting off on how his hands travel my body, like now that he has permission, he's going to use his all-you-can-touch pass to be a greedy bastard. Fine. Let him.

Because I'm doing the same.

We roll around, first me on top, then him, until we're so worked up, the only thing that will satisfy me is to be inside him.

I suppose it's not the only thing. But it's what I want. And I think it's what he wants, too.

"Can I ride you?" he asks.

"Absolutely." Whatever he needs. I smile and reach for a condom and some lube. "But wait a sec. Get on your stomach."

He obeys immediately, and I take a moment to admire him. Lean, but with a bubble ass that must be genetic. "I don't know how you get that ass without squats, but I'm here for it."

Scott laughs. "I hike."

"Magic hikes, I guess."

I trace a finger down his crack very gently, and when I get to his entrance, I squidge in some lube. Carefully, I work him open until he's relaxed.

"Ready?" I ask, checking to be sure.

He nods. "Please." His voice has gotten husky.

I kiss his shoulders, taking my time. I let myself linger, because he shudders under my touch and I know he loves it.

He might be starved for touch.

Hell, *I* might be starved for touch. And having one hand occupied in readying him while the other caresses him feels like the best of both worlds—the sublime and the profane.

It also feels romantic, even though I have a finger up his ass. Because yes, parts of sex are base, but other parts connect us to each other.

When I get another finger in, he groans, and I feel it when his body adjusts to me again.

"Want me?" I whisper.

"Yes." His simple statement makes me shudder. I gently withdraw from him and sit, propping my back on the pillows. I could lie down, but I don't want to.

I want the closeness.

I want the intimacy, even if it scares me.

Because it scares me. It proves I'm alive.

When I have a condom on, Scott climbs up onto my lap and hovers over my hard cock, which is now like steel. I'm exceedingly ready for this.

He lowers himself down on my dick, all the way, and then we're staring at each other, our mouths almost close enough to kiss.

I want to curse, it feels so good, but that might wreck the moment.

His face shows agony and pleasure competing, and he breathes harshly, trying to get used to me.

"We don't have to do this," I assure him.

"I'm fine. Just give me a minute."

"Take your time. You're doing so well. You feel so fucking good."

After a few moments, I can tell his body has accepted me, and he leans in to kiss me, no longer distracted.

It's a deep kiss, lots of tongue, and again, I'm scared.

Now that we're kissing, it feels like I'm the one opening myself up to him.

He moves carefully up my dick, then back down, his cock bobbing in front of him.

We both groan.

"You're incredible," I grit out.

"*We* are." Scott's tone is reverent, and I almost can't take the way he's looking at me. Almost.

Except I let myself really see his blue-green eyes. Notice the little crow's feet at the sides from smiling so much, despite his youth. Feel the softness of his hair when I brush my hands through it.

"That's it." I let him pick the rhythm, but after a bit, I start rising up to meet him, and he groans louder.

"Fuck," he says. "This is the best—" He cuts himself off, since you're likely not supposed to make comparisons while you're in bed with someone, but I don't care. Part of the romance with Scott is that it's okay to be imperfect.

"Yeah. Agreed."

Soon our movements get artless and out of sync.

"You good with changing positions?" I ask.

He nods and pops off of me. With a kiss, I guide him onto his back. He gets the hint immediately, lifting his knees up toward his shoulders. I thrust into him, and we both moan. I shove a pillow under him, thinking the angle will be better for his prostate, plus it'll give me more access, and he whimpers. "Oh, *fuck*. That. Right *there*."

"Good," I say. I lean down, kiss him, and get to work.

I've held off my orgasm this long, but now I want to get him there. I'm almost thinking I should stop fucking him and suck him off, when he tenses and starts coming untouched, and it's the most beautiful thing. His eyes flutter open, then closed, then open again, and he lets out a moan of pure rapture. It's so fucking hot.

And with that, I'm done. I dig my hands into his hips and shove my cock in deep, pulsing in great waves inside him.

He's fucking mine.

19
SCOTT

Did that really happen?

Curling into Luke as he tugs me closer, both of us still naked in his bed, though cleaned up now, I try to calm my racing heart.

I think … it did.

I think Lucas Lagomarsino made love to me. Not a quick fuck. Not something where he used me to get off, then remembered me as an afterthought.

The first time Luke was inside me, he made love to me. He made me feel precious.

And this hookup arrangement is so much more treacherous than I thought it'd be. Because I've been trying to tell myself I'm not going to fall for him.

If he keeps this up, I'm going to be in big trouble. How could I not give my heart to this guy who acts all gruff but who's a total marshmallow inside? Someone who gives those he cares about *everything*.

Hell, he even gave his ex-wife custody of his child because he thought it would be better for them, then upended his life so she could take her dream assignment overseas.

And he's going to be leaving when she gets back. I need to remind myself of that regularly, so I don't get too attached.

"What's your life in Manhattan like?" I ask.

Luke is silent a moment before answering. "Very different. The world I built there isn't like this."

"Do you have some fancy loft with a doorman?"

He rubs his chin.

"You do, don't you?"

"Yeah. I'm not there much, though. I work constantly, so I don't have time for anything else. I go out with coworkers sometimes, but frankly, it's pretty lonely."

"I was lonely, too," I admit. "I was just trying to survive, and while I have a lot of friends …" I don't want to finish that sentence. Because I shouldn't say how I feel about him. I'm pretty sure that would scare him off.

I also wonder when he's going back to New York. And what's going to happen to us.

And I really want to know more about his past. "Why did you decide to live in New York?"

"The short answer is for work, but the longer answer is more complicated." He sighs. "I already told you that my parents fought all the time. As a kid, whenever I'd hear them yell, I'd go escape to my room and do whatever. Play video games, read, watch a movie. Anything but be around all that tension. I hated it, and I never wanted a child of mine to have a bad home life like I did growing up. They weren't abusive to me, or even neglectful. It was just … not loving. My mom was miserable, and my dad buried himself in his work."

I feel sorry for little-boy Luke, but I don't interrupt. I like it when he opens up.

He gives a rueful laugh. "Somewhere along the line, though, I got the idea that getting married—especially getting married to a woman—was what I was supposed to do. I somehow imagined I could have the healthy marriage my parents never did. When Kira and I got together, I think I wanted the idea of her more than I wanted her. But then she ended up as miserable as my mom, and —just like my dad—I buried myself in work."

I thread my fingers through his and pull him tighter to me.

"After the divorce, I figured I might as well do what I'm good at: make money."

"You're good at lots more than making money," I whisper. "And that's rough. It seems like you were trying not to hurt Kira, even though it didn't work out."

"Right. I failed at that."

"You need to stop calling yourself a failure. You have a great daughter and a wonderful job."

"I have more than that," he murmurs, and I cuddle into him.

Luke kisses the back of my neck and whispers good night, and soon his breathing evens out.

But I stay awake for a long time, reliving what just happened. And wondering what it means.

The following day, Addi is back, and snow is predicted. Every year, the first snowfall is magical. The sky goes pale gray, and then the world is blanketed in white, the fluffy stuff silencing the noises all around. Everything becomes sparkly and clean and pretty.

So maybe my sappy heart doesn't only like fall, it likes the spell cast by winter, too.

Addi and I tear outside the moment we see flakes start to fall. I barely remember to put gloves and a hat and a jacket on her, but I do my job, shouldering into my own jacket once she's wrapped up. Addi stands in the front yard with her tongue out, trying to catch snowflakes. Meanwhile, I'm running around, whooping like a kid.

Eventually, she gets bored of standing still and chases me. I slow down so she can catch me, and we pause for a while, letting the snow fall on us. I don't know practical statistics like how much is forecast, but I hope to never lose my appreciation of snow's beauty.

When the door opens and Luke emerges, his smile is easy.

"Look, Daddy!" Addi says, showing him a tiny snowball she made. She takes off to run around some more, while I just want to gaze at him. His dark lashes catch the snowflakes, and I don't think he could look any more desirable.

When Addi's back is turned, he leans in for a quick kiss. "You look cute with snowflakes in your hair," he whispers.

"You look amazing with them on your eyelashes." I kiss him one more time, but when Addison approaches, we take a step apart.

I'm not sure we're kidding her, since she likely saw him hug me on Thanksgiving. She's surely seen him touch me. It's getting harder and harder to hide our affection for each other.

And it's getting more and more confusing.

"Mr. Landon and Mr. Ty said they were going to have sleigh rides when it started snowing," Addi says.

"We'll have to make sure to go on one," I reply. Then, realizing I might have overstepped, I look to Luke. "I mean, if that's okay with you."

He grins. "Sure, we can go on a sleigh ride."

"Yay!" Addi cheers.

Luke turns to me, his face happy. "You're going to get me to do all this frivolous stuff, aren't you?"

"Yep. It's fun."

He leans in conspiratorially. "I'm starting to agree with you."

"No kidding?"

"No kidding. Speaking of fun, do you have plans for your birthday?"

"I haven't made any, no." While my family always had parties when I was little, they nevertheless felt overshadowed by the December holidays, and once I wasn't living at home, the celebrations stopped. Having someone remember me, separate from Christmas, warms me inside even though I forgot to put on my own gloves.

He reaches out and grips my belt loop, tugging me close so he can whisper in my ear. "Don't make plans."

I shiver, and it's not from the snow.

It's the afternoon of my birthday, and I'm sitting on the couch playing with my phone when I hear the car pull up. Luke took Addison out, I'm not sure where, since he gave me the day off.

I furrow my brows as Luke walks into the house alone.

"Where's Addi?" I look around as if she's going to peek out from behind him.

He sets down his keys and phone and strides into the living room. He gives me a grin that's almost predatory. "She's staying the night at Julia's house."

I blink. "All night?"

"All night." His deep tone makes my body heat up. Is he thinking what I'm thinking?

"We don't have to watch a kid?"

"We don't have to watch a kid," he assures me. "And it's your birthday." With each sentence, he moves closer to me.

"Are we going to do something?" I whisper. I'm picturing taking all my clothes off right here, since there's no one to barge in on us.

"Oh yes," he says. "But first, I'm taking you out."

"What?"

"I think I need to take you on a date."

"You're … you're asking me out?"

"Yes. As my date. For your birthday. Do you want to go out to dinner?"

I nod like a hula girl on a dashboard. "Yes."

He pulls me up and tugs me to him, then kisses me. The kiss goes slightly wild, and he grunts deep in his throat. "We need to take advantage of the fact that we can go out, just the two of us," he says, as if he's reminding himself.

"Okay," I whisper against his lips. "What should I wear?" I look down at my dark blue T-shirt and jeans.

"What you're wearing is fine." I think my face must drop, because he holds up his hands. "If you'd rather get dressed up, then by all means do so."

"Where are we going?"

"Clifton's."

It's the fanciest restaurant in the state. I have no idea how he managed to get reservations on short notice, but I'm not complaining.

"I can't wear jeans and a T-shirt there."

"Pretty sure you can. This is Vermont. Fleece is a uniform."

I shudder. "No, thanks."

After one more kiss, he steps back and swats my ass. "Then go put on something you like."

I stride away with my dick at half-mast, and he slides off to his room.

Taking my time, I put on a dress shirt in a blue so pale it's nearly white, a maroon jacket, navy chinos, and my polished shoes. It's amazing what you can find at a consignment shop.

I haven't had occasion to get dressed up in a long time, and I feel good.

When I step out, Luke is waiting for me in the living room, his feet up on the coffee table, playing on his phone. He's put on brown jeans, a white shirt, a light gray tie, and a dark gray sweater.

I stand there staring at him. With his dark hair and tan skin, the crisp shirt looks spectacular, and the cashmere sweater shows off his trim waist.

"We'd better leave," I announce, "or we're going to have something entirely different for dinner."

He stands up and takes my hand, and at first I'm disappointed he doesn't kiss me. But then I realize it might be for practical purposes, because if he did, we might not make it out the door.

We get in his Range Rover, and he maneuvers us through the

twisty roads until we get to the famous restaurant hidden away in the woods.

When we park, he looks at me. "Stay there."

He gets out and goes around to get something out of the back, then comes over to open my door and holds out a boutonniere, smiling.

"Why did you—" I start, as he leans in to pin it on my lapel. It's a white rose.

"I thought you might appreciate it," he says. "Happy birthday." He kisses my cheek.

My cheeks flush as he takes my hand.

I can't believe this is the same man who pooh-poohed the idea of flowers. He's learning and changing.

He has romance in him. I've been seeing it. I'm seeing it right now.

I can't help stroking the soft blossom, knowing that it's something beautiful and alive that he chose for me. Something frivolous that will die soon—but that he bought me nonetheless.

We walk into the historic home that's been converted into a romantic restaurant. Each of the rooms holds just a few tables.

We're seated but not given menus.

"Um," I say, looking around.

The waiter appears, a middle-aged man wearing a black apron over a black dress shirt and black slacks. "Welcome to Clifton's. Is this your first time here?"

"Yes," I say, but Luke shakes his head.

"You've been here before?" I ask.

He gives me a quick nod. "With Kira, before Addi was born."

His words make the waiter look at us differently. Like at first he thought we were a couple and now he thinks we might be friends.

Except Luke reaches across the table and takes my hand in a claiming move that is nowhere near platonic.

Okay, then.

"Well, you're in for a treat," the waiter explains to me. "Is there anything you're allergic to or don't care for?"

"I'm not allergic to anything," I say, "although I'm not a fan of seafood."

"All seafood, or just shellfish?"

"I'm okay with fish, but not a fan of oysters, that sort of thing."

"Have you ever had them?" Luke asks.

"No, actually."

"You might surprise yourself."

"Then no," I say, deciding to be bold. "I don't have any preferences."

"And I'm fine with everything," Luke says.

"Wonderful," the waiter says. "I'll be back with your starters."

The waiter leaves, and I stare at Luke. Then I slowly look around. The room is lit by candles and gentle lamplight. The tables are covered with classic white tablecloths and accented with arrangements of white roses in low vases. The silver is polished to a high shine, and as I put the crisp napkin in my lap, I realize this is going to be a wholly different experience than I've ever had before.

"What's the plan?" I ask.

"It's a chef's tasting menu. The chef makes what they want."

"That's it?"

"Yep. It's their opportunity to show off, so it's usually fantastic."

The waiter comes out and pours fancy water for both of us, and then we get wine. I didn't even know that Luke ordered it, but maybe it's paired with the food.

Which now starts to arrive.

Tiny, edible pieces of art that look like they are more designed to be photographed than eaten.

But then I take a bite, and I learn the word synergy. Because something about having food be utterly beautiful and taste amazing is blowing me away.

This is the most romantic date of my life.

Luke keeps the conversation going, getting me to talk about my siblings, and I open up to him more about how wrong things went with Edsel. "I guess I just really wanted someone to love me, and we were not on the same page at all. I read the signs all wrong."

"What an ass," he says. "He doesn't know what he's missing." Then he gestures to the next tray of delectable morsels. "What do you think?"

He looks like he's holding his breath, waiting for me to pass judgment on the food. On him.

"Luke, this is incredible. Don't get me wrong. I'm appreciating every second of this. But you don't have to spend money on me for me to like you." I grin. "I like you just as you are. You don't need to bribe me."

God, words are not working for me right now, even though they're ostensibly one of my jobs. But he gives me a gentle smile. "This isn't because I have to. It's because I want to. Sometimes money can buy you experiences you can't get otherwise. And it's fun. We don't often have time to ourselves. I want to make tonight special for you."

I'm touched. "What if we get a call from Addi, or Julia's mother, saying to pick her up?"

"That could happen," he says. "That's why I gave them Kira's parents' number as a backup."

"You did what?"

"I figured that, while we should be available in an emergency, things that are less than an emergency shouldn't require our attention."

"I am amazed that you gave up that much control."

"I'm not going to make a habit of it," he admits. "But I do want tonight to be good."

"It already is," I say, eating another bite.

The pace of the dinner is such that I never get too full. And it's an *event*.

I love events.

I'm starting to realize I could genuinely fall for Luke—as opposed to typical me, who thinks I'm in love with everyone immediately.

This? Luke giving me things he doesn't much care about but he knows I'll appreciate?

This is more than a meal, and he isn't showing off. He's doing this because he's getting pleasure out of seeing me enjoy it.

That's quite a present.

20

LUKE

What am I doing?

I'm so torn.

I want to be with Scott. I want to spend time with him, celebrate him, give him things he'll appreciate. Let him have a wonderful birthday.

And I'm starting to enjoy all these outings with him, with Addi, with both of them together.

Yet I know tonight is the worst idea I've ever had. Like, period. Except for getting together with Kira ... though if I hadn't done that, I wouldn't have Addi, and she makes any shit worth it.

It's the worst idea because I'm starting to get all kinds of dangerous feelings. What happens if I fail again? Like I did with Kira?

And I'll admit that I never thought I'd end up in a real relationship with a man. Somewhere along the line, I got the idea I wasn't supposed to. Except, as I look at Scott across from me at this romantic dinner table, I wonder if I've been thinking about being a couple all wrong.

As much as I don't want a relationship—that's my brain talking—my body definitely votes to keep him. And there's something simmering inside me: a desire deep in my soul that wants him in all ways, because I feel a connection with him.

I feel like Scott sees me. He gets past the bullshit and understands the parts of me that I hide.

I don't know if I like it, but I also don't know if I can keep the feelings I've been denying from breaking through. Because he makes me smile. He makes me feel good. He wakes up parts of me—body, soul, heart, mind—that I've ignored.

I want him like no one else.

After we've polished off a sublime crème brûlée, I hand the waiter my black Amex and smile at Scott. I don't know if anyone has ever made me smile more—except Addi, but that's different. With her, it's that she's mine and she's so cute.

With him ... well, perhaps it's somewhat the same. I think I want him to be mine. And he *is* so cute.

Scott has a fundamental innocence about him. He's been through some tough things but still has this sunshine quality. He came through his trials soft and friendly, not hard and bitter.

Not like me.

Partway to the car, Scott stops suddenly, and I almost bump into him. He puts his hands on his hips and turns.

"What?" I ask, feeling defensive.

"You surprise me. That's all." He leans in, his forehead pressing against mine. He smells sweet, like the dessert we both ate. "I think there's a big heart underneath your prickly exterior. Thank you for the perfect birthday dinner."

I don't say anything, not wanting to agree with him, even though I'm pretty sure he's correct. Instead, I capture his mouth with mine, and he feels so right.

His lips part, and our tongues collide, then dance. It's messy, and it fucking turns me on. There's no finesse here. We're just connecting.

Scott's hands reach down and grip my ass, holding us together, and that turns me on, too. *He* turns me on, period.

The wind ruffles his hair, and I rake my hands through it, forcing his head back so I can deepen the kiss.

We break apart on a gasp. "If we don't go somewhere else," he mutters, "I am gonna be getting my knees very dirty, very fast. And it's cold out."

"God," I groan, as the image of his mouth wrapped around my dick makes me harder than that half chub I've been sporting all evening.

He licks his lips, then licks mine. It's a silly move, but I love it. And we're making out again in the dark, tall trees around us.

"What else do you have in mind tonight?" he asks.

"I was trying not to maul you," I admit. "I wanted to wine you and dine you before I fucked you."

"How do you know it wouldn't be me fucking you?"

I stare at him.

He bursts out laughing. "I'm kidding. I'm a bottom, pretty much exclusively."

I've always topped—and the club boys all seemed fine with that—but I might have been willing to switch things up if that's what Scott wanted. I let out a startled breath. I've never considered doing that with anyone else before.

Scott continues, "I do need you inside me, though. Like, right now."

"Then let's go." I tug him along, and he hops on my back for a piggyback ride. He's heavy but not too heavy, and I end up carrying him, wobbling a little under his weight, all the way to the car.

Where I make sure to open his door first before getting in myself. And if we peel out, well, shit happens.

We're barely in the door before he's kissing me, taking off my sweater, tugging at my pants. I didn't know I'd be undressing before him, but that's fine.

And then he's on his knees, licking my dick, and I get very, very hard.

"Don't wanna come this way," I mutter. "You're too good at that, and I'm too turned on."

We look at each other and shed the rest of our clothes, then kiss again, only this time we're fully naked, bodies pressed one to another.

His skin is soft and warm, and his slim body looks healthier than when he first got here.

"You're so damned hot," he says against my neck.

"I could say the same thing about you."

In sync, we move to the couch and collapse on it.

He reaches down and strokes my dick, and I do the same for him. That's what I need. I need touch.

His touch.

I want *his* hands on me. It's not just sex or kissing. It's touch and affection.

And Scott is so affectionate. He traces a finger along my jaw and then follows it with his mouth.

I can't contain my shudder. I can't control my panting breath. I can't conceal the way I can't get close enough to him.

His mouth is hell-bent on exploring my body, but that wasn't the plan. "I'm supposed to be doing that to you," I murmur. "It's your birthday."

"Shut up and take it, boss," he says, grinning, as he kisses down my midsection. "*Hotsexyboss*."

The word "boss" shouldn't do it for me. Because it's wrong to be fucking my employee.

Except he's so much more than an employee. And this might be more than fucking. Especially with the way he's taking his time with my body. It's like he's trying to memorize it.

I haul him up by his armpits so he's straddling my belly, knees on either side, his dick jutting up.

"C'mere," I say, gesturing for him to move closer to my face. "I want to suck you."

"Shit," Scott mutters. "Okay." Carefully, he scoots up so he's straddling my shoulders, feeding his dick between my lips.

I love the taste and feel of him. I love *this*. I want to get him off this way.

But when it feels like he's about to blow, he pulls back. "I need you inside me," he says. "Please." He crawls off me, flopping onto his stomach, bending over the couch with a knee pulled up so he can finger his ass.

"Let me do that," I say, kissing his neck. I get up and make a dash for supplies.

I press lubed fingers against his hole, entering easily. He lets out a contented sigh and wriggles, letting me finger-fuck him.

After a while, he looks over his shoulder. His "Please" fucking guts me.

I rip open a condom wrapper and roll it on, then add more lube. It's messy, but this is a situation where more is better.

With a kiss to the back of his neck, I mutter in his ear, "This what you want, gorgeous?"

"Yes," he says. "Fuck. Yes."

I line up against his entrance and, with care, guide myself inside him.

Scott's back is beautiful. But his ass is world class: round and firm and perfect.

He gets on his hands and knees, and I love this position. I can do anything to him.

As I thrust in and out, it's even better than the last time, because I'm getting to know him better. I'm learning what makes him squirm, what makes him moan.

And I really love how he seems to unfurl in response to praise.

I'm starting to remember that I used to be a nice guy before I got divorced and moved to New York. Because even though I said I was okay with leaving Addi behind, I really wasn't.

My life is better these days, though, and it's all because of Scott, who is becoming essential.

"You good?" I ask.

"Yeah," he pants. "I am. Fuck. This. Yes."

I grin against his neck. "Want to ride me?" I murmur.

He nods, and I pull out, then get on my back, lying lengthwise on the couch. Scott straddles my hips, then impales himself on me before he starts to move.

I throw my head back, because it feels so good I can't stand it. I don't know what I'm doing with him. I just think I can't let him go.

But when I look up again, my eyes lock on his. "You ride my dick like a jockey, and you look so fucking hot doing it."

After a few more thrusts, he comes on a cry. I push into him a few more times, chasing my orgasm until it hits me, and when the aftershocks finish, he collapses over me.

When we recover, we quickly shower together, washing off the come and lube. Then we go to my room.

We lie in bed, tangled up in each other.

After a moment, I lean over and open my bedside table drawer, pulling out a small, wrapped box. "Happy birthday."

His eyes go to saucer size. "What's this?"

"Your birthday present."

"You already gave me that amazing dinner. And you didn't have to get me anything at all."

"I know. But"—I shrug—"someone around here has convinced me that it's nice to do things for someone else, even if it's not required."

He sits up, cross-legged, still naked, and turns the box over in his hands, clearly delighted.

"Open it."

"Okay." He lets out a breath. "I just want to enjoy it, you know? Savor the moment."

My heart skips a beat, because I may have gotten this exactly right.

He pulls off the paper and opens a box with a classic men's watch inside. He gasps. "It's beautiful."

I kiss him. "Read the inscription."

He flips it. "It says …" He squints. "It says, 'Enjoy this moment.'"

"That's what you've taught me to do."

His eyes well up. "Thank you. So much. This is the best birthday ever."

21

SCOTT

"Scottybear!" Murph says as Addi and I walk into the bookstore part of Vino and Veritas. Though Murph's normally a bartender, he occasionally picks up shifts over here. Addi skips off to take a seat at the story circle, and I stop to chat while Murph restocks books.

"Hey," I say wearily.

Murph's face drops. "What's wrong?"

I shrug. "Nothing."

"Uh-huh. Yeah, that's a lie. Tell me."

No one's near us, and my thoughts come out in an ugly rush. "I slept with Luke and he took me out for a romantic dinner and gave me a nice present for my birthday and now I think I'm in love with him, except I can't be in love with him, so this is more complicated than the simple hookup I thought it was."

Murph puts a hand on his hip. "Puh-lease. This was never going to be a simple hookup for you. It was always going to mean more."

"Then why did you push me into it?"

"Because I had a feeling that he might be into you, too."

"Based on what evidence? Overhearing me talk with him on

174

the phone? One conversation you two had, where you were my reference?"

He looks sheepish. "I guess it started because I was excited to see you with someone who wasn't Edsel. Anyone would be better than him. But then I saw the look on your face after you met him, and Luke sounded like someone you should get to know."

"But I'm just going to get my heart broken."

"Do you know that?"

"I always do."

He studies me. "Hmm. I'm not sure I have any advice here."

"Thanks," I say sarcastically.

"Well, okay, I'm always full of advice. I think you have to figure out if he's worth opening your heart to. For real. Not just the idea of him, but him as he is. Does he have flaws?"

"So many. He grunts a lot and is kind of brusque. He can be emotionally withdrawn, although I assume that's because he's been hurt." I sigh. "I also think he's been brainwashed into believing he needed to be the man of the family and have his daughter and wife and all that—and since it didn't work out like a Hallmark movie, he thinks he failed."

"Ah. He needs to understand that the only way to fail is to give up. Life's about picking ourselves up and trying again, not condemning ourselves because we aren't perfect to begin with."

"Yeah." I look at Murph with warmth. "You're right."

Just then, there's a rustle, and a tall person with long, ash-blonde hair, wearing a pink sateen pantsuit with a tie belt, emerges from the back room. Her shoulders are thrown back, and she steps confidently, in four-inch heels, out to a group of children. Time for drag queen story hour. In addition to Addi, the veterinarian's son is here, along with a few other kids I recognize.

"This should be interesting," Murph mutters.

"Why?"

"Well, children are a danger to drag queens. They might break a nail or muss her hair. But I'm sure Miss Shenairy Position will be as fabulous as she always is."

As we watch, the queen sits daintily in a chair, crossing her slim legs at the ankles, although the look she gives is as fierce as a viper. "I am going to read you a story about a caterpillar who turned into a butterfly."

The queen pulls out the book with a flourish, perches a pair of glasses—rhinestone ones, very pretty—on her nose, and begins reading *The Very Hungry Caterpillar* in a dramatic fashion—oohing and awwing and commenting on the caterpillar's choices of food.

"Isn't that a silly thing for the caterpillar to eat?" she says. "Wouldn't it be more practical for it to have green leaves?"

"But what if it wanted the candy?" a child asks.

"That's the thing, child. You need both. We need the sweet, and we need the bitter. We need romance, but we also have to pay the bills. How do you think Miss Position got to be so fabulous?" She gestures at herself. "She has to be able to buy her jewels."

"What happens inside the cocoon?" another child asks.

"Growth. It's messy. But it's necessary. For a while you think nothing is happening. And then, eventually, you emerge as a colorful, sparkling butterfly."

The children all stare at her, rapt.

And I think about what she said. Sweet and bitter.

I've spent my entire life clinging to the sweet and pretending the bitter doesn't exist.

But maybe I need to change my approach.

I don't want to admit it, because if I do, I'll be living in the real world. The world of bills and taxes and the DMV and dentists and whatever else adults have to deal with. Not the world of nonstop sexy men and sunsets and champagne toasts.

It hits me like a slap in the face. New Scott was going to change. Like Scarlett O'Hara. And I wasn't going to let men get to me.

I'm doing better. I have a job and am making money—but I haven't dug into any of my debts. Though at least I'm current on the payments to the mechanic.

So maybe I can take the next step.

When I get home, I take a deep breath. Time to face my bills. I've still been shoving everything in a drawer. Too bad no one sends anything else—like love letters or ginormous sweepstakes checks. But if I keep avoiding this, it's never going to get any better. In fact, it'll probably get worse. I'll end up being sued or something.

I set all the envelopes out on a table in my suite and arrange them by return address. Then I take a deep breath and start opening them. While some are worse than I thought, a few aren't bad at all. I can pay some of these.

On a notepad, I start writing down what I owe and to whom. It's a lot. Going through credit card bills is like Monday-morning quarterbacking all my bad decisions. From food I had to buy on credit to the treats for Edsel, there's a lot here to be ashamed of. Once I'm finished with the physical mail, I go through unopened emails and online statements.

Fuck.

My face burns, but I force myself to keep going, opening the messages that make my hands shake, clicking into accounts that scare me.

I don't know how long I've been sitting here when there's a knock at the door, and I spook.

"Scott?" Luke opens the door before I can respond, and I want to run and hide. I want to sweep all the bills onto the floor or throw them away.

But that's something I used to do.

"What's going on?" Luke asks. "Oh, sorry. You're paying bills. I'll come back." Then he notices the tears in my eyes. "What's wrong?"

"Nothing." I sniffle.

"Bullshit."

I look at him, and my heart cracks. Maybe I'm being reckless, but I can't deal with this on my own. And I trust him. "I have a lot of debt, and I don't know how I'll ever pay it off."

"Want to talk about it?"

God help me, I do. I nod. He sits at the table next to me and holds my hand, waiting for me to gather my thoughts. Finally, I say, "I never told you I was about to be evicted before I got here."

He inhales sharply. "What was the reason? Not paying rent?"

"Yeah." My voice cracks. "I wasn't making enough money to pay my rent, and the money I had, I spent on frivolous things. Then I didn't have any money, so I felt bad, and when I got a little, I spent it on frivolous things again."

"Scott, I'm so sorry. I can't believe you were that close to being homeless." He pushes his seat back and tugs me to him. I end up in his lap, his big arms wrapped around me. I don't feel like a child, though. I feel comforted.

I snuffle into his neck. "I didn't know what I was going to do. Maybe move back home? But besides that meaning I was a complete and total failure, I wouldn't want to put more strain on my parents."

Luke cards a hand through my hair, and it feels so soothing. "You aren't a failure."

"Oh no?" I shove the paper I've been scribbling on at him and get off his lap to go back to my seat. He frowns as he reads it.

"Why haven't you contacted your creditors to try to work something out? Or at least made minimum payments on some of these?"

"I just told you. I'm bad with money."

"Being 'bad with money' is a result, not a cause. Maybe no one ever taught you about it. But so much of it has to do with what you think you deserve."

"I never thought you'd be into new age concepts."

"It's not new age. It's reality." He furrows his brows. "What's really going on here?"

"It's simple avoidance."

"Okay, what—or why—are you avoiding?"

"Because it sucks! I don't want to deal with it. There's no place in my dreams for paying a dental bill."

He sighs and stands up, holding out his hand. I take it and let him pull me to the bed, where he sits with his back to the head-board, positioning me between his legs.

He kisses the back of my neck and puts his arms around me again. "If something doesn't match your dreams, that's not a judg-ment about you as a person. It's just a data point. It means you're not where you want to be yet. It doesn't mean you won't get there someday. You can have everything you want—just not immedi-ately. But you shouldn't give up because it isn't the way you want it right now."

I twist around to stare at him.

"What?" His big eyes are soft and worried.

"That's huge," I whisper. "I've felt like I was a failure every time I looked at my bank account. I didn't have the balance I wanted, and I felt like I could never get there."

He rearranges us so I'm straddling his legs, and then he holds my face and kisses me. "So you never got there, because you were focusing on how bad it was. You can't get something good by focusing on the bad. You have to focus on the good."

"It seems so bleak," I mutter.

He kisses me again. "I understand how it could seem that way. But everyone has to start somewhere. And how many people do you think are exactly where they want to be? Very few. Everyone has ambitions."

"Where are you getting this from, Mr. Grump?"

He smiles and boops my nose. Playful Luke? Where did he come from? "I read about it a long time ago."

I still feel lost. And dubious. "I just don't see how things are going to change, unless I win the lottery."

"But that kind of thinking is what keeps you stuck. It's keeping you from making some small changes with a big impact. You have to stop thinking that problems are magically gonna go away and start figuring out ways to solve them."

I stare at the depressing numbers spread all over the table.

Luke gestures to it. "How much of this did you spend on yourself? Not very much, I suspect." He kisses me again. "I think you're afraid you won't be loved for who you are. So you buy people things. But you don't have to buy someone's love. I've been told that just spending time with someone you care about is enough."

"Hmm," I say.

"C'mon." Luke scoots off the bed and hauls me up so I'm standing next to him. I like the symbolism. Rather than coming down to my level, he lifts me up.

And while I'm embarrassed to have shown him the worst part of me—the part I'm most ashamed of—it's also freeing. Because I'm not one to keep secrets—except for surprises.

Our tongues dance together, and I finally feel like I might have a chance to become new Scott: mature, confident, and someone who faces the tough things he needs to.

When we pause, we sit down at the table again, and Luke helps me figure out how to pay the first few bills.

The sleigh bells jingle rhythmically as we glide through the silent forest, the cold biting our noses. Addi sits between us as we huddle under heavy fur blankets.

We met Landon and Ty at Lost Acres Morgans to take the first sleigh ride of the season. Luke has joined me a few times to watch Addi's riding lessons—not because he thinks I need supervision, but because he's starting to spend less time working and more time with his family. Even if he has a tough time admitting that to himself.

Transport like this feels really special—old-fashioned, like the hot-air balloon ride. It's also leisurely, so we can enjoy the scenery ... and cuddle up with each other. In the twilight, surrounded by snow, it feels bewitching.

"I'm not sure how you talked me into this," Luke says quietly. "But it's nice."

"It's fun, Daddy," Addi says. "And I like the horses."

"I know, baby."

He has his arms around her, but his hand grazes my shoulder.

"It *is* fun," I agree. Luke starts to lean toward me, then stops.

Addi tugs on his sleeve, her big eyes sincere. "Daddy, it's okay if you kiss Scott."

"What?" he says.

"I know you like each other. It's okay if you kiss him."

He grins sheepishly. "I'm not sure I need your permission, little lady. But I'll keep that in mind."

He looks at me and raises his eyebrows. *She figured us out.*

I can't help my wide smile back.

So we snuggle in more, and the rhythm of the bells almost puts me to sleep.

Almost.

When the ride is done, we thank the driver as she pulls up to a platform so we can disembark. Because it's on Luke's side, he gets out first, then helps Addi. I clamber over, and he extends a hand, even though I don't really need it.

I take it, though, because Luke's a gentleman.

When I step onto the platform, he inspects my face, then glances at Addi. So quickly I don't anticipate it, he kisses me chastely, then takes her hand in one of his and mine in the other so we can walk back to the car.

But to me, that kiss moved mountains. Because it means there's more between us than just employer and employee.

Maybe there's an "us" here—one that's real and that he can show to the world.

New Scott is very confused, but old Scott cheers.

22

LUKE

This time, when I meet Landon for coffee, he's already sitting at a table where he can see the door. We're trying a different café, and it's busy, with plenty of people in line ordering drinks.

Since it's midmorning, it feels odd for me to be out—like I'm playing hooky. I should be working.

But yesterday, Scott came home from Addi's riding lesson saying that Landon mentioned hanging out with me. So he shooed me out the door ten minutes ago, telling me I need friends. He's probably right, not that I'll admit it.

I give Landon a chin lift and order my drink, joining him after I've doctored it up with cream and sugar.

"Good to see you," I say, shaking his hand and taking the seat next to his.

"You, too." Landon seems slightly more relaxed than the last time we met, which is good. I understand why he feels the need to watch his back, but I hope he knows he doesn't have to do it with me.

After I take a sip of coffee, I set my mug down and look around. "How's life treating you?"

He shrugs. "It has its ups and downs."

"Same." Although, frankly, things are more up these days than down—and definitely better than they ever are in New York. "How're things at the stables?"

"The horses are great. Ty is great to work for. You should come riding sometime."

I make a face. "Maybe. I think that's more of an Addi hobby, though."

Landon gets a sly look on his face. "That nanny of yours hasn't talked you into it yet?"

I laugh. "I'm surprised he hasn't tried, but I'm sure he will." I can see the question on Landon's face, although I know he's not one to pry. "I'm not going to be around long enough to bother, though."

"Why do you say that?"

"Kira will be back soon, and I'll be going back to New York."

"Does that mean Scott will be out of a job?"

"Dunno." The idea of Scott being a nanny to Addi without me around is unpleasant, to say the least.

So is the idea of returning to Manhattan and late nights in the office, loneliness, and anonymous fucks in bars. So I add, "Scott and I might be dating. I think."

He raises his eyebrows. "You think?"

"We are," I admit. "Except I don't date. It's all fucked up. He's my nanny, but we're also kind of maybe sort of in a relationship."

"Kinda maybe sort of?"

"I'm just not sure if it's real. He's a hopeless romantic. The kind of guy who'll send you a singing telegram and forget to pay his own rent. I genuinely like him, but I don't want to get his hopes up."

"Why not?"

"Because I'm not relationship material. Kira told me that, and she's the smartest person I know."

"She's also your ex-wife. She could also be feeding you a bunch of bullshit."

"I don't think so."

"I dunno, man. Sounds pretty convenient for her to blame you for all the problems in your relationship. It takes two."

His words pull me up short. All this time, I've believed I was the one who fucked up our marriage.

Maybe it was no one's fault, though. I'll take responsibility for my failings, but maybe we simply weren't right for each other.

What would happen if I could start over and get the things I really want?

Scott in my life, for starters. For more than a short-term fling.

"Maybe it wasn't just me?"

"Seems likely."

I grin at him. "You're pretty smart."

"I am?"

"Yep. And it's good to see you." But if he can ask about my private life, I can do the same to him. "Did you get up the nerve to ask Ty out?" I ask, taking an educated guess. I can read between the lines.

"Well ..." He grins. "Let's just say we know each other a little better now."

I sip my drink. I can see the traces of the kid I knew, even though his exterior screams trouble. "Glad you're getting some. Ty seems like a good one."

"He is."

We spend the rest of the time talking about nothing and everything, and ... Scott was right. I'm grateful to have a friend in town.

The next weekend, Scott and I stroll around a Christmas craft festival in booths on Church Street, letting Addi run ahead and look at everything. The air is crisp, and people are in heavy coats and hats, drinking spiced cider, mulled wine, and hot chocolate. Carolers in Victorian outfits sing on corners, and vendors stand over braziers of roasting chestnuts that they pass out in brown paper cones straight out of Europe.

I feel like I'm in middle school, because I really want to hold Scott's hand.

"What's your favorite holiday?" I ask. "Christmas? No, I bet it's Valentine's Day."

Scott tilts his head. "Actually, I think the most meaningful holiday is a couple's anniversary. My parents always make a big deal out of theirs, and they've been #relationshipgoals to me. They've shared and built so much love, and despite raising all us kids, they always take the time to do something special for just the two of them. But, okay, I like Valentine's Day, too. I know people feel pressure to spend a lot on things they maybe don't appreciate or can't afford." He shrugs. "I guess I think it's special that we take time to celebrate love. Even if I don't know if I'll ever get the real thing."

Danger.

Because he sounds so forlorn, and his words make me want to reach out and tug him to me.

So I do. Even though I shouldn't.

I wrap my arm around Scott, and it feels right.

We catch up with Addi, who is eyeing tidily wrapped boxes of candy and chocolate fudge. Scott's eyes are as wide as hers, and he reaches out and holds her hand. So now he and I are arm in arm, and she's holding his hand, and something shifts inside me.

Because I can see this happening in the future. I can see the three of us out doing things, fun things.

I've already been conflicted about going back to Manhattan once Kira returns. A big part of me doesn't want to miss out on any more of Addi's childhood. When I think about my life in New York, it feels empty. No mess, no laughter. No spontaneity and no ridiculousness. No friends and no company.

And I stiffen. Because this isn't just about Addi.

I want to stay here because I like having Scott in my arms.

I don't know what's going on between us, though. Any logical person would say that we're all wrong. I'm too old and grumpy. He needs someone as enthusiastic as he is. I don't get my heart involved. He's all heart.

Maybe I need to stop overthinking and just enjoy him while I have him. I can worry about our goodbye later.

When we get home, Addi's so tired she almost falls asleep in the tub. She curls up in bed, and we turn off her light.

Scott disappears for a while, putting away the Christmas presents he bought. I wander around the house and realize that I don't have to do anything. He takes care of it all.

So I go and find him. Because if our time with each other is limited, I want to make the most of it. Also, touching him in public, where we had to be restrained, made me want to not be restrained at all.

I can't seem to stop myself. I just … want him.

Scott feels like a party about to happen. He feels like a celebration.

And for someone who spends most of his time looking at numbers, being free from all that is a revelation.

When I find him in his room, we're unrestrained. I rip off his clothes so fast I almost tear them. In between our hard kisses and brutal grabs, he pants, "This time I want you to fuck me hard and fast."

He's a vision with his hair askew, cheeks flushed, lips swollen.

I smile against his skin. "I'm good with that."

When we're both naked, my clothes kicked somewhere in a corner of his room, I can't wait for skin-to-skin contact. I take handfuls of his ass, rubbing our achingly hard cocks together. Then I pick him up and throw him onto the bed, where he lands with a strong exhale.

"Fuck, you're sexy," he whispers.

I kneel on the bed, studying him. Seeing the way he writhes under me. "Show me how you touch yourself," I order.

He obeys immediately, his hand sliding up and down his erection, and he moans, his eyes intense and locked on mine.

"That's it. So good. It's so hot watching you."

Scott grimaces, but it seems like pleasure, not pain. "If I keep this up, I'm going to come."

"Then stop." He reaches for me, his hand sticky with precome, and tugs me down for a kiss.

After a moment, I grab the lube. I press one finger into his ass, using plenty of fluid. I want him to be slick and ready.

Once he's stopped clenching so much, I wiggle in another finger, opening him. As I do, I'm taking in his gorgeous body, telling him how every part is beautiful. Then I look up and notice that his eyes are red-rimmed.

I pull my fingers out immediately. "What's wrong?"

He bites his lip. "Nothing. Keep going."

"Did I hurt you?" My other hand dances along his hip and up the side of his torso, caressing him.

Scott shakes his head vehemently. "No."

"Are you sure? We can stop. Or go slower."

He lets out an annoyed sigh. "It's fine. I just have the feels. That's all."

Oh.

I don't know what to say, so I kiss him. Because I might have the feels, too. Except I can't tell him that.

Kissing my way back down his body, I place my fingers back where they were. "You going to open for me?"

"Yeah." His voice is husky. "I'm ready. Do what you will. Please. Fuck me." He turns over so he's on his hands and knees.

It's not lost on me that this is a less emotionally vulnerable position—although it's vulnerable for him.

"I love it this way," he assures me.

"Okay." I pause. "You really are so fucking tempting."

"Get on with it," he whines.

LESLIE MCADAM

I chuckle. "Yes, sir." Lining up my dick with his entrance, I push in without further preamble. He inhales sharply, so I give him a moment to get used to me. Then, "Oh my god," I say, pulling back. "I forgot a condom. Hang on."

"No." He reaches to grab my wrist, stilling me. "We're both negative. It's fine." He can sense me hemming and hawing. "I trust you," he insists.

"Okay." I'm not arguing.

Because there's only so much I can resist him. Especially when I feel that tight, wet heat. Especially when I need to be inside him.

I thrust again, and this time I reach around and jack his cock. He groans, and I start a brutal rhythm, making sure he's still with me.

But then … I kiss his neck and withdraw.

"Flip over," I whisper. "I need to see you."

Again, he obeys promptly, and this time, when I enter him, I look down. Our tattoos go together, and it feels like something in my heart is slipping into place, too.

If I keep this up, I'll fall for him, but I don't know how to stop.

Christmas comes and goes. I knew that the holidays would be tough on Addi, with her mom gone, so she and I celebrate at Kira's parents' house in an attempt to have her around as much family as possible, especially grandparents who spoil her silly with presents. Scott spends the day with his family, and when he returns, I give him a pair of cuff links to go with a vintage shirt of his, and he gives me a set of romance books that I'll definitely be reading. He also gives Addi a framed picture of the three of us in the hot-air balloon, which we hang on the wall in her bedroom. I don't think Kira will mind.

But every time I pass the family portraits in the hallway, I wish we could hang it there.

During the break between Christmas and New Year's, I

contact a realtor, and she starts showing me houses in the Burlington area.

I don't tell Scott, though, because I don't want him getting his hopes up.

But I can't go back to New York—at least not on a permanent basis.

I want to be close to my daughter. I want to watch her grow up. I want to be here for her.

And … I want more time with my boyfriend.

Because even though we haven't said the word, it's what we are. What else do you call it when you spend all day together and can't get enough of each other? When I want him in my bed every night?

What if this could work?

Kira's been right the whole time in one regard: from a financial standpoint, I don't need to work. I've socked away enough savings for the rest of my life—that's what happens when you focus on nothing but money for fifteen years.

Even if I don't want to quit my job, I've been doing fine with this work-from-home thing. And I don't miss Manhattan at all.

I like being here. It feels like home, even if this house isn't mine.

When the realtor shows me a home for sale not two miles from Kira's, I can't help but picture a life in it—one with room for Addi to grow, and an office where I can work. It's on a big, secluded piece of property.

There's a large bedroom with an expansive view of the mountains, and it seems like that's where Scott and I are supposed to be.

Except … that thought scares me a little too much.

Still, I tell the realtor to put in an offer. For Addi's sake, I'll need a place so I can visit frequently even if I go back to New York.

23

SCOTT

On New Year's Eve, Luke and I climb the stairs of Murph and Jason's stately Victorian, which has been divided up into apartments. Addi's at a sleepover with some friends, and I'm looking forward to an evening of adult conversation. In contrast to the snow falling outside, inside is cheery and cozy—and we're not even at the party yet. Music and voices spill from the top floor. Luke holds two bottles of champagne, while I'm carrying a cake.

I'm a bit nervous, because this is the first time Luke is meeting my friends. And what is he meeting them as? My boss, or my boyfriend?

Maybe it doesn't matter.

I'm also trying not to think about the last time I was here, when I was trying to get together with Murph. How times have changed.

Murph opens the door before we get to the landing, waving excitedly. "Hello, hello! Thank you so much for coming! You must be Luke." He rushes out, the noise of the party on full blast behind him.

Luke grins and shakes his hand. "Nice to meet you. You're Murph?"

"Righty-o." My petite friend is wearing the skinniest white

jeans ever invented, an oversized pale blue sweater that falls off his shoulder, and a huge grin. I can tell that all sorts of mischievous plans are forming behind that sweet face of his, and I go to pull Luke into the party.

Except Luke is rooted to the spot, nodding slowly. "Your voice sounds familiar …"

"That's because we've talked before! When you were hiring Scott. I'm David Murphy. I, uh, worked with Scott."

Luke's eyes widen in recognition, and he laughs. "Great to put a face with a name, then."

"Likewise," Murph purrs, and even though I know how in love he is with Jason, I want to shove him. He turns to me, reaching out an arm. "Come on in. Jason's been cooking all day."

"Did you help?" I ask, giving him a hug.

"No, my job is to look pretty." Luke and I both stare at him, and he bursts out laughing. "Of course I helped. I'm not a useless sponge." He makes grabby hands at the champagne. "I am, however, in charge of drinks. Let me keep this chilled."

"It's all yours," Luke says, handing him the bottles. It's real champagne, from France. I don't know much about wine except the label is fancy, and I'm pretty sure they were expensive, since money isn't an issue for him.

Must be nice.

When we walk inside, the party is in full swing.

Jeremy runs over and reaches out a hand to Luke. "Hi, you must be Luke. Scott's told us so much about you. I'm Jeremy Everett, and it's very, very nice to meet you."

I laugh so I don't groan, because while I knew I'd have to do a ton of introductions, I'd forgotten how inquisitive my friends are.

Luke takes it in stride, though, shaking his hand. He seems genuinely interested in meeting him. Before I can do anything, Jeremy's escorted Luke off to meet everyone else while I'm left holding a dessert.

Still, as I look around, I feel a tremendous sense of warmth and goodwill. I'm here with a guy I've been seeing for a while. While we haven't said we're doing anything beyond hooking up, it feels like there's more to us than that, and if it's just me thinking so, I'll be shocked.

Once Luke meets everyone, he comes back over to me and puts his arm around my shoulder, and that one show of affection in front of all of my friends means more than anything he could say. Because if he wanted to keep me on the down low, he wouldn't have done that.

"Murph," I call, "where on earth did you get that sword?" There's a real sword taking pride of place over the mantel, along with some photos of Jason and Murph smooching all over the place. It looks like they went to Vegas. And some trip across the Southwest?

"That's Jason's. Ask me how he wields his sword."

Everyone laughs, while Jason blushes. "Please don't," he says.

"Oh my goddess," Murph exclaims. "I have the best idea." He turns to Luke. "Can we saber your champagne?"

I have no idea what he's talking about, but Luke seems to know. He chuckles. "Sure."

"What's that?" I ask.

"You'll see," he says. "I mean, I've done it with a butter knife before, but since we have a sword, we have to do it right."

Murph retrieves the sword and hands it to Jason, who does look relatively comfortable holding it, then runs and gets one of the bottles of champagne from the refrigerator.

"What on earth are you doing?" Aaron asks. "Do we need to have everyone sign a liability waiver?"

"Nah." Murph waves a hand. "If you get a clean cut, it's no big deal. And even if you don't, the pressure from the champagne keeps any shards from getting in the drink. I can't do this at work for customers because, you know, breaking glass is generally frowned upon. But here, we're all good. Do the honors, shmoopie."

With one hand, Jason grips the champagne, and with the other, he holds the sword. In one smooth movement, he hits the top of the bottle, right under the cork, with the base of the blade, and it pops off, cork and all.

Fizzy liquid spills out, but Murph is quick to catch it in two bright-colored glasses. They're not champagne flutes but are very cool. "Want to try it?" He hands them to me and Luke.

I look dubiously at my glass, but it appears to be full of champagne and nothing else. "Promise you're not feeding us ground glass?"

"Promise," Murph assures me.

Luke's lips tickle my ear when he comes up behind me. "This is exactly the sort of gesture you love, isn't it?" He wraps his arms around me.

I shiver. "So much."

"Think it's safe to drink?"

It feels like he's asking something more. Like whether it's safe to try new things with him. Or to be with him. "Yeah."

I've never felt both safer and more unsettled than I do with him.

Luke and I clink our glasses, and in that moment his eyes are shining, and he's smiling, and I'm laughing at how ridiculous and over the top my friends can be. And I'm more in love with him than I've ever been with anyone, because he's going along with this. Because he's amiable with everyone. Because he knows I like events, and sabering champagne surely counts.

Murph distributes the rest of the champagne, and we all hold up our glasses.

"To a new year," Jason says.

"To good friends," Jeremy adds.

"And to love," Murph says, snaking his arm around Jason's waist.

"Cheers," we all say, and take a sip. Since Luke doesn't let go of me, he sort of drinks his over my shoulder. Then he kisses my cheek. "You like?"

"Yeah," I murmur.

But what I really like is how affectionate he is with me.

I don't know if this can last, but I hope it will.

All through dinner, Luke's the perfect ... *boyfriend*. He's interested in my friends, attentive to me, and has his own personality and opinions without being a jerk about them.

He needs to stop, because old Scott is threatening to reappear and think this means more than it does.

When the clock counts down to midnight, Jason says, "Open the door and let the new year in!"

Murph races over to do it, and we all feel a slight whoosh of cooler air. Then he zips back into Jason's arms, leaping up and hooking his legs around Jason's waist. They kiss hard, but before I have a chance to be jealous, Luke is spinning me around and kissing me like he means it.

It makes my heart feel things that aren't safe at all.

But I love the sensation anyway.

When we get home, it's late—or early in the morning on January 1.

A brand-new year.

Luke and I crunch across the fresh snow in the front yard and go inside.

Even though this isn't my house—or really even his—it feels like home. I don't know what I'll be doing once Kira comes back, but I'll figure it out, I guess. Maybe I should start applying for new jobs.

While I want to tell Luke I love him, it's not the right time, so instead, I crawl into bed with him.

I can't say the words, so I use my body, telling him with my kisses. In the physical act of joining with him, I tell him everything.

That's maybe all I can do.

We go through January in a post-holiday haze, Addi returning to school, Luke burying himself in work, me trying to sort out which bills I can pay and which ones I can't.

And I spend every night in Luke's bed. I've given up using my own.

Even Addi knows we're together. She knows we sleep in the same bed, although we avoid getting hot and heavy in front of her. Still, she knows we kiss, and we cuddle on the couch when we're watching a movie.

By the time February rolls around and maple sugaring season approaches, all I care about is that it's almost Valentine's Day. Luke accuses me of loving every terrible chocolate and bad card, and he's right.

Addi's at school, and Luke's come shopping with me. I can see him holding his tongue as I peruse the over-the-top display. We buy boxes of valentines for Addi to give to her classmates, along with doilies and construction paper and candies, and I surreptitiously buy him a card. It's actually one I designed, so it makes me happy to see it in stores.

"This seems like a waste of time," he says, but it sounds more like a hollow protest than his usual objections do.

"I dunno. You might enjoy this stuff as much as me."

He gets the "Scott is amusing me" look on his face as we trudge back to the car in the snow.

When we step in the door, I pull out my laptop to try to write another card, but all I can think about is him.

Maybe I just need to tell him in a straightforward manner—not by writing him a poem or sending him a singing telegram or anything old Scott would do. Old Scott would hide behind romantic gestures as a way of avoiding getting hurt—because they weren't real. They were just pretend.

He walks in while I'm midthought and must notice the expression on my face. "What is it?" he asks.

"Nothing."

LESLIE MCADAM

He sits down beside me. "I don't believe it's nothing. What's up?"

I square my shoulders and look at him. While I would want to tell him this on a mountaintop at sunset or on a cruise ship amid sparkling Mediterranean waters, I suppose telling him in his kitchen after lunch and before I need to go pick up his kid is real life.

And I should be embracing real life, not some fantasy world.

"What?" he says gently. "Are you okay?"

I nod. "I love you." It comes out low and fast, almost in one word.

Luke freezes. That clearly wasn't what he'd been expecting. He opens his mouth and closes it, then opens it again.

His face falls, and so does my heart. He gets this pained look on his face and reaches out to hold my hand. "I ... I don't know what to say."

"You don't have to say it back," I start. "Fuck. I did this wrong. I can't ... I'm sorry. I just didn't want to keep it from you."

His next words make my heart sink even farther. "Scott, the last thing in the world I'd want to do is hurt you. But I don't know what I'm doing here." He squeezes my hand, and I squeeze it back. "Your parents are loving people, and you've had their healthy relationship modeled for you your whole life. I'm the product of a family filled with bitterness, and my divorce shows that I make bad decisions. I have no fucking clue how to be a good partner."

"You've been amazing—"

"But I'm not relationship material. At least, not long term." His voice is pleading. He pulls his hand away, stands, and starts to pace. "I'm thinking of *you*. You're fun and kind and lovable, and any guy would be lucky to be with you. You deserve someone who can give you your heart's desire. You deserve someone who can make you feel cherished."

"*You* make me feel cherished."

He tugs at his hair. "But it's only a matter of time before I let you down. I'm not someone you should fall in love with."

Even though I know it's juvenile, I roll my eyes. "Well, too late."

"Think about it. Do you and I make sense on any level? Even if what we have is working now, do you think it could last?"

I stand so I can tug him to me, but he steps away, so I ball up my hands at my sides. "*Yes*. I think we could work. And I'm willing to take the chance."

Except ... does he really not believe in us? To my horror, a tear falls down my cheek, but I wipe it away.

Old Scott and new Scott are having an argument right now. Old Scott wants to be in love with everyone and everything. New Scott doesn't want to fall in love with someone who won't love him back.

Except new Scott thought he had a chance at real love. And maybe he was wrong.

The devastation on Luke's face is gutting me. "I care too much about you to take that chance with your heart."

Fuck that. Anger flares in me. "What kind of bullshit is that? Either you care about me or you don't."

"I do care. But ..."

I take a step forward. "But what?"

He looks away. "But I'm too much of a fuckup for you."

Oh, he's not getting away with that. "If you're a fuckup, what does that make me?"

"You're delightful."

"Then why won't you let yourself love me?"

"I don't know," he whispers.

We stare at each other, chests rising and falling. I hadn't realized I'd been holding my breath.

Finally, I say, "You know what, Luke? I think you're scared."

His eyes go wild. "Of course I'm fucking scared. How could I not be? Love hurts. I can't get it right."

"Love can also save you."

"I just don't want to get it wrong with you," he says.

I need to leave. I'm not going to debate this with him. I'm going to let him have a chance to think.

I wipe my eyes, then stand up, close my laptop, and say, "I'll go get Addi. We'll come back before dinner. I'll give you some time to yourself."

And I flee.

Addi bounds out from her classroom, chattering about the day, and it's all I can do not to cry.

If I just fucked everything up with Luke and have to leave, I'm going to have to leave Addi, too. And I love her as well—I realize that now.

"No riding lessons today, but do you want to go on a hike?"

While there's snow on the ground, the Maple Falls trail doesn't require snowshoes.

She nods. "Will there be unicorns?"

"I haven't seen any, but that doesn't mean they don't exist. I've heard that the waterfall is frozen, though. Want to see it?"

We're both in heavy coats and sturdy shoes, and I have my usual backpack with snacks, water, and supplies. "Let's go," she says.

We drive to the familiar trailhead and park the car by the ranger station. It's a cold day, but not as cold as it gets. "Are you warm enough?" I ask her.

She nods. "I want to see the unicorns! And the fairies! And the frozen waterfall."

"I think we can do one of those."

Addison and I take off walking, the trail familiar, although it looks a little different than even a month ago. The snow is thicker in some areas than others, but it's well-marked enough that it's easy to see the path. We go around the turn and down and then see the spur to the waterfall. "Want to keep going?" I ask. "Or do you want to head back?"

"I want to see the waterfall."

I let out a sigh of relief. Because I'm not ready to go home. I'll do anything to avoid the awkwardness of having to face Luke after what I told him. "Be careful when you walk. Make sure you stay close to the hill and away from the edge."

Addi and I continue through the woods until the trail junction to the waterfall—with her little legs, we walk slowly. Although in the few months she and I have been hiking together, she's gotten faster and doesn't stop for every little thing anymore. Part of me is sad about that, but mostly I like that I can get in a bit of exercise with her.

I'm really going to miss her.

When we get to the well-worn path down to the river, the banks covered in snow, she points. "Look!"

The waterfall has frozen over, forming huge icicles. I take in a sharp breath. "It looks like a wizard put a spell on it, doesn't it? Maybe there really are unicorns. It seems like the kind of frozen palace they'd like."

"Can we go touch it?"

"No, I don't think that's safe."

"Okay," she says. "Want to go back?"

"Sure." I can't think of another thing to do out here, and I'm going to have to face Luke eventually. I turn, but my foot catches on a root hidden under a thinner layer of snow, and I trip and start sliding down an icy ravine. Automatically, my hands reach out for branches or something to stop my fall, but I keep going to the bottom.

Pain lances through my ankle as I crash to a halt eight or ten feet below Addi.

"Scott!" Addi cries. "Are you okay?"

"Yeah," I say automatically, until I move my leg and realize that no, I'm not all right at all. I try to stand, but when I put weight on my ankle, it crumples under me.

Addi peers down at me, eyes wide.

"Stay back from the edge," I say. "Maybe it'll be better in a minute." I try my best, wincing, but I can't step on my foot.

And I can't figure out how to get out of this ravine.

"Do you have an owie?"

"Yeah, baby. I definitely have an owie. Let me see if I can get us help."

But when I pull out my phone, there's no service.

You told Luke you were good in an emergency, Scott. Now's the time to act like it.

LUKE

I'm such a fucking fuckup.

Scott hasn't been gone for two minutes before I text Landon. I'm not the kind of guy who discusses my feelings, but Landon doesn't judge, and I think he'll be sympathetic.

Luke: *You around?*
Landon: *Yeah, what's up?*
Luke: *Can you talk?*

My phone buzzes immediately with a call from him, and I smile despite myself. Tough guy, my ass.

"What's going on?" His voice sounds wary, like he can't tell whether my news will be good or bad, or what it's going to require from him.

I sigh. "All kinds of shit." I proceed to tell him how Scott said he's in love with me and I don't know how to deal with that because it was never supposed to be more than convenient hooking up except I caught some inconvenient feels. And how I fucked up by hurting him, even though the whole point was that I didn't want to hurt him.

When I finish, Landon's sigh matches my own. "I'm gonna lay down some truth for you, okay, Lucas?"

He doesn't wait for a response.

"You're being a complete and total fool. Scott's a great guy. He says he's in love with you, and I'm willing to wager you're in love with him." I sputter, but he talks over me. "Even if you think you're not. Because if you didn't have big feelings for him, you wouldn't be calling me. You wouldn't care."

I don't say anything. Because … is it possible to have Scott be my partner?

"Let me ask you: is Scott someone you want to come home to every day?"

"*Fuck.*"

He chuckles. "I'll take that as a yes. Is he someone you can see a life with in a few years?"

I already know the answer to that. Of course he is. "This sucks." I sound like a sulky jackass.

"When's the last time you cared about someone else? Besides your kid."

"It was Kira."

"Right. It was Kira. And she left you, and you're still hurting from it. Even though it's been, what did you tell me? Five years?"

He's right. I've been punched in the gut that long. I can tell he knows he's right from my silence.

"Listen. I spent enough time locked up to realize life's too short to waste. Don't fuck around with his feelings. Admit yours. Go. Find him. Do something to let him know you love him."

I told Scott not to focus on the negative with his finances. But I've been doing the exact same thing with my love life.

I need to take my own advice. Stop focusing on the bad and pay attention to the good. Then the good will grow.

Still … "I have no fucking clue what to do."

"I notice that you didn't deny that you love him."

Huh. "Guess I didn't."

And when I think about it, a life with no Scott Malone in it—

no sleigh rides, no stargazing, no sabering champagne, no romance book club, no flower arranging, no make-believe with my daughter—isn't a life I want. He cares for Addison as much as if she were his. He takes care of me in so many ways.

Scott's never been temporary, and I should never have thought of him that way.

If I'm honest, I'm not sure I ever did.

He brings joy to my life.

"You deserve to be happy," Landon says, somehow in sync with my thoughts. "Next time you see him, tell him. Don't wait."

I hang up and pace around the house. I fucked up big-time, and I hurt Scott's feelings.

The thought of hurting him makes me ache. I need to think of a way of telling him I want to be with him.

Love? Maybe.

Mostly I feel a deep sense of relief, like I've solved some major mystery. I want him around, and whatever it takes to achieve that, I'll do.

I haven't thought I'm the kind of guy who anyone stays with long term.

Except …

I want to try. I was so fucking lonely in New York. And Scott's brought a spark into my life that I don't want to lose.

Instead of working on the next regulatory filing I have to get done, I find myself researching bed-and-breakfasts to surprise him with a romantic getaway as an apology—and to tell him that I love him. Even if I'm still afraid this will all end badly.

———

I'm absorbed in my computer when my cell starts ringing. I don't recognize the number, but it's local, so I pick it up.

A woman's brisk voice says, "This is the Maple Falls ranger station. I'm looking for Addison Lagomarsino's father."

It feels like my stomach got hit with a bowling ball. "That's me."

"Your daughter is safe," the woman assures me. The bowling ball rolls away, but adrenaline still spikes through me. "She's here at the station."

I'm already moving, looking for my shoes, my keys, my wallet, my jacket. "What do you mean, she's there? Where's Scott? I mean, her nanny?"

My jumbled-up feelings are making my mind race to all sorts of scenarios, each more improbable than the last: Scott got in a car accident and couldn't pick her up from school. He ran away from me and took her with him.

What the hell is going on?

"Addison is here with me. She came to the ranger station by herself—"

"By herself?" I growl. What happened to Scott?

"She said that her babysitter had gotten hurt and it was an emergency. They've called search and rescue for him."

"Search and rescue?" I repeat weakly, getting in my car. "Tell me where to pick her up. Where is he? I'm driving right now."

She gives me the address.

Before I hang up, I ask, "Tell me. How is Scott Malone? How badly is he hurt?"

"We don't know. The search party hasn't reached him yet, so we don't have a status update."

I hang up and scream. What the hell were they doing? I know they go hiking, but today? In the snow?

I attempt to not drive recklessly, because the last thing I want is to go off the road. But I need to see my daughter. I need to know that Scott is safe and happy. He should be planning a party, not lost in the woods.

Fuck, this is bad.

I try calling him, but there's no answer.

I park at the ranger station near a large snowbank and race into the building.

"Where's Addison?" I almost shout, slamming both hands on the front counter.

"Are you Lucas Lagomarsino?"

"Yes." I fish in my pocket for my wallet and throw the receptionist my ID. My logical brain is glad they're not just releasing my kid to anyone, but *oh my god hurry already*.

"Come this way."

She leads me into a conference room that was apparently last decorated in 1973, with a metal table and plastic chairs, but it's the most perfect place I've ever seen, because Addison is sitting in there, wrapped in a blanket, drinking a glass of water.

"Daddy!"

I rush over to her, but she seems totally unharmed. There are no tears. Her hair is squashed under a knit cap, and her nose is red from the cold, but she's bright-eyed and seems proud of herself.

I let out a breath I hadn't realized I'd been holding.

She goes into my arms easily.

"Baby girl," I whisper. "Are you okay?"

"I'm fine, Daddy," she says cheerfully. "I did all the things I was supposed to. Scott told me I would be a hero." She starts saying something about how she was supposed to hug a tree but this was one of the times when she couldn't do it, and I have no idea what she's talking about.

"How is Scott?" I ask.

"He fell down."

"Where?"

"In the woods." Her lip trembles. "On the trail by the water-fall. He couldn't walk."

I whip around to the ranger standing at the doorway. "Scott Malone. Where is he?"

"Sounds like they've found him. Search and rescue is indicating that they are with him right now." She holds out a radio, twisting the volume dial so I can hear the exchange.

"Subject is a Caucasian male, early twenties, fallen down a ravine on the waterfall spur of the Maple Falls trail. He's awake and aware. Oriented to time and space. He appears to have an injured ankle or lower leg."

She slides the radio back onto her utility belt.

"Okay." I let out a sigh and realize my hands are trembling. "I'll wait for him."

"I think you need to take care of your daughter," the ranger says. "It could be an hour or more before we're able to bring him back, depending on the injury. They're likely going to have to hoist him out, because it's not passable by snow machine."

I look at Addi, who is shivering. Her boots are wet, and her gloves and jeans are soaked through. She needs to be warm and dry before she gets sick. And while it tears my heart out, I have to assume the professionals will do their jobs.

Still. "Have him call me the minute he can," I order.

I take Addi home, stick her in a warm bath, and get her into cozy clothes. I try calling Scott again, but he doesn't answer.

Feeling sick to my stomach, I pull Addi into my lap on the couch and ask, "Now, tell me what happened, but slower this time."

25

SCOTT

I'm propped up on a rock, my ass freezing and my leg in serious pain. I tried to walk on it again, placing sticks in my boot as a splint, but it was no good, and I couldn't get any purchase on the icy hill.

And I'm fucking worried about Addison.

She knows the trail. We've been on it so many times before. She knows how to get to the ranger station safely. It's not that far, and the trail is clearly marked.

I'm still worried, and I regret everything I've ever done in my life.

From going on this hike to letting Addi go for help by herself to telling Luke I loved him.

What was I thinking?

He's going to be so pissed at me. I put his precious little girl in danger. I should probably just quit, but I don't have cell phone service to call him.

Finally, I hear the faint noise of a motor getting closer and closer, and eventually a snow machine busts through the branches and stops on the trail above me.

I struggle to get up and then sit back down hard when I realize who it is. My rescuer gets off of his search-and-rescue vehicle and takes off his helmet.

As if I weren't humiliated enough.

"Scott?" Edsel calls. "Are you okay? We got a request for help."

"I'm fine," I grumble. Then I cringe. "Okay, I'm not fine."

"What happened?"

"I fell and hurt my ankle. I can't walk on it." I look up at him. "Please tell me Addison found the ranger station."

He smiles. "She did. That's how we knew to come."

Brave girl. "Okay, can you take me to her?"

"Her dad already came and picked her up."

I'm relieved, but I also feel like Luke is going to call me into the principal's office for such an epic screwup.

Who on earth would let a little girl go off by herself in the woods? No one.

Except I know Addi was listening to all our lessons, and obviously she got help for me. I still feel terribly guilty.

Meanwhile, Edsel is getting out ropes and a harness to pull me up. "Can you put weight on your foot?"

"No. That's part of the problem."

"Okay. Hang on a moment, and I'll take a look at it."

Edsel gets to work rigging up a belay system anchored by a nearby tree and efficiently makes his way to my side, where he sets down a medical pack and stoops to inspect my injury. I try not to wince, but it hurts.

"Let's stabilize your leg, and I'll take you back to the ranger station. From there, we can get you to medical care."

I'm mortified, but I let him splint my leg, and then he puts a harness around me. Using the rope, he climbs back up, then hauls me up to the trail. He helps me hop over to his snow machine and wraps me in an emergency blanket. My jeans are soaked from sitting on a snowy rock for so long, and I'm freezing.

He radios in, and I sit behind him, shaking and dirty, feeling awful in every way possible.

Before we take off, he turns around and inspects me. "Scott, I don't think things ever could have worked out between us—and sneaking into my house like that was way out of line—but I know you're a good guy at heart. I hope you find someone who appreciates you for your whimsy."

I sigh. "Thanks. Me, too."

———

At the station, the rangers take one look at me and decide I need to be transported to the hospital. Since I can't drive, I'm getting a ride in their SUV.

On the way, I see I have thirteen missed calls from Luke and twice as many texts. I know he must be angry. I've never seen him lose his temper, but I know how precious Addi is to him. I figure I'd better get this over with, so I hit the button to call him.

He answers immediately. "Luke?" My voice sounds creaky.

"Scott! Oh my god. What happened?" He doesn't sound mad, only panicked.

"I'm fine. First things first: how's Addi?"

"She's fine." I can almost hear how he's choking back words. It makes me scared and nervous. "She said you told her she'd be a hero. Can you please tell me what happened?"

"She and I go hiking on this trail all the time. This time, though, I fell and hurt my ankle, and I couldn't walk on it. I didn't see any other option, so I sent her to get help."

I'm definitely going to get fired. But he doesn't say anything about that, not yet. "How are you feeling now?"

Pain level seven. "Not that great. They're taking me to the doctor's." Hospital. Whatever.

"I was so scared," he admits in a low voice. "I thought something horrible had happened to you. I thought something horrible had happened to Addison—even though the ranger told me right away she was fine."

"I'm so glad she's okay. I'm very sorry I made you worry."

LESLIE MCADAM

"It's not your fault." He sighs. "Can I go with you to the doctor?"

"I don't think it would be much fun for Addi. It's okay, I can handle it." I want him to come, but I'm scared of what he's going to say when I see him.

"Are you sure?"

"Yeah, I can figure it out. I might need a few days off, though, depending on what the doctor says." That's my feeble way of raising the question of whether I still have a job.

Because I fucked up majorly.

Addi's voice sounds in the background, and he calls, "Yeah, sweetheart. I'm coming. Hang on." Then, into the phone, he says, "Okay, sorry, Addi needs me, and I have to go. I'll make other arrangements. Call me later and let me know how you're doing." And he hangs up.

Other arrangements?

Other arrangements, like, he's going to hire someone else while I'm recovering?

Did I just get fired?

───

At the hospital, after an X-ray—which will surely be another scary bill—I learn that the only thing broken is my heart. Apparently I have a bad sprain and need to keep my foot in a boot for a while. Once I get that thing on and some painkillers, though, I'm mobile again.

Except ... I don't want to go see Luke. Maybe I'm chickenshit, but I told him I loved him when he doesn't love me, and then he had to go pick up his kid because of my accident. Something bad could've happened to her, too, and it would've been my fault.

I text Luke that I'm going to go see Murph.

Luke: *If that's what you want to do. I hope you feel better. We need to talk.*

"We need to talk" never means anything good.

Murph picks me up and takes me to the car I'd left at the ranger station—Kira's Subaru. Luckily, it's an automatic I can drive with my foot in a boot. I follow him to his house and hobble up the stairs, then collapse on his couch.

To Murph's credit, after he gets me into some sweats of Jason's and flies around making me hot tea, he sits quietly and listens while I babble out all my stress and fear.

"I let Luke down. He trusted me to watch his daughter, and I had to ask her to walk through the woods on her own. She's six! Anything could've happened to her."

"Nothing did. And it was an emergency. She knew the trail. You did the best you could. That's all you could do."

"Still, she could've been hurt. Badly. She could've gotten frost-bite or hypothermia or gotten lost or fallen herself or been eaten by wolves."

Murph taps my knee. "None of those things happened. Stop dwelling on imaginary catastrophes and focus on what did happen: You're safe. She's safe."

I sigh and stare out the window. It's gotten dark.

"Do you want to stay here tonight?" he asks.

"I shouldn't. Although tomorrow's my day off. If I even still have a job."

"And maybe you need a break from him."

I nod.

Scott: *We do need to talk, but right now I'm at Murph and Jason's. I think I'm going to spend the night.*
Luke: *Okay.*

I stare at that one word. What does he mean, "Okay"? "Okay" as in don't worry about it? Or a seething "Okay" that he can't do anything about right now, but I'll have it coming to me when I get home?

Not that his house is my home.

Setting my phone down, I look at my hands.

"Hey," Murph says quietly. "What's going on?"

I gulp. And tell him everything. I end by saying, "I do think I'm in love with him. Not the love I write about in greeting cards. Not Valentine's Day love. Something quieter but stronger."

"Love can be very quiet," Murph says. The warm certainty in his voice makes it obvious he's thinking about Jason. "It can show up in just supporting each other. Or the way he takes care of something or notices something—filling your gas tank or buying your favorite flavor of ice cream. It doesn't have to be all those big gestures from the movies."

"I know. Even though I always wanted the big gestures from the movies."

"And that's one thing we adore about you, Scottybear." He tilts his head. "I'm not so sure he doesn't feel the same way about you. Because I saw you two at New Year's, and let me tell you …" He fans himself. "The chemistry off you could ignite our fireplace without tinder."

"But what if that's just sex?"

"He was affectionate with you, and he respected your opinions. He seemed to be entertained by you, and he always made sure you were taken care of. It looked like more than sex to me. How do you know he isn't in love with you?"

"Because he didn't say it back. Instead he said all these things about not being a good long-term bet."

"Yeah, he's smitten. He just doesn't know it yet or doesn't think he can trust it. What do you think about his daughter?"

I sigh. "I've fallen in love with her, too. I can't imagine what my life would be like without Addison in it."

Murph gets up and grabs a blanket and a pillow for me, tucking me onto the couch, even though it's nowhere near bedtime. "I wonder what would happen if you both let go of what you think a relationship should look like and focus on what you actually have."

My phone buzzes with a text.

Luke: *How are you feeling now?*
Scott: *I'm okay. It's a sprain, but it'll heal. I'm mobile. Ambulatory. You know—I can move.*

I send him a photo of the boot on my foot.

Luke: *I'm glad it wasn't worse. Are you in a lot of pain?*
Scott: *No, although they gave me meds.*
Scott: *I know you want to talk, but before we do, can I have a little distance to think?*
Luke: *Yeah.*
Luke: *I don't want that, but if it's what you need, okay.*
Luke: *You matter to me.*
Luke: *I really want you to come home to me. It's lonely here without you. I have so many things to tell you.*
Scott: *I want to come home, too, but I'm feeling really guilty.*
Scott: *I fucked up, putting Addi in danger.*
Luke: *Look, I might be overprotective, but I'm focusing on the fact that you're both safe.*
Luke: *And I appreciate the fact that you taught her so much about how to be independent and smart.*

Well, hmm. Maybe I haven't totally messed everything up. His next text warms me as much as Murph's blanket.

Luke: *I miss you.*
Scott: *I miss you, too.*

26

LUKE

I feed Addison dinner and settle her in her room to play quietly until bedtime. I'm astonished she's not exhausted. I am, and I'm not the one who had to walk alone through the snowy forest. But she seems fine.

Along her woodland wall, she props up a few dolls, along with some stuffed animals.

She's muttering to herself, but I catch her words. "Oh, no! Scott! You're hurt!" A toy fairy flies over, clutched in her hand. "I'll save you. I know what to do. I can do it all by myself."

The more I listen to her, the more I appreciate how Scott has helped her to know things well beyond her years.

The fairy doll flies off, and Addi looks up at me. "Hi, Daddy."

"Hey, pumpkin. How do you feel?"

"Okay. Is Scott okay?"

I swallow. "I think so. He told me he wanted to spend the night at his friend's house."

"Like a sleepover?"

"Something like that."

"I like having him here," she says.

"I do, too."

But my stomach sinks. Because even if I'm in love with him—

which, Landon is right, I am—there's no way we'll work. I'm not the kind of person he can have anything lasting with. I can't give him the kind of romantic love he wants.

Except, a little voice says, *you tried. You gave him a romantic dinner. The first time you were inside him, you made love.*

"Can we call Momma?" Addi asks.

"Sure." We're used to calling at strange hours because of the time difference. I pull out my phone, and soon enough we get Kira on the video call.

"Hey, baby," Kira coos. "What's going on?"

"Scott and I had an adventure."

"What happened?"

Addison tells Kira about their hike and her rescuing Scott.

Kira sucks in a breath. "Is everyone okay?"

Addi nods gravely. "Yes, Momma."

"It appears that Scott taught her trail safety," I offer.

"Jax, too."

"Who's Jax?" I ask. Does Scott know everyone in town?

Addi answers, "Scott's friend who lives in the forest." I assume she means *works*. "He told me about bacteria and to not eat anything in the woods."

I let out a breath. Scott appears to have been far more responsible than I gave him credit for. And I already trusted him with my daughter's life.

When Addi's done with her story, Kira looks at me. "Addi, can I talk to your dad alone for a moment? I promise I'll talk with you again after."

"Okay." She snuggles into bed, and I kiss the top of her head.

"I'll be right back," I tell her, and I take the phone down the hall. "What?" I ask Kira.

She sighs loudly. "Some things never change. It's nice to talk with you, too, Luke."

I pinch the bridge of my nose. "Sorry. It's been a stressful day. How can I help you?"

215

"I got news that they accepted my story. I'm going to leave soon. I'll probably be home in a week."

"Good," I say. "I'm glad."

Except I'm not. Because now I really need to figure out what I'm going to do next. And how that can involve Scott, because the thought of leaving him behind to go back to the city makes me sick.

She's staring at me intently. "What's wrong?"

Who better to ask than the horse's mouth? "Do you remember when you said I wasn't relationship material?"

Kira jerks her head back. "What?"

I press my lips together, not wanting to repeat myself.

"Let me guess," she says. "You and Scott?"

"Yeah. We have … a thing. How did you know?"

"Luke, you answer the phone shirtless when he's around. You get this dopey grin when he says something sweet. You've got it bad for him."

"Yeah," I admit. "I think I do. And it sucks, because I don't know how to make a relationship work."

She shakes her head. "I fucked you up."

I snort. "Pretty sure I fucked myself up."

"Maybe. But when we split up, I was … disappointed, and frustrated, and I lashed out. But just because we didn't work together doesn't mean you can't have a relationship with anyone." She smiles. "From what I can see, Scott's really good for you."

"How can you tell that over Skype?"

"I know you, and I can see how he brings out the person you used to be before you got all *responsible adult* and into financing the world. He's playful; you're serious. You need someone to care for. He needs someone to spoil. You're probably perfect for each other. You'll make him be responsible, and he loosens you up. Tell me this: do you work less than you used to?"

"Yeah."

"And you seem to be out more with the family, doing more things."

The family. She means Addi. Or is Scott part of that, too?

He is. Scott's part of my family.

"True," I say slowly.

"I hate to break it to you, but you're already in a relationship with him."

My heart jumps at her words. Because maybe, just maybe, it's possible. At least, I'm willing to try.

"I'm sorry, Luke. I did you a disservice. The things I said during the divorce, that was my ego speaking. But we're both older and wiser now." She peers at my face. "Why do you look so stricken?"

"He told me he loved me, and I argued with him. Tried to talk him out of it. And then he got hurt—physically—and now I feel like a total asshole, and I don't know how to fix it."

"You're always going to be a bit of an asshole, but you can tell him you're sorry and that you love him."

"But then what do we do? You're coming home. Are you going to need him as a nanny?"

"Probably not. But that doesn't mean you have to break up with him. Take him with you to New York."

I raise an eyebrow. I hadn't thought about that. "I've actually been looking at places here in Vermont."

Kira smiles. "That works, too. Then you can see Addi more often."

"Yeah." And that makes my heart happy.

"Just ... don't cut off the one thing in your life that brings you joy."

Things.

Flying in a hot-air balloon with my partner and my daughter. Snuggling under a blanket on a sleigh ride. Watching movies and passing popcorn back and forth. Telling stories. Watching them play dress-up. Tucking her in at night, and joining him afterward.

Without him, I never would have taken the time to look at the stars. Or drink coffee with my old friend. I would have just spent my life imprisoned at my desk while other people went out and had fun.

"Enjoy this moment," I whisper.

"What was that?" she asks.

"Nothing. I think … yeah. I don't have the answers. But I'm going to try asking the questions."

"Like, 'Will you be my boyfriend?'" she says in a teasing tone.

"Yeah." *Or more.* I catch her eyes. "Thanks, Kira. I owe you."

"You don't. You gave me these months to focus on something that really mattered to me and that matters to the world. You're pretty fucking cool, Mr. Lagomarsino."

"'S the right thing to do," I mutter. I clear my throat. "And I know it's too late, but I'm sorry. It takes two to have a relationship, and I know I hurt you in ways I don't even fathom. I take responsibility for my part in it not working out."

"Thanks." She nods. "That means a lot to me."

After a long moment, I say, "I'll give you back to Addi."

Addison chats with her momma a little longer, super excited to hear that she's coming back next week. When they're done, I sit down at the edge of her bed.

"Hey, kiddo. Today was quite a day. Are you sure you're all right?"

"Yes! It was fun. I want to be a forest ranger when I grow up."

"I can see you doing that. It wasn't too scary for you to go for help by yourself?"

"No. I knew the way." Her simple statement reaffirms my belief that Scott has been teaching her life skills this whole time. He has a lot of knowledge to impart. So, he's lacking in financial skills. But that's the one thing I'm great at. Maybe between the two of us—three, including Kira—we can help Addison grow up to be well-rounded and amazing.

I let out a sigh.

"Daddy, are you sad?"

"Why do you ask that?"

"Because Scott is hurt, and you haven't seen him."

"He'll be okay," I say, hoping it's true. "He needs to be with people who love him."

"Daddy, *we* love Scott."

We *love Scott.*

What the hell is wrong with me? I thought if I closed myself off from the possibility of a relationship, no one could get hurt, least of all me.

But I was ignoring the fact that Addison already has a relationship with Scott.

And so do I.

If I screw this up with him, I don't think I'll ever recover. Because now that I'm thinking clearly, I know: he's it for me. I'm all in.

"I'll tell him," I say in a raspy voice.

"We should make it a game," she says. "Scott likes games."

I stare at her. He once told me he wanted a grand gesture.

I put my head in my hands. How the hell can I pull this off?

She puts a small hand on my arm. "You can do it, Daddy. Just make it so he has to find you."

A plan starts to form in my head. Scott is this amazing guy who dreams of being important enough to someone for them to want to romance him.

And tomorrow is Valentine's Day.

It's perfect.

His leg is hurt, but from his texts, it sounds like he can get around okay. I'll have to make sure things are easy for him. Maybe I can get some assistance in carrying this out.

"Let's come up with a plan," I say. "Do you want to help? What are some of his favorite things?"

She grins and claps. "Yes, Daddy! Let's play a game with him!"

What I'm thinking of is something he's wanted his whole life, and I can give it to him.

FedEx is wonderful. This should work.

I hope.

Because if it doesn't, I don't know what I'll do.

27

SCOTT

Although it's my day off—and Vino and Veritas is all decked out in pink and red for Valentine's Day—I'm squirreled away in a corner tapping on my laptop, designing a sympathy card.

Because that's the mood I'm in—and because I need the money. I'm frustrated with myself because I did the same thing I always do: made up something in my head that doesn't exist in the real world.

After all, even though Luke seems to be amazingly okay about me sending Addi off alone to get help, I'm pretty sure that when we talk, he'll be singing the same song as before: I shouldn't fall in love with him, etc. etc. etc. Too late, *hotsexyboss*. Too damned late.

But he messaged me saying that he and Addi were busy with something and he'd talk with me later this evening. So I guess we'll see what happens. He asked about my leg, and I assured him that it was doing better already.

Murph's busy, and most of the regular patrons are deep in their own conversations, so I try to get some work done.

If I'm honest, I need a moment to think.

Where do we go from here? I'm in love with him, but he either doesn't feel the same way or won't admit it.

Can I live with the way things are? What we've been doing is amazing, but I want more. I don't want to be in love with Luke while he sees me as nothing more than a fuck buddy—no matter how romantic he's trying to be.

Not if he's only doing it for my sake rather than because he really feels it.

I don't know what to do, so I go with avoidance.

Although since that tactic didn't work for my finances, it's not likely to do any better for my love life.

I'm so focused on the card design that I don't register the scrape of chairs and noise of movement until a prickling sensation travels down my spine.

The bar has gone quiet, and four men stand in a semicircle in front of me, all wearing red-and-white-striped jackets, white pants, and straw boater hats.

I glance around, confused.

The tallest one, who sports the most luxurious mustache I've ever seen, asks, "Are you Scott Malone?"

I nod. *What the hell is going on?*

"Lucas Lagomarsino thought that you were feeling blue. He wants to play a game with you. It requires you to solve some clues."

My jaw drops, and a feeling suffuses me like I've been coated in warm oil—hedonistic, comforting, all-consuming. One of them pulls out a harmonica and plays a note. Then they start to sing "Like I Love You" by Lost Frequencies, a cappella.

Oh my god. Luke is doing the Grand Gesture! The *one thing* I always wanted someone to do for me.

Enjoy this moment.

I'm so excited I can't stand it, and I listen to them harmonize, totally rapt, sure my mouth is hanging open unattractively. So, of course, Murph has his phone out and is recording my reaction—no doubt to send to Luke.

What has Luke done?

"What do I have to do?" I ask when they finish.

The mustached man smiles and hands me a red heart with a

doily pasted to it. It's clearly Addison's work, misshapen and handmade. It says, in Luke's writing, "To find what you seek, go to the place that's lost."

"A place that's lost? That makes no sense. Places don't get lost." The only thing I've lost recently is Luke's heart. But going to his house doesn't seem like the right answer. I look around. "Murph?"

"Don't ask me," he says, holding up a hand, still recording.

We've attracted a crowd, some of whom are offering suggestions, each more outlandish than the last.

Lost. A place.

Lost Acres Morgans!

I scramble out of my seat as fast as I can, given the boot on my foot, throw down money for my bill, and yank on my coat. I give the barbershop quartet a group hug. "You guys are the best. I'd love to stay and listen to you sing some more, but I have someone to find."

They grin and hold out their hands like I'm part of the show. "Good luck!"

I get to the car—I still have Kira's Subaru—and take off to Lost Acres Morgans. When I get there, I don't see anything unusual, but as I limp toward the stables, Landon strides out, giving me a rugged smile.

"Hey, Scott. Luke asked me to give you this." He hands me a pink envelope decorated with star and heart stickers.

"Oh my god. He's having me go on a scavenger hunt," I whisper excitedly.

"Yeah." His eyes squint with amusement.

"Did he tell you where it goes?"

Landon just raises an eyebrow.

"You're not going to tell me even if you did know, I gather."

He nods in acknowledgment.

"Thanks." I open the envelope carefully and see nothing but a childish drawing of stars on another cutout paper heart—this one pink.

Stars. Stars. Stars.

"The field where we went stargazing," I yelp. "Thank you, Landon!" I cry as I hop back to my car.

"Good luck out there," he calls.

I drive to the grassy area by Luke's house, now covered in snow. When I pull up, I recognize the car already parked there.

It's my dad's car, and he's got Addison with him.

I've barely opened my door before she's racing over to see me. "Scott!" she cries, arms spread wide.

"Hey!" I unbuckle myself and get out, returning her hug and then giving my dad one as well. "What are you doing here?"

"Luke asked me to watch Addison for a bit. I'm happy to help." Dad looks pleased. "Seems you found a good one with him, so maybe you don't need me as a wingman anymore."

"No, maybe not."

"Is your foot okay?"

"Yeah, it's fine. It'll heal."

I'm too impatient to focus on myself, so I'm grateful when Addi says, "We have a clue. Want it?"

"Absolutely." My throat grows thick with emotion.

She hands me another envelope, and I pull out another heart— red this time. In Luke's writing, it says, "What's large and blue and green but isn't on the earth or of the earth?"

"Blue and green like the earth?"

She nods.

I think about it. "Water. Trees. Um. But what isn't on the earth. The sky." Then inspiration hits. "Our hot-air balloon was green and blue."

Addi claps her hands. "Right! You have to go to where we flew." Then she claps her hand over her mouth. "Did I give you too much of a clue?"

"No, I think you just helped a little." I kiss the top of her head and give my dad a hug. "Thank you both!"

"You're welcome," they call after me as I get back in the car.

I head for the launching place for the hot-air balloon ride, keeping an eye peeled for state troopers. I wouldn't think anyone would be at the site at this time in the afternoon, but I see our operator sitting in a van, drinking something out of a thermos and playing with his phone.

"Your boyfriend asked me to give you this," he says when I drive up and roll down my window.

My eyes bug out. "Boyfriend?"

"That's what he said."

I can't help my huge smile. "Oh my god, he's the best!"

"He was insistent that I stay until you came. Thank him for me. He paid me a hundred bucks to wait for you."

My heart beats faster. "My man is being extravagant? Heavens."

"He seemed like he was in love."

That makes my heart freeze up and then melt all over again. "Thank you!" I say, taking the envelope from him.

I open it, eager to see the clue. This time, the heart is decorated with a label from a champagne bottle. The same brand we had at New Year's.

I tear off to Jason and Murph's place, no longer being careful with the speed limit. When I get to their porch, I'm buzzed in immediately.

Will Luke be waiting for me at the top of the stairs?

Except before I can get a few feet inside, Jason trots down. "Don't hurt yourself. Luke left something for you." He hands me an envelope plastered with stickers and hearts.

"Thank you," I say. "He's making me go all over town."

"Sounds like fun."

"It's so much fun. Oh my god. He's reminding me of all these things we've experienced together."

Jason grins at me. "He's a keeper, then."

"He *so* is."

He gestures at the envelope. "Are you going to open it?"

I nod and rip it open. The clue inside is a photo of crème brûlée.

"Oh my god. The restaurant where we went on a date for my birthday."

Jason winks at me. "Go get him." He pauses before climbing the stairs. "Do you want a hint as to where this is going?"

"No. Yes. No. I don't know."

"Let's just say my sister is in on it, too."

That doesn't help. I don't know Jason's sister.

"Okay. Um. Thank you!" I shout as I hobble back to my car.

It's not a regular meal hour, but when I pull up in front of Clifton's, the maître d' comes outside to meet me. "Are you Scott Malone?"

"Yes."

He hands me another envelope. "Here's a note that was left for you."

"Thank you," I whisper. Written on the heart inside is an address I don't recognize. Each other clue has sent me somewhere we've been these past few months. But this one is new to me.

I furrow my brows.

"Everything okay?" he asks.

"Yeah," I say. "It's fine. I just don't know where this is." I plug the address into my GPS, thank him again, and take off, wondering if this is the final clue or if there's more to it.

The GPS takes me to a part of town not far from Kira's house, but it's not an area I'm very familiar with, mostly because it's super nice, with large, well-kept homes.

I pull up to the address, which is on a hill, with a view of Lake Champlain and surrounded by trees. I can't see any other houses around.

I hobble toward the simple but lovely two-story white clapboard house, but before I can knock on the door, I see the envelope taped to the door handle.

My mouth goes dry. I open the envelope and find an ornate key and a note.

"You're the lock I never knew I was looking for, and I hope

you'll accept the key to my heart—and to your new home with me."

Luke is giving me a key. Unlike with Edsel, I didn't have to swipe it.

I take the key and fit it into the lock. It turns easily.

I hold my breath and step inside.

LUKE

For the past hour, I've been pacing, giving myself pep talk after pep talk.

I can do this.

I've faced down corporate mergers and angel investors. I've given presentations to the harshest critics. I've invested in companies that have flopped and ones that have soared.

But I've never invested in my own relationship, and that's what I'm doing here. I'm investing in Scott, and I'm investing in me. I hope this move will pay dividends ... or at least not bankrupt me.

Also, I feel foolish. I mean, given what I'm wearing?

I breathe slowly, trying to calm my nerves.

What if this doesn't work? What if I went through this whole rigmarole just to have him say no? That he's decided he doesn't need me. Doesn't want me.

I shouldn't have opened my heart.

What if—

I could drive myself to drink with what-ifs, couldn't I?

My phone buzzes.

Landon: *What does he think?*

Luke: *I don't know.*
Landon: *Are you panicking?*
Luke: *No.*
Landon: *Really?*
Luke: *Yes. I mean no. I mean, yes, I really am panicking.*
Landon: *Hang in there, man.*

I hear the front door open

Luke: *He's here. Bye.*

I put my phone on a nearby table and stand there. I look down my front. I know I look ridiculous. But I did it anyway, because I think he'll like it.

When I raise my eyes, Scott is standing in the open doorway, key in hand, the expression on his face completely unreadable.

Is it awe? Disgust? Confusion? Yearning?

I have no fucking clue.

All I know is that I want to run to him, but I'm gonna let him make the choice. His foot has a huge black boot on it, but otherwise he looks unharmed—and beautiful.

I clear my throat. "Um. Hey. I have something to say—"

He runs to me, limping slightly, and wraps me in his arms. Then he kisses me soundly.

I almost fall over.

Our tongues tangle, and my cock hardens, which is difficult in these tight pants—and what I'm wearing underneath. I don't exactly have a lot of room for my junk in this getup.

When we break apart, both breathless, he says, "I can't believe you did all that for me. I can't believe you made me run all over town. I can't believe you're wearing a fucking Chippendales costume."

I look down at my bare chest, the bow tie and cuffs that were delivered this morning. "I, um, wanted to—"

He grins. "That was so much fun!" But then his face falls,

uncertainty flashing across it. "Does this mean you want to keep me around?"

I get down on my knees before him. "It means I love you, Scott. I wanted to show you in language you understand: romance. You've taught me that making an effort to show another person how much I care about them isn't a waste. It's fun, and it's a way of showing love. And life doesn't need to be so serious all the time. And ... I fucking love you, okay? So ... did you like it?"

"Yes!" he says, beaming. "It was a dream come true. You made today an *event*. You know that? I loved every moment of the scavenger hunt."

"That's what I was hoping for." I'm feeling entirely *not* myself. I'm never this shy. Or awkward. Or uncertain.

Except with love.

I told him. But he seemed to let it pass.

My face drops. He looks at me, and then understanding dawns. "Oh my god, Luke, I love you, too. Still. Always."

I blink. "Yeah?"

"So much. So much that it hurt me to stay away from you. I didn't want to, but I ... I was afraid. And, with Addi and all, I thought you might need to calm down."

"I was calm. Or—not calm. I was terrified that something had happened to you, but I couldn't drag Addi all over the place." I grin sheepishly. "And then, while I could have just called you or come over to Murph and Jason's to tell you I loved you, I thought you might appreciate a bigger gesture."

"I appreciated it so much," he whispers. "It's true?"

I stand and hug him, whispering against his neck, "Yeah, it's true. I love you. I realized it right after you said it, but I didn't believe it could work. I did a lot of thinking, though, and"—I feel myself redden—"I hope you might want to be my boyfriend for real. And maybe move in with me? If that's not too fast."

Suddenly I'm worried I'm so far beyond the realm of what's realistic that I've lost all sense.

But then I remember who I'm talking to. The king of imagination.

"It's not too fast. We've been living together for months."

"And I thought, if you want, we could split our time between here and New York. There's plenty of space in my loft. You might like it there."

His face drops. "I don't want to be a burden on you."

"You could never be." I let out a breath. "I was thinking, what about going to college? Do you want to do that? Then you could figure out what you want to do in the long term. You're good with kids, and you're good with emotions. Maybe you could be a child psychologist or write children's books or—I don't know. If you want to still write greeting cards, that's fine, too. I don't want you to feel like you have to do anything I suggest. I just want you to be happy and know you have options."

He blinks back tears. "Why would you do all this?"

"Because I love you. I don't know when it happened. Maybe somewhere in between you cleaning paint off my kitchen floor and us all going stargazing. But you are something else. Watching the way you take care of Addi inspires me to be around to help her grow up. You're the love of my life. I love you down to your core. I love the way you make decisions with your heart, without thinking, because there isn't a bone of malice in your body. I love the way you always choose love."

He smiles shyly. "Do you really mean that?"

"Yeah," I croak. "I mean that. And I hope you'll forgive me for being an ass when you told me you loved me."

"Yeah, of course. You just needed a moment." He grins. "Just make sure to enjoy *this* moment, too." Scott takes a step away from me and glances around the room. "What is this place?"

"Jason's sister helped me find it."

"He mentioned something about that to me. I didn't understand what he was talking about."

"She's a realtor. So ... I bought this place, and it came furnished. If you don't like the décor, we can change it out."

He shakes his head. "You're incredible." He bites his lip. "But I feel like there's this huge power imbalance between us. You're older, richer, wiser. I'm a kid with no money or skills."

"Don't sell yourself short. Why don't I invest in you? Invest in your education. Help you do whatever it is you want to do. That way you won't have to depend on me—even though I wouldn't mind if you did. I have plenty for us to live on."

"It sounds too good to be true."

"Most romantic things sound too good to be true, right? But that doesn't mean they are."

"Okay," he says. "This is a lot to process."

"While you process, come to bed. I need to show you how I feel about you."

Scott grins. "I think you've been showing me this whole time."

I pause. "You're probably right about that. I can't seem to hide myself when I'm naked with you. You bring out the real me."

The me who wants to praise. Who wants connection. Who is a lover, through and through.

"Yeah, I can see that." He kisses me. "We work together."

"I think I should put you to work," I say. "Work on sucking my cock."

He laughs and follows me into the main bedroom, which I now see as our room.

I stroke my fingers under his jaw and kiss him softly. "How do you want it?"

"I want to be on my knees," he says, as he kneels before me and goes to unbutton my pants. But then he notices that there's no button. He tilts his head to the side, and in one move, rips them off.

I'm left in nothing but a thong, and Scott is both laughing and hard.

"Give us a spin," he says. I oblige, although it's embarrassing.

"Holy hell, are you hot in that. Joe Manganiello has nothing on you." Scott smacks my ass and then kisses it. Then he runs his finger along my crease. "This is some kind of fantasy come true, and I do *not* want to wake up from it."

I look over my shoulder, but before I can do anything, he's spread my ass cheeks and moved the string and is licking my hole.

"Oh god," I groan. "Do that again."

He slides my thong down and then pushes me to the bed. I writhe, seeking friction for my cock, but the cheesy satin sheets I ordered to go along with the stripper theme are more of a tease than anything else.

"You're the best thing that ever happened to me," I pant. "I fucking love you."

Scott grins against my skin and keeps licking me, his hand snaking under me to grip my cock and give it a few light strokes.

"Fuck. Scott. Yes, please. Keep doing that. Wait. Oh god, no. Stop."

He pulls back immediately. "What's wrong?"

"Nothing's wrong, but if you keep that up, I'll come, and I want to come inside you."

"Okay," he whispers and starts shucking off his clothes as fast as he can. There's an awkward moment with the boot, but he deals with it.

I turn over on my back and start lubing up my cock. "I love you. Come let me fuck you."

"I want it fast," Scott whispers. "I want to feel you." Without any ceremony at all, he straddles me and comes down on my cock, the head breaching the ring of muscle and then the rest of me slipping inside him.

We're nose to nose. Scott takes a moment to adjust, managing the burn and the pain. "I should've prepped you," I start to say.

"I'm fine," he wheezes.

After what is likely just a minute but feels like an eternity, his body relaxes around me.

"Okay," he murmurs, and he does an experimental bounce on my dick.

"Fuck, yes. You always look so gorgeous on my cock."

Once he gets the angle right, we really get going, me surging up to meet him every time he goes down.

Before long, we're covered in come, satisfied, and in love.

For the first time in my life, I don't feel empty. I feel whole. I feel cherished. I feel like I have someone to cherish.

And I'm happy.

29

SCOTT

We're walking through the farmers market on the first day that truly feels like spring, picking up fresh eggs, bread, delicate peas, and jams and honey. Luke is carrying a basket that I keep filling up, while Addison runs ahead, too excited for words.

When we get to a stall filled with flowers, Luke stops to talk with the proprietor. Before I can get a word out, he's purchased bouquet after bouquet of flowers, setting them in a separate basket to take home.

How my man has changed.

He gives me a shy smile and takes my hand, his other laden with produce.

"We should put this in the car," I say. "It's too much for you to carry. Here. Let me go do that, and you stay with Addi."

"Okay." He passes me the flowers and the food, and I return to the Rover, where I place everything in the back and retrieve another tote in case we keep shopping. When I return, they're watching a band play and drinking hot cider.

You'd never know this is the grumpy man I met months ago. Now he has an easy smile and spends more time with his daughter than ever.

Kira's back from her trip, and while they've kept the custody deal the same, when we're in Vermont—which is most of the time —they've come to an arrangement where they help each other out and are both active in parenting Addison.

There's even a photo at Kira's house from St. Patrick's Day, the four of us all dressed in green, looking at the camera and laughing. Kira had it framed and added it to the wall of family photos.

Because, yeah, I'm now part of their family.

When we sat down with Addi to explain the change in our relationship, she didn't bat an eye.

"Baby girl," Luke had said, gathering her into his lap as he sat on the couch in the living room of his new home. *Our* new home. "I love you so much."

"Me, too," I'd said.

Addison nodded like being loved was what she expected, which made my heart sing.

"While Scott started out as your nanny, he's become my boyfriend. We wanted you to know that instead of him just being your babysitter while Momma was working out of town, he's going to be living with me—and with you when you're staying with me."

"Forever?" she asked.

Luke looked at me. "Yeah." His voice was rough, and it made my eyes sting with tears.

Because yes, forever. I nodded at her, and she tilted her head to the side. "That's good."

"Do you have any questions about it?"

Addison bit her lip. "Can Scott still play with me when I'm at Momma's house?"

He grinned. "I'll ask your momma, but I'm sure we can work something out."

"Okay. Will he find me a unicorn?"

"I'll get right on that," I said, kissing the top of her head.

Since formalizing our relationship, we've been having a lot of fun: boat trips on Lake Champlain, signing Addi up for horse camp this summer, planning more excursions around the Big

Apple so we can explore all the sights Luke never took time to enjoy before.

I've applied to Moo U and have looked into community college classes. I might study creative writing since I love words.

But life is so good now. Luke smiles and leaves me notes for no reason. He frames the cards I give him—ones that I wrote. He goes for walks with me along the lake or on our favorite trails, sometimes with Addison and sometimes just the two of us. He gives me little presents, too—and I do the same for him sometimes—but I no longer feel like I have to buy anyone's love or affection.

While he offered to pay off my bills, I refused. However, I did accept his help coming up with a payment plan and negotiating away some of the late fees and interest charges. If I keep this up, I'll be out of debt in two years, which is amazing.

I'm going to keep it up.

Imprescott Designs, a local letterpress shop and design studio, has hired me part time, and between that and the designs I submit to the greeting card companies, I have more than enough coming in, especially when Luke insists on taking care of all my current expenses. I know he loves me, and this is how he demonstrates it. So I try to balance letting him show his affection with not wanting to take advantage of him.

In my pocket is a key to his house—our house. But more importantly, he gave me the key to his heart.

Enjoy this moment.

EPILOGUE: LUKE

The sun is rising, and there's a cute man sleeping in my bed. I gaze at him with fondness as I walk back into the bedroom of my Manhattan loft. Scott's curled up in a ball, his face buried in a pillow.

I'm holding two champagne flutes, an open bottle of bubbly, and fresh-squeezed orange juice.

I set everything down and pour each of us a mimosa. Crawling in next to him, I pull the blankets over us and tug him to me.

"Hey," he says sleepily, pressing his ass to my interested dick. "Morning."

"Morning." I kiss the back of his neck and run my fingers through his hair.

Scott turns over, still in my arms, and gives me a kiss. Then he pulls back, a quizzical look on his face. "You look awfully awake. What have you been doing?"

I reach over to the bedside table and hand him a drink. "Making these."

"Ooh! Yummy." He sits up, grinning, and we rearrange ourselves so he's sitting between my legs while my back is propped up against the headboard.

Scott leans against me, and as he sips his drink, I murmur, "This is one of the first things I thought of when I saw you."

"Having me in your bed?"

I chuckle. "No. Well, yes. But specifically, having Sunday morning mimosas with you and, uh, cuddling."

He squeezes my thigh. "Oh my god, you really are a romantic!"

Grinning against his neck, I kiss it. "Don't tell anyone."

"Your secret is safe with me."

In the year since we've been together, Scott and I have come to New York many times and done all the things I never bothered to do when I was working so much: Broadway shows, baseball games, riding the Staten Island Ferry for no reason except to enjoy being on the water. Sometimes it's just him and me. Sometimes Addi comes with us. Sometimes Kira comes along with her new boyfriend, Ray. We're a family bonded by blood, promises, and friendship.

Oh, and love. Lots of that.

When we're in Vermont, we frequently visit Scott's family in Stowe or catch a high school football game with his dad, who I've become friends with.

"I have a few plans for us today," I say.

He turns around. "Do you?"

I nod. "Someone once told me that a couple's anniversary is the most important holiday."

Scott frowns. "But ... we're not married. We don't have an anniversary."

"Today is the anniversary of the day I met you. I figure that counts." I lean in for a long, deep kiss. "What do you think?"

He blinks, looking dazed. "Yeah, that works. Okay." He settles back against me, and we finish our drinks.

When we're done, I take our glasses and set them back on the bedside table. Then I gently push him up and smack his ass. "Time to get going."

"What are we doing?"

I grin. "That's for me to know and you to find out. Except, one hint: you once told me your favorite things were sunrises and sunsets."

Scott hops out of bed fast and reaches out a hand to pull me with him. "Really? You have a surprise planned?" He rubs his hands together.

"I do. Get dressed."

Our shower takes a little longer than strictly necessary, but when we're both clean and presentable, we take the elevator down to a waiting town car. The excitement on Scott's face as we get in the back is palpable—and catching.

"Are you going to tell me what we're doing?"

"Do you want me to?"

"No way."

I wrap my arm around him and kiss the side of his head. I can't get enough of him, and I don't see that ever changing. His view of the world is so sunny, and he reminds me of everything I love in life that I'd forgotten about. I love paying attention to my daughter and being out in nature instead of always squirreled away in an office. I love that Scott comes up with fun things to do every day. I love *him*, to the bottom of my soul.

When the driver pulls over in front of a trendy breakfast spot, Scott's eyes light up. "I've heard about this place. How did you get reservations?"

I shrug. "I have my ways."

After a leisurely breakfast, we spend the day being tourists, going up the Statue of Liberty and eventually having lunch in Little Italy.

"What a marvelous day!" Scott says as we stroll through Central Park hand in hand, headed to the Met.

We've had a big day already, but neither of us is tired as we each pick a gallery we want to see and spend time really looking at the art. Instead of trying to absorb everything, we go deep.

Then, when I've timed it right—I hope—the town car takes us to the Empire State Building.

Scott's excitement is palpable. "Oh my god! I've never been here!"

I bought tickets in advance, so we head straight for the elevator to the observation deck. I'm a little worried, because the sun is getting lower, but we make it up before it dips too far.

When we get there, we hear, "Daddy! Scott!" and Addison comes flying at us for hugs. I pick her up and say hello to Kira and Ray. Kira gives me a conspiratorial look. "You made it," she murmurs.

"Yep." I'm starting to get nervous, my mouth dry. But I can do this.

I set Addison down, and she starts telling Scott about what she's done that day. Together with all the other tourists, we ooh and aah at the panorama spread out before us. Kira gives me an encouraging smile.

"Look!" Scott says. "The sun is about to go down." We walk over to get the best view, and my pulse is racing.

There's a rustling behind us, and Scott's parents make their way through the crowd, but he's too entranced by the view to notice. His dad winks at me and gives me a thumbs-up, then puts his arm around Aimee.

While Scott's watching the sun dipping below the horizon, I fish out a box that I've been carrying around all day. For more than a day, actually, because I didn't want him to find it by accident.

And then I get down on one knee.

When Scott realizes what I'm doing, he gasps and covers his mouth with his hands. He glances around wildly, noticing his parents, and his eyes widen.

My heart beats so fast it might burst out of my chest. I reach up and tug one of those hands to me.

"Scott," I whisper, my throat scratchy, "I love you. I'm not really one for a big speech, but I wanted to bring you to a romantic place and give you a romantic day because not only did I think you would like it, but I like it, too. You've reminded me of who I really am, and you make all my days better. They're full of joy and so much love, and I want to be with you for the rest of my life. Will you marry me?"

Scott nods repeatedly, his eyes teary, and whispers, "Yes."

My heart soars, and he tugs me up for a kiss. Our family—and all sorts of strangers—clap, and when we break apart, I slide the ring onto his trembling finger.

"You already had the key to my heart," he says.

"And I promise to keep it safe, always."

ACKNOWLEDGMENTS

In August 2021, I wrote the following to the folks at Heart Eyes Press:

About halfway through writing Undone, *a character walked in the room hoping to woo Murph, who was destined for Jason. Scott's the kind of ridiculously romantic guy who stands in the rain with two bottles of wine and a red-checked picnic basket, hoping to find his one true love. He'll serenade you or send a singing telegram, take you up in a hot-air balloon ride, and do all sorts of over-the-top, hopelessly romantic gestures.*

Candlelit dinner? Yes.

Roses? Yes.

Pay his bills on time? Not so much.

Scott wouldn't leave me alone. Perhaps he deserves a chance at his own story. Thanks for considering.

As you can see … they said yes. My sincere thanks to Sarina Bowen and Jane Haertel for giving Scott that chance. Luke and Scott were really fun to write, and I hope you love them as much as I do.

Thank you to the helpful folks I'm surrounded with: Kristy Lin Billuni (Sexy Grammar coaching), Mary Carr (alpha reading and helping me work out Luke's personality), Megan Dischinger (beta reading), and Heather Roberts (all the things). Thank you also to Phala Theng and Julia Heudorf for your thoughtful comments. Thanks to L.A. Witt for collaborating on Landon and Luke's friendship and all the emails back and forth. Thanks to Garrett Leigh and Victoria Denault for being an amazing part of this project. Thanks to my proofreaders, Virginia Tesi Carey, Jerica

MacMillan, and Katy Cuthbertson for finding all the errors (any left are my own fault).

I'm eternally grateful to my cohort of mm authors: J.E. Birk, Rachel Ember, and Charley Descoteaux, who are equal parts cheerleaders, problem-solvers, and shoulders to cry on.

Extra special gooey thanks to my editor, Alicia Z. Ramos, who cares about my words and molds the story into resembling what I actually intended. And to Cory Stierley and Brock Grady for the cover photo.

And thank you to my family. Let's just say that Scott's coming-out story is rooted in real life. I'm so glad for all the love and respect we have for each other.

Made in the USA
Middletown, DE
15 September 2022

10498522R00151